BRIEF CASES

By the same author:

An Eye on the Whiplash and Other Stories

C.

Brief Cases

HENRY MURPHY

ASHFIELD
Press

This book was typeset by KRISTIN JENSEN for

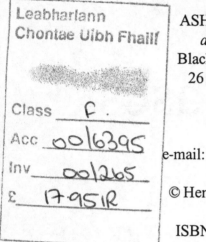
ASHFIELD PRESS
an imprint of
Blackhall Publishing
26 Eustace Street
Dublin 2
Ireland

e-mail: blackhall@tinet.ie

© Henry Murphy, 1999

ISBN: 1 901658 236

A catalogue record for this book is available from the
British Library.

This book of short stories is a work of fiction. The names,
characters, cases and incidents portrayed are entirely the product of
the author's imagination. They do not, nor are they intended to,
resemble any person, living or dead, or any actual case or incident.
Any perceived resemblance is coincidental.

Printed in Ireland by
Betaprint Ltd

Contents

Henry Murphy lives in Greystones with Mary and their children. He is a practising barrister.

Acknowledgements

Shortly before *An Eye on the Whiplash* was published, I appointed a small but discerning jury to read it. I wanted to have their advice as to whether or not I should proceed with it. The members of the jury were Jack Fitzgerald, the late Mr Justice Peter Shanley, Frank Murphy and Mr Justice Francis D Murphy. I was delighted when they gave it their imprimatur.

This time around I would like to have been able to appoint the same jury but alas, Peter is no longer with us and so the jury had to deliberate without him. When I went to Peter's Chambers two years ago to collect *An Eye on the Whiplash* from him and to hear what he had to say about it, he advised me very strongly to change the ending of the last story so that Dermot could go out on a winning note. Indeed, he more or less dictated the variation off the top of his head. Rightly or wrongly, I decided to leave it as it was but I hope that Peter will be happy with Dermot's progress in this volume.

Many thanks to the Two Franks and to Jack for travelling with me through *An Eye on the Whiplash* and now *Brief Cases* and for their advice and enthusiasm along the way. I would point out that the responsibility for any remaining mistakes is entirely theirs.

A very special word of gratitude is owed by me to my publisher, Gerard O'Connor, for adding *Brief Cases* to his list of titles and for all his guidance and encouragement in relation to these two books.

It was a pleasure to work with Kristin Jensen and to drink coffee with her in the IFC as we discussed the fruits of her accomplished editing.

I would like to thank Leonie Lawler and Tony Mason of Blackhall Publishing for their contributions to this publication.

Thanks to Mel O'Rourke at Creative Inc. for the splendid cover.

Nivés Collins was vital in the business of converting my indecipherable dictation into a typed text and in the matter of correction.

According to my wife Mary, she works full-time in the home. In addition, she has to answer questions like, "How do you spell alickadoo?", "Give me another word for eclectic" and "Have you read the first story yet?" Like Arnold's phone calls, these queries tend to arrive around 6.25 pm. When she announces which is her favourite story, she is interrogated as to what is wrong with the other ones. Mary is my first critic and really I think that if it passes her examination, it can't be too bad. Thank you Oz.

Henry Murphy
October 1999

for
Mary

The Opening

When I first met Arnold I was in my second year at the Bar. He was, in my estimate, in his late-forties, early-fifties. His efforts to roll back the years were a dismal failure. From the time when, as a physical hulk, he had been a formidable centre three-quarter for University College Dublin where he specialised in upper body strength – Adonis was a disappointment in comparison – he had transferred his allegiance to sumo wrestling. (The thought of Arnold in the sumo wrestler's g-string was one thought too many for most.)

While at UCD, insofar as he read at all, he read rugby and attended the occasional lecture in law. It wasn't that the law lectures were occasional, merely his attendance. It was his intention to become a solicitor, and in the fullness of time that ambition was realised without even his closest friends knowing how. It is certain that there are many gentlemen around the country successfully practising medicine on account of their prowess on the UCD rugby field and it is thought by some that the same might be said of Arnold, were one to substitute the practice of law for medicine.

He was neither the best of solicitors nor the worst, though in fairness he probably ran the latter a very close second. Neither efficiency nor punctuality were his hallmarks. Nor, it had to be said, had he imbibed of the pool of wisdom. In truth, it was hard to know how he got by. One client in particular was very important to him – Mr Wilkinson's insurance company. Mr Wilkinson was his captain back in those physical, fun-loving days and Mr

Wilkinson never forgot who scored the winning try in the dying moments of their rain-drenched Colours match. Were Mr Wilkinson to fold his insurance tent in the morning and join the Jesuits, it is extremely doubtful if Arnold would have been able to support himself from whatever of his practice remained after Mr Wilkinson's departure.

Perish the thought that Mr Wilkinson should join the Jesuits, for Mr Wilkinson was a friend of my old man in the golf club and it was on that account that somewhere in the course of my second year at the Bar I received my first brief from Arnold (in fact, my first brief from anyone) on the instructions of the very-important-to-both-of-us Mr Wilkinson. I remember every moment of that first case, but having hashed it once in an earlier tome, I will not rehash it here, save to say that it did not herald the commencement of my career quite as I would have wished, and for some weeks I did not hear from Arnold or Mr Wilkinson. If Mr Wilkinson lived in a continuing state of loyalty to Arnold, there was no reason for him to be loyal to me – I hadn't scored a winning try – except it was my old man who got him into the golf club when he, my old man, was captain there. In accordance with that strain of loyalty, Arnold returned on the instructions of Mr Wilkinson. Perhaps it was going to be some time before Arnold would contact me on his own initiative and for his own purposes, but on Mr Wilkinson's behalf we began to strike up something of a team. At least that was the way I saw it. That's not to say that I was his first port of call, but when he was stuck for a barrister to represent Mr Wilkinson's insurance company – in other words, when he had unsuccessfully contacted every other barrister whose name was known to him – he tended to turn in my direction. For which profound thanks.

Whatever Arnold did between nine and five and indeed well after, he did from No. 203 Gardiner Street. I say well after because he rarely contacted me in the Law Library during office hours. It was much more usual for him to phone me at home at any hour of the night, and he always seemed to know the precise moment when I was settling into something – dinner, a football match on the telly, Rachel – because the call invariably arrived at that very moment. And another thing, there was something sacred to Arnold about twenty five minutes past the hour. For example, most people arrange their consultations for, say, half past nine. In the morning. Not Arnold. Twenty five past nine, sharp, for a "detailed" consultation. It didn't mean that he would turn up at that time himself, but I certainly had to. And as for phoning, the calls would come in at twenty five past six, or eight or ten. Twenty five past whatever hour suited Arnold, regardless of my convenience.

Arnold enjoyed the assistance of his secretary, Samantha, whose role was not confined to the office. By that I do not wish to convey any romantic liaison between the two, though now that I think of it, it may explain some of Arnold's later phone calls. I simply mean that from time to time, she crossed the city centre and joined us in the Four Courts. It will be obvious that not all of Arnold's cases were sure-fire winners. Many, indeed most, were iffy enough and the iffier they were, the more likely that I would be attended in court by Samantha rather than by Arnold, who at least had that degree of street wisdom and sense of self-preservation that, if we were unlikely to win the case and the costs that accompany victory, he would send Samantha down and he would go off and close a sale.

Samantha was a popular visitor to the Four Courts. For one thing she did not adhere to the dress code for court. The dress code stipulated, fuddy-duddily, that clothes should be worn. Now admittedly Samantha had the technical argument that as she was a secretary, not a solicitor, the code did not apply to her. Occasionally, in deference to the code, she would wear what purported to be a skirt, a flimsy pleated thing compared to which the conventional tennis skirt enjoyed all the modesty of a nun's habit. Chewing her gum and maybe or maybe not plugged into her walkman, there always seemed to be a lot of documents to be taken out of Arnold's briefcase. Between that and frequently having to stand up in court (Samantha would be seated opposite me with her back to the judge) to hand in documents to his Lordship, which necessitated the most intricate (and hence revealing) bodily contortions, the concentration of even the most impervious of my male colleagues – and God knows there are enough of those – was sorely tested. Intellectually, Samantha, no more than her boss, added little to the proceedings.

If Arnold's office is on the third floor of No. 203 Gardiner Street, above a fast-food joint, a gymnasium that blasts contemporary music for most hours of the night and day from its open windows, and the headquarters of the Communist Party of Ireland, whose star, much like the building itself, peaked some considerable time ago, my office is a much more grandiose affair. In a Library at the rear of Mr Gandon's Four Courts, my colleagues and I have our modest seats. The Communist Party would approve at least of the communal nature of our facilities. If little else. It is to this Law Library that Arnold and his colleagues come in search of their barristers and it is from here that my colleagues and I service the courts of the land. In recent years the number of barristers has grown so that there are now nearly as many barristers as there are books, which is not to suggest any shortage of the latter. Within this Library, not only physical but also intellectual facilities are shared, as the brains of the leaders of the Bar are picked and plucked by the likes of me.

It is this very Law Library, of which I have been a member now for six years, that has given us such judicial luminaries as Judge Rogers and Mr Justice Fleming, before whom my colleagues and I at the behest of the Arnolds of this world give the constitutional rights of our unsuspecting clients an airing.

Too early in my career at the Bar I married Rachel, and too early in my career with Rachel she became pregnant with twins. Accordingly, there were certain extra-curricular pressures that made it necessary for me to rocket to fame and fortune. The rocket was turning out not to be quite as turbo-propelled as I had hoped, notwithstanding my ambition and application, and it was just as well we had the safety valve of Rachel's thriving matrimonial practice. For the moment at any rate.

If you were to believe Rachel, she didn't lose too many cases, but in my experience, no matter how good a barrister you are, there are certain cases that just cannot be won. Unfortunately, if you get too many cases that fall into this category, you may never get the chance to reveal how good a barrister you are because you will attract the reputation of being a losing barrister and solicitors will abandon you. This was precisely my fear at this early stage of what I was still nervous about calling my career. I had had a number of cases but not much success. Indeed, my only success was that case about the young fellow who got alcoholic poisoning and sued the innkeeper who served him the drink. As I had a touch of alcoholic poisoning myself as a result of a celebratory dinner in King's Inns the night before the case, I missed the fact that the young lad was still under age when he collapsed from drink – he wasn't eighteen until midnight – but the point was not lost on the judge, the wise judge, who held that, while it wasn't the strongest case to have come before him, there was just enough there for him to decide in favour of the plaintiff and indeed in favour of me, thereby breaking my duck. This one win in the wilderness needed company. I went in search.

The Lord Edward

According to Rule 6.1 of the Barristers' Code of Conduct, "a barrister may not do or cause to be done on his behalf anything for the purpose of touting, whether directly or indirectly or which is likely to lead to the reasonable inference that it was done for such purpose". For completeness, Mr Chambers says that, elsewhere than in Scotland, to tout is "to look out for custom in an obtrusive way", whereas in Scotland it means "to pout", unlikely to be what the Bar Council had in mind as coming within the scope of its prohibition, though perhaps worthy of consideration when the Code is next up for review. And a tout is "a low fellow, who hangs about racing stables, etc. to pick up profitable information".

I do not know why vertically challenged male barristers who hang about racing stables and the like are singled out for specific mention, but, presumably, the law being so attached to precedent, it goes back to some nineteenth century scandal when perhaps a diminutive colleague prosecuting a doping or racing fraud trial confused his duties in the pursuit of a conviction and spent the evenings of the trial slinking from stable to stable, picking up information to be used profitably in court the following day.

This is pure surmise on my part. Leaving the racing types out of it for the moment, you probably have a fair idea from the foregoing what it is precisely that the Bar Council wishes to prohibit in the interests of maintaining standards. I cannot be sure, but I imagine that to call around to a solicitor's home for the purpose of requesting work would come within the prohibition. So, too, would sitting in the reception of a solicitor's office and refusing to leave until one is given a few briefs. Attending post-accident operations would probably not be permitted by the Bar Council and, in any event, the Medical Council might have something to say about the practice. Likewise, attendance at funerals in fatal cases would surely be frowned upon.

The wining and dining of solicitors and claims managers in the Lord Edward is not specifically mentioned in Rule 6.1 and may therefore constitute a grey area, not being such a flagrant breach of the Code as those listed above. Presumably, if a colleague were to be hauled before the Professional Practices Committee for such activity, the *contra proferentem* rule, which provides that a clause will be construed against the person insisting on it, would be invoked.

It's funny how often it is left to one's friends to make the cruelest remarks.

One day over lunch we were talking about this very rule. Rumour had it that a leading Senior Counsel had brought Claims and Assistant Claims Managers to New York for the weekend to see Ireland beat Italy one nil in the World Cup.

"It sets a very bad example for the entire Bar but, in particular, for the Junior Juniors," said Rory, who like the rest of us had only recently crossed that first Rubicon of a barrister's life and who, unlike the rest of us, was already feeling protective of the Baby Bar. The rest of us were less altruistic, more interested in our own skins and felt that the Baby Bar and the Bar Council between them could adequately look after the interests of that section of the Bar from which we had just emerged. Even in the few short years since our arrival, things had changed and the freshers were much more outspoken in their demands than their more deferential predecessors.

Fergus was more practical.

"What chance have the rest of us if this is going on at the top?" he added in the full knowledge that his touting expeditions would be, of necessity, of a more local character. Passport not necessary.

As always, the highest moral ground is reserved for the worst offender. Brendan, in truth a recidivist, added aggressively, "This kind of thing should be stamped out. Once and for all. It's a scandal. The Library is too small a place for this sort of activity.

Does the Bar Council do nothing?"

There were few days that Brendan was not lunching in the company of a Claims Manager, and fewer the days that the venue was the downstairs brasserie in the Four Courts rather than the culinary hot spots of Temple Bar. His single and entirely coincidental concession to the Code of Conduct was his insistence on the presence of a solicitor.

Foolishly raising my head above water, I offered, "There's nothing wrong with the odd cup of coffee of course, but there has to be a limit. Lunch in the Lord Edward and tickets for two to New York are just not on."

Brendan, who was by now clearly suffering from a severe dose of retrograde amnesia, had an ideological difficulty with my contribution. "Now hold on Mac, that's just where you're wrong. As Shaw said, 'We have established what you are, it's just a question of your price.' The principle is the thing. Whether it's New York, the Lord Edward or..." he paused, searching for a more democratic example of the fall from grace, "in your case, touting on a dollar a day, the principle is equally offended." The lunch table, overflowing with my erstwhile friends, thought this hilarious and an appropriate note on which to return to the forensic skirmish.

What Brendan was referring to, with no great subtlety, was my occasional coffee in Bewleys with my solicitor, J Arnold O' Reilly.

Sometimes at the end of a day in court, Arnold would say to me that he had a case he wanted to discuss, but that he had left the papers in the office and would I like to walk back with him? This was an expedition I was inclined to keep to myself – or tried to in any event. I had no doubt that in time I would not have to walk all around the city centre in a psychophantic quest for a holy brief.

As often as not, Arnold would suggest interrupting this odyssey for a coffee and ring-doughnut in Bewleys. Of course I would pay, but I never regarded it as touting, only courtesy, that's all. Common courtesy.

There was nothing limited, whether in time or place, about Arnold's eccentricity. For example, it extended to his café life. His unusual traits were not revealed to me all at once. Rather, were they unfolded one by one, over time.

The first I can recall was his preference for stirring his coffee with a pencil rather than the more conventional method of using a spoon. Of course, on the first few occasions he sought to excuse it, saying that he had forgotten the spoon and was too lazy to go back for it. Alternatively, he sought to conceal it, stirring furtively and with great speed when he thought my attention was elsewhere. Eventually, however, he abandoned the disguise and stirred quite openly with his Faber Castell.

No sooner had I got used to this quaintness and began to treat it as normal than another was introduced – the second untouched cup of coffee. He always ordered two cups of coffee, one for himself and another that always remained untouched, as if it was for someone else, Mr Wilkinson perhaps. I never was to get an explanation for this particular wantonness.

In fact, you could say that Arnold slipped very easily into the Bewleys ambiance. Ten minutes in the place would show you what I mean. It was crowded with men and women on their own except for bags, hundreds of bags, rooting endlessly in them for uncertain purposes. Women and men moving from table to table for no clear reason. The oddest of books being read. Even odder poems being written surreptitiously. I once saw a man shaving behind his newspaper.

I have never satisfied myself if it is the fact that every oddball is a customer of Bewleys, or if every customer of Bewleys is an oddball. It is one or the other; there is no half-way house. By accident or design, the oddest of God's creatures gather here under one roof. Don't get me wrong, I am a great fan, indeed, addicted to the coffee. When I go away on holidays I suffer withdrawal symptoms for the duration.

On Sundays, you will find these loyal patrons of Bewleys in the Pro-Cathedral for the Palestrina Mass. It is no coincidence that the quietest hour of the week in Bewleys is on Sunday morning between eleven and twelve. If you don't believe me, take yourself off next Sunday to Marlborough Street. You will see that I tell no lie. Familiar faces trailing familiar bags from statue to statue, caressing each one with lingering fingers in a manner bordering on the indecent, all the time uttering pious ejaculations in that see-saw monotone of repetitive prayer. Confidence in the correctness of my theory about what the Europeans would call this "transmigration" of population between Bewleys and Pro-Cathedral was given an unexpected boost when on one occasion I saw a worshipper tucking into a coffee and ring-dough-nut in front of Our Lady's altar.

In an age when office technology has been hijacked by computer, fax and e-mail, it never ceases to amaze me how far behind the times Arnold's office insists on remaining. Arnold obviously shared the view of my colleague who believed that the fax should be linked to the shredder.

If you visit one of the posh offices, you will find a user-friendly reception area manned (if that is the right word) by a number of gloriously mini-skirted and obscenely young females, say between fifteen and twenty, or maybe twenty-five, or alternatively by a number of older models, sophisticated and superior in much the same way that a vintage wine outclasses its rivals. They will all speak as if they have just come from their latest elocution lesson, address you, no matter how much their senior, by your Christian name and point you in the direction of a chair fit for the principal partner where you will chortle away an hour or two with *Business and Finance* or some similar commercial glossy. The consultation will be a piece of cake after this introductory session.

When the time comes, the personal assistant to the personal assistant will conduct you to the elevator, where you will be handed over to a first year apprentice, who in turn will elevate you to an upstairs corridor the length of an indoor athletics arena where you will eventually be introduced to the senior partner's assistant, a qualified solicitor of twenty years standing, who will usher you into the boardroom, called after the late founder of the firm and presided over by his portrait, where your ultimate host and the final link in the chain is already in animated conversation with the client.

Introductions will only just have been accomplished when the firm's catering manageress enters, an even more magnificent creature than those manning (or is it personning?) the reception area below, who wishes to know if tea or coffee is the beverage of choice and if tea, whether herbal or ordinary, and if coffee, whether decaffeinated or not. Her curiosity satisfied, she withdraws.

Ten minutes later, a different tea and coffee lady enters for distribution purposes. Insofar as it is possible to discuss affairs of state while pouring tea or coffee and making suitable enquires as to sugar and milk while passing around tennis-club sandwiches, the consultation continues. If there is any danger of serious discussion going on too long, a relay of behind-the-scenes apprentices and assistants are unleashed to distribute volumes of additional and hitherto unseen paperwork.

An afternoon or so later, the senior partner, for no reason that is immediately obvious and at a moment when some progress is at last being made, brings the rendezvous to an end and arrangements are made for a follow-up meeting.

Not so Arnold or Arnold's establishment, a mile or so and a century or two to the north of the boardroom just visited.

On Arnold's office door is a sign bearing the inscription, "J ARNOLD O'REILLY & COMPANY, SOLICITORS, COMMISSIONER FOR OATHS, NOTARY PUBLIC". On the other side of the door, a small square area is cut off from the remainder of the office by a six-foot-high panelling, which has a clouded window in the middle with a bell alongside.

Obviously, it is intended that, in order to get attention, the visitor should ring the bell. For as long as I have been coming to the office – and by now I have a path worn thin – I have noticed that the one thing you do not get on ringing the bell is attention. I have begun to wonder if my visit might not be more quickly acknowledged were I to ignore the bell in the same way that those on the other side of the cloudy window do. A response in anything shorter than the time it would take to run a marathon is exceptional.

A slave to precedent, I ring the bell more in hope than in expectation. A rosary later, the two little windows part company in a reluctant manner that suggests that intercourse with the public represents a lowering of professional standards. The sole receptionist is revealed, whose salt-white appearance suggests she has not been outside that building for any moment of her sixty-five years.

God knows the reason for the delay. Throughout, I can see her shadowy movement through the clouded glass, can hear her type, open and close the filing cabinet, answer the phone, blow her nose even. I am tempted to raise myself on my toes and, resting my chin on the top of the panel, enquire as to why I am not receiving some priority.

The salty soul looks at me with great intensity, as if her life depends on finding some feature of recognition. For a moment or two she looks as if she might be on the brink of a great breakthrough, only to give way to the utter futility of the task and all the time she is as familiar to me as my mother.

As if meeting me for the first time, she enquiries my name, my business and with whom I wish to meet, oblivious to the fact that, she aside, the only remaining possibilities are Samantha and Arnold.

I patiently release the innermost secrets of my visit and am told to take a seat while she sees if Mr O'Reilly is in. This is a little surprising on two counts. First, there is no seat and secondly I can actually see Arnold through the open door of his office and it seems highly improbable that he could be sitting in his office unbeknownst to his receptionist.

In time, she returns and escorts me to Arnold's room, not far from where I have been standing while this Pinteresque drama unfolded. No plenipotentiaries, no elevator, no long corridor, no boardroom dedicated to the founding father. Neither a computer nor e-mail in sight. Not even a filing cabinet. The single concession to late twentieth century technology is a dictaphone or two.

On some occasion in the embryonic stage of our relationship, when my perception of Arnold was still tinged with awe, I asked him how he coped with the voluminous paperwork that must be an integral part of the practice of a busy solicitor. Arnold, not recognising some of the assumptions that underlay the question, took a little time to reply, "The dictaphone was a great invention." *The cute whore*, I thought at the time. *Cards close to his chest*. No way was he going to allow this precocious beginner into the secrets of his success. How innocent I was then.

On this occasion, things were different, as they usually were if I entered the office in the company of the principal, indeed sole, partner.

"Good afternoon, Mr O'Reilly."

"Good afternoon, Mr McNamara," intoned the principal, indeed sole, receptionist as she opened the door to her inner sanctuary. *How about that for a change?* I thought to myself. *Instant recognition.*

Once in the office, Arnold threw me a large brown envelope using the spin pass that had become fashionable in recent years and completely forgetting that while I may enjoy certain accomplishments, manual dexterity is not one of them. Instinct for survival rather than any suppleness of limb prevented the missile from going to ground.

No matter how long one is at the Bar, there is always an excitement about opening the large brown envelope, surpassed only by the opening of the small brown one. Admittedly, the longer one is at the Bar, like other things in life, the shorter the excitement. In this instance, the excitement was short-lived due to the following instruction from Arnold.

"Mac," (Arnold had taken to calling me 'Mac' recently) "you could do with a win. It's not that there has been anything wrong with your performances, or that you are in any way to blame for recent results, but you need a win. There are a lot of fish in the sea and, take Mr Wilkinson for example, he understands the system and knows that not all cases can be won, particularly on the defendant's side, but he does expect to win occasionally. He'll tell me to brief someone else." Arnold concluded his pep talk rhetorically, saying, "You don't mind me talking like this to you, do you? Just marking your card."

What could I say? Nothing. I read the Civil Bill.

Indorsement of Claim

The plaintiff, Priscilla Connolly, who resides at 85 Robinson House, Robinson Square, in the City of Dublin claims £30,000 damages for personal injuries, loss and damage suffered by her by reason of the negligence, breach of duty, breach of statutory duty and nuisance on the part of the defendant, Park Beauticians Limited, its servants and agents in and about the carrying out of certain landscaping works in Robinson Square on or about the 1st day of November 1992, in consequence whereof the plaintiff, who was in the playground of the said park at the material time with her children, was injured when, as she made her way from the slide to the swing, she stepped on some autumn leaves which, unbeknown to her, concealed a hole the size of her hand, and was thereby caused to fall to the ground.

The Civil Bill went on to give the predictable details of negligence and also particulars of personal injury, in short a broken ankle, and some out of pocket expenses.

So much for her story.

Arnold was rather excited about his different version of events the self-same afternoon. One thing that could be said in Arnold's favour was his unswerving loyalty and commitment to his client. Not for him to see the weaknesses in his client's case or the strengths in his opponent's. Someone else, Counsel perhaps, could draw attention to these. And perhaps that was Arnold's value to Mr Wilkinson. Claims Managers had enough advisors pointing out the pitfalls. It was nice to have someone on your side occasionally.

Apparently some work was going on in the playground around the time of Ms Connolly's accident and the Office of Public Works, whose park it was, had engaged Park Beauticians Limited, a firm of landscapers, to do up the park. It was their employees who were responsible for this leaf-filled hole which, it had to be admitted, did in fact exist.

Thus far, and thus far only, did the two versions accord. Park Beauticians Limited, now the defendant and Arnold's client in these Circuit Court proceedings due to be heard in a fortnight's time, had an entirely conflicting account of the plaintiff's mishap.

Around four o'clock, the two employees who were carrying out the landscaping were about to knock off for the day – a little on the early side it had to be said. There was no one else around at the time, apart from the plaintiff and her three children and as far as she was concerned she had the place and her version of events to herself.

Little did she know that her fall was observed, and her fall was not within an ass's roar of the swing and slide. It was a good fifty yards away as she noticed her three-year-old making for the gate and she gave hurried chase. As she pursued the exiting child, she tripped over the kerb that separated grass from path. She took a nasty tumble. Happily, the child heard her mother's scream and returned immediately. A good Samaritan passing outside the park heard her screams also, came to her assistance and organised an ambulance.

In a nutshell, that was the confrontation that lay ahead.

"Now Mac, you can't say I don't give you good cases. The coconut case may have been one against the head for an assortment of reasons, but there doesn't seem to be any hidden agenda here, no potholes as it were. A chance to restore the balance. Mr Wilkinson will be pleased."

There is nothing worse than a case your solicitor and client think you can't lose. With my brief under my arm, I made my way back to the Library.

Arnold's phone calls stepped up in the interval between my visit to his office and the case. Six twenty-five most evenings. In addition, every time he came down to the Four Courts during that fortnight, he called me out to offload some entirely irrelevant development and, *en passant*, to add something about the importance of a win, particularly having regard to Mr Wilkinson's aversion for fraudulent claims. At this rate, I would be lucky if I wasn't in St John of God's by the time the case was called. Luckily, this had been quite a busy term and I had not had too much time to think of the pressure I was being put under in relation to Ms Connolly's case.

"You didn't think life was fair, now did you Mac? These things are sent to try us. Anyway, you are getting far too worked up about your cases. The good barrister doesn't care whether he wins or loses. He is a professional, hired to do a job. He does it to the best of his ability and a good result is but a bonus."

My best friend Mark and I were discussing my case over breakfast in the Barrister's Restaurant. This was a recent change in my schedule – an earlier DART and breakfast in the Library. This way, I beat the traffic and now that I had some paperwork to do – don't get me wrong, I still had plenty of free time – it gave me an opportunity to do it in the Law Library rather than have to hawk it home in the evening. Once the Library filled up for the day there was precious little chance of working at your desk.

The first thing I had done when I came in was to consult the Legal Diary on the pillar to find out what judge I had drawn. O' Brien. Of all the judges on the Circuit Court Bench, why did it have to be O'Brien?

"It's easy for you to talk like that, with your father a solicitor and your cosy Chancery practice, nice long cases, nice fees, not at the whim of insurance magnates. You are not exactly what one might call 'on the hazard'," I said.

"Easy on, Mac, no need to get personal. It isn't all plain sailing on our side of the Bar, you know."

"I know. You're right, I am a bit worked up. Arnold has me this way with all his talk of needing a win. I've read the papers several times. If my witnesses are telling the truth, then this is a fraudulent claim. It would be a nice one to bring home. As Arnold says, 'Mr Wilkinson would be pleased.' But who do we draw? O'Brien. The most pro-plaintiff judge in the Western world. It just isn't fair."

"You're right about O'Brien anyway. But there is nothing you can do about that. Tell Arnold and Mr Moneybags about him. Tell them his reputation. Tell them the case of the fellow who went into the supermarket and lay down on the ground and started calling for an ambulance and was whisked off to hospital. How could he have known that the entire drama was being recorded on an overhead security camera? O'Brien was shown the video and yet he reserved his decision overnight to see if there was any way he could find for the plaintiff. Tell them that with this judge the outcome, even on your own evidence, is far from certain and that it may be necessary to appeal."

Mark was right. I left my fry untouched and went off to the consultation.

We only had the two witnesses, Connors and Brady, and the doctor on standby. I was hoping we might not need him.

Connors was all right, but I didn't like Brady. Too opinionated. Too belligerent.

"Mr Brady, would you mind telling me your account of this woman's accident?" I asked innocently, as I had asked a hundred witnesses before him, totally unaware of the passion brewing in the breast of Mr Brady.

"In fact I would mind, Mr O'Meara."

"McNamara," I interjected quickly. This fellow had better be kept in his box.

"All right then. McNamara. I do mind. First of all, this man here," referring irreverently to Arnold, "told me to be in here at twenty five past nine, which I was on the dot. It is now five past ten. I had to get a taxi to be in here on time. If I had known it was not going to happen until now, I could have walked and still been early."

"Mr Brady, I can assure you that you will be refunded your taxi fare," interposed Arnold, switching to his placatory mode.

"Secondly, Mr O'Meara, sorry, *McNamara*, I spent a lot of time some months back preparing a statement and would have thought you would have read it before now," Brady continued, with no intention of being prevented from completing his litany of complaints.

"I can assure you that Mr McNamara has read his brief very thoroughly, Mr Brady," said Arnold, unnecessarily coming to my rescue. "This is just his way of getting you to tell your story in your own words, as if you were in the witness box."

"Exactly, Mr Brady, I have read every line of your two page statement."

"There you are, you see? It's three pages."

"Quite so, three pages. Of course. I would just like you to tell me now in your own words," I said, echoing Arnold.

"Why can't you just hand my statement to the judge?"

Because you are not an imbecile and you're perfectly capable of giving your evidence orally, I almost replied, but said instead, "Because that's not the way the courts work in this jurisdiction. However, it's a very interesting idea and the next time I am talking to the judge, I'll mention it to him. I'm sure he'll do something about introducing it immediately." I couldn't help myself from being cheeky.

"There's no need to get sarcastic, mate." I wasn't sure if he said 'mate' or 'Mac'. Both were unacceptable coming from him. "I was just trying to be helpful."

Mr Brady then treated us to a faithful recital of the contents of his three page statement. No one could be in any doubt about the fact that it was learnt off. One had the distinct impression that, as with a familiar prayer, were he to be interrupted he would never be able to pick up where he left off and would have to return to "go".

This fellow was clearly going to be a disaster. If he recited his evidence, the judge would pay no attention to it and one way or another he seemed fated to antagonise him, either by being argumentative or by being smart. I left Arnold to suggest to him how he might give his evidence without making it obvious that he had memorised it word for word. Coaching, like touting, was out. At least for Counsel.

How much luck can one have? As if O'Brien wasn't enough,

I had Brady on top of him.

We hurried to the call-over. Court Nine. O'Brien already sitting.

"*Connolly v. Park Beauticians Limited,*" announced the registrar.

Someone I didn't know, didn't even recognise, was on his feet as I made my way to the top of the crowded court.

"I appear for the plaintiff, my Lord. Or, at least my master, Mr Handy, does. I wonder my Lord, could your Lordship say not before two o'clock as my master is detained in the High Court, but he informs me it will finish by lunch hour at the latest?" requested the devil.

As I forged a path through the crowd, I didn't know whose audacity impressed me more, master or devil.

"Certainly," said the judge.

"But my Lord," I said from behind a colleague's back, "I'm for the defendant and all my witnesses are ready. This is the first I've heard of this application. If we lose our place, we may not got on today."

"I'm sure, Mr McNamara, you wouldn't like to take your colleague short."

Handy, I thought to myself, *I'll take him any way I can.* "Of course not, my Lord. It's just that I wouldn't like to lose my place."

"Very well then, not before two o'clock. Who knows, Mr McNamara, perhaps there will be some developments in the meantime," said his Lordship, smiling a knowing smile. O' Brien liked settlements.

"May it please your Lordship." And the case not yet started. Mr Brady wanted to know if it would have made a difference had I been in the courtroom on time.

The nerve of Handy. No prior communication. Simply send the devil in and ask for the case to be put back. Now what would have happened had I made that application as Counsel for the defendant? I could hear it now – "I'm afraid, Mr McNamara, the inconvenience of Counsel has never been accepted as grounds for an adjournment. If you aren't ready to go on at eleven o'clock, there are nine hundred other Juniors in the Library and I am sure at least one of them could be ready, willing and able in the time-honoured formula."

Nothing for it but to go for a long coffee. One of the most tedious duties is coffee with the witnesses. Even Arnold had that much *nous*. Mr Wilkinson would be a different matter of course, but because of the determined stand he was taking on this case, he had not even bothered to show. Arnold sent Brady and Connors off for a coffee and we delayed to give them a head start. Of course, as luck would have it, the only free seats were guess where? Right beside Connors and Brady, so I had to listen to Brady's insights into the legal system for the next half hour. At the first moment I slipped away, as the private investigators say, on a pretext.

Between coffee and two o'clock, I had plenty of time to think, mostly badly, of Handy. Like Browne up in Letterkenny, Handy was a bit ahead of himself. Not just the fact that, while junior to me, he had a devil of his very own, the first of his year to take on this status duty. I wouldn't like to minimise that fact either, but that performance that morning was another example. We were a bit short in the tooth to be sending the fledgling devil in to ask the court to wait until we were ready. And still it worked. Mainly when other people did it. I was sure that O'Brien would have wiped the floor with the young lad, but no. *Au contraire*, as the Europeans would say. Quite *au contraire*.

Handy had a cherub-like face and, at a push, looked as if he might be sitting the Leaving Cert that June. Superimposed on such youthful appearance was a pair of glasses, entirely unnecessary, entirely unprescribed, solely for ageing purposes. Self-confidence that didn't just border but trespassed on the arrogant oozed from every pore. From year one he had the infuriating habit of summoning his colleagues by finger to his perch by the pillar where, conspiratorially, he would share with them the amount of the extravagant cheque and the identity of the posh office from which it had come.

I was seething by the time I encountered him at five to two outside Court Nine. Every pound of jealousy and resentment which I had felt for him had assumed actuarial proportions by the time I got to speak to him.

"Where the hell were you this morning, Gerard? We were all set to go. What do you mean by sending your devil in to put it back and without as much as mentioning it to me? I was made to look a complete fool in front of my solicitor and client," I said without drawing breath.

"Sorry, old man," replied Gerard, without much sign of repentance.

"Well, that doesn't explain anything. Where were you?" I was anxious to stitch this one in.

"You don't want to know," Handy replied.

"Oh yes I do," I said in pantomime fashion.

"Well, if you really want to know, I had two other Circuit actions on and a motion in the Supreme."

He was right, I didn't want to know. He had made more money already today than I had made all week, for heaven's sake.

"Your devil said you were detained in the High Court. Misleading the court on top of everything else."

"Don't be pedantic, Mac."

"Well, you could have mentioned it to me," I added lamely.

"Okay, I will next time," he said with the air of one who knew that it was likely to be repeated sooner rather than later. "What about this one?" he enquired, anxious to move on.

"Not a hope," I said. "My fellow hasn't even bothered to come down. Strict instructions to go the whole way."

"Seems straightforward enough. Fell in a hole. Your hole. Broke her ankle. Say twenty thousand?" Handy summarised.

"Two different cases, it would appear," I shot back.

"Not a hole in sight. Your client fell as she was dashing to prevent her child from going out the gate."

"My lady seems honest. Obviously, I'll take a discount for the risk...God, she's got a great pair of legs."

"I beg your pardon?"

"Geraldine, wonderful legs. She's just gone by. I'd give a big discount for a go at her," said Gerard, sharing his fantasies.

"I see. Well I can't speak for Geraldine," I said, eventually getting onto Handy's wavelength, "but I can tell you that there is not a penny for Priscilla," I emphasised, secretly glad that my instructions coincided with my desire to make life as difficult as possible for Handy.

"*Connolly v. Park Beauticians Limited*," the crier announced as he threw his head out the door. We gathered up our papers and our fantasies and went within.

"No developments, Mr McNamara? How long will this take, Mr Handy?" asked Judge O'Brien in deference to the long-established judicial commitment to getting home as early as possible, now known elegantly as case management.

"Should easily finish within the hour my Lord. Except for one problem."

"What's that, Mr Handy?" asked the judge.

"My doctor, my Lord. I am afraid he is operating this afternoon. He was here this morning."

"So were we," I couldn't help myself adding *sotto voce*, meaning it was just about audible to the Bench.

"Most unfortunate, Mr Handy," said the judge in reference to the waste of the doctor's time, not mine.

"With your Lordship's permission, I will call him first thing tomorrow morning."

"Very well," said his agreeable Lordship. I couldn't get over the ease with which Handy was getting his way. The omens were not exactly sparkling in my direction.

Handy called his engineer to give us the distance from various blades of grass to different ESB poles.

Garland was the doyen of the Forensic Engineers and took himself frightfully seriously. To say that he didn't suffer fools gladly would be to suggest, in his case, that he was tolerant. He barely suffered himself. The judges loved him. He was precise, reliable and didn't waste time, except in moving to the witness box. Nothing hurried about that. If he had been the central witness in a tribunal of inquiry, he could not have conducted himself with greater gravity. Once installed, he settled himself with great deliberation, donned his glasses and spread his map and photographs before him.

Counsel might now address him.

Handy brought him through his photographs of Robinson Park, most of which consisted of shots of the playground area, ending up with a few close-ups of the hole into which it was alleged the plaintiff fell. Then the map with every conceivable elevation of the hole.

Naturally, all the measurements were calculated in metric, so it was necessary to convert into feet and inches. Really, it was an awful pity that this wasn't a more important case. He deserved better. This would have been one of the run-of-the-mill cases for Garland, who was anxious, having been hanging around all morning, to get away to another court or another investigation.

There really wasn't anything to cross-examine Garland about, particularly as our case was a complete conflict of evidence in that we were saying the accident happened elsewhere in the park.

However, a small registered message arrived from Arnold just as I was about to say "no questions". It read, *ask him about the dimensions of the hole*. It was difficult to see why we should ask any questions about the hole, but in fairness to Arnold, I supposed what he had in mind was that if we lost in relation to where the accident happened, then we could fall back on contributory negligence for failing to see the hole. Not good tactically because really we had to go for broke. The accident either happened where she said or where we said. No half-way house. Not all of this occurred to me instantaneously, not clearly anyhow, but I had my instructions.

"Just before you go, Mr Garland," I said, stopping the witness in his departing tracks. Garland had enough experience of giving evidence and being cross-examined to expect that there would be no cross-examination here. However, he hadn't allowed for Arnold.

Unwisely, I delayed him. "Mr Garland, as I think you are aware, the defendant's case is going to be that the accident happened elsewhere in the park?"

"Yes, I am."

"In fact, I think we can see where the defendant places the plaintiff's fall in one of your photographs. Yes, there in photograph number twenty-two?"

"Well, I haven't been informed as to precisely where it is your witnesses say she fell."

"I think you can take it from me that it is shown there in photograph twenty-two. There's a gate visible to the left of the photograph."

"That is correct."

"Well, it was in the vicinity of that gate that my witnesses say she fell."

"If you say so."

"How far is that from the playground area?"

"About fifty metres."

"Talking about measurements for a moment, I would like to know the dimensions of the hole in case the judge accepts the plaintiff's account, in which event contributory negligence would arise."

"Mr McNamara, I already gave that evidence. I gave the dimensions of the hole in metric and in feet and inches. Also, the dimensions appear on the map. However, if you insist, I will repeat myself. Please pay attention this time."

Oops. Thank you, Arnold. But how did I miss it? Garland proceeded to repeat himself, with exaggerated deliberation, adding unnecessarily, "Now did you get it this time?"

"Thank you, Mr Garland," I said sheepishly.

If Arnold handed me fifty notes I wasn't asking Garland another thing. Garland retired.

Ms Priscilla Connolly made her buxom way to the box. If she had dressed herself up to the hilt to impress the judge, it was a waste of time. Completely lost on O'Brien. Not that he was the other way, simply that on the Bench, unlike some of his colleagues, he concentrated on the task in hand. From the point of view of impressing him, it was sufficient that she was a plaintiff. Male or female, young or old, rich or poor, it didn't matter to O'Brien. If you were plaintiff, he would do the best for you.

If her appearance was lost on O'Brien, not so on Handy, whose nickname, needless to say, rhymed with his surname. Handy removed his bifocals to appreciate in full the dimensions of the witness.

Priscilla told the court that she lived with her partner and three children. No sign of the partner and no need to mention two of the three children who were running up and down the side aisle, only stopping each time they reached me to giggle and point at my wig. Presumably that was Priscilla's mother sitting beside her.

This was a confident team. Handy, Garland, Priscilla. Not as much as a scintilla of uncertainty. She crossed her legs in compliance with Handy's unspoken wishes and proceeded to give her evidence as one born to the witness box.

Most convincingly, she told the court about going to the park with her three children, spending time in the playground. Shortly before she intended to depart, she had just been pushing her eldest on the swing when she moved to the slide to receive her descending youngest. She trod on the hidden hole with fateful consequences. As luck would have it, who was passing by the park at the time but her mother, who arranged for an ambulance. She detailed her injury.

By the time she finished her evidence-in-chief, there was no doubt about where the judge's sympathy lay.

"Ms Connolly, I must put it to you that your accident happened elsewhere in the park," I opened, opting to go to the heart of the matter immediately.

"Why?" came her obscure reply.

"Why what?" I asked, uncomprehending.

"Why must you?"

Oh, I see. A smart aleck. Well, Priscilla, this may not be a clever tack. "Because my client requires me to," I responded.

"Well you client wasn't there, was he?"

This was too good to be true. Surely, the witness was digging her own grave. In front of many other judges this cheek would not go down well, but before O'Brien, who was pro-plaintiff, I couldn't be sure.

"In fact, he was. At least his employees were. Two of them. Saw the whole thing, Ms Connolly. Your accident happened fifty yards from the playground when you spotted your youngest making for the gate and you gave chase. Isn't that right?"

"Lies, a pack of lies. No question of it happening that way. As God's my witness, it happened as I said."

I couldn't have asked for better. I hoped O'Brien was taking it in.

"There was no one in the park when I fell, except my children. If your two heroes were really there, why didn't they come and help me?" Priscilla asked after an interval.

"They can deal with that when they're giving evidence. The fact is they were there and saw where you fell and it was not in the playground. Now tell me, Ms Connolly, how many children did you have with you?"

"I told you. Three."

"And what time did you arrive in the park?"

"I told you that, too. Were you not listening?"

Clearly she had been listening. And learning, too. From Garland. "Well, Ms Connolly?"

"I'll tell you once more, Mr McNamara. But only once. Pay attention this time."

While I didn't think these answers were doing her case much good, they weren't exactly flattering me either. I felt I should do something. "My Lord, I would ask you to direct the witness to control herself and answer the questions."

O'Brien didn't answer for a moment. I assumed he was deciding how to warn the witness.

"Frankly, Mr McNamara, I think the witness has a point. She has given all this evidence and I see no reason why we should have an action replay of all that is said."

I see. Well, so much for trade unionism and backing your own. Not so long since you were down here O'Brien. And what's worse, it looked as if she may not have been damaging her case in his eyes.

I backed off and asked one further question to keep Arnold's paper supply happy.

"My witnesses will say, Ms Connolly, that the person who came to your assistance was a good deal younger than your mother?"

"What age do you think my mother is?"

"I take it that you disagree?" I asked, resuming my seat.

I was happy enough with my cross-examination, but there was a long way to go. Oftentimes in these cases you were at your strongest before you went into evidence. Always, in fact. For the moment, the plaintiff's confident start had at least been slowed. In light of the manner in which Priscilla gave her evidence under cross-examination, O'Brien surely must have a reservation.

"Come up, Mr Connors," I invited.

Connors was grand, neither defensive nor aggressive. He neither said too much nor too little. Calm and restrained. The scales were moving in our favour. A pity Mr Wilkinson wasn't here to see it. However, on a head count, it was still the plaintiff's word against Mr Connors'. The battle was too finely balanced. It needed another witness to tilt the scales in our favour.

"Mr Brady please," I announced, concealing my hesitation about calling this witness.

I was worried about how to control Brady. He was one of those know-all witnesses you get from time to time. No sooner in the place than he is full of theories as to how the courts should be run. Get rid of the wig and gown for one. Start at nine o'clock like everyone else for another. "And why do you need both solicitors and barristers anyway?" And other tedious questions tediously asked, as if for the first time. At the slightest attempt at the forbidden coaching, I was assured, "I have been here before, you know. This isn't my first visit. And I have seen you lawyers on the telly. You don't hold any fear for me. I can handle myself."

Armed with this assurance, I feared the worst. I didn't have to wait long. "Mr Brady, do you recall the afternoon of the first November 1992?" I asked innocuously enough.

"Why do you ask me? You know I do," Brady replied. Getting us off to a poor, if predictable, start.

"Because this is the way evidence is presented, Mr Brady."

"I know all about presenting evidence, Mr McNamara, and I can tell you that I am none too impressed by what I have seen here this afternoon."

"Thank you, Mr Brady. If you would just confine yourself to answering my questions. I think you were in Robinson Park?"

"Why do you keep asking me questions you know the answer to?"

"Were you or were you not in the park, Mr Brady?"

"Sort of."

"What do you mean 'sort of', Mr Brady?"

"Well, in fact I was in a hut," replied Brady.

"In a *hut*, Mr Brady?" I asked, unable to conceal my surprise. There was nothing about a hut in his three page statement.

"Yes Mr O'Meara, in a hut."

"*McNamara* please, Mr Brady."

"Very well, *McNamara*."

At this stage I could conceal neither my surprise nor my exasperation. I could see Park Beauticians Limited going down the tubes. But what else could I have done? I had to call him. The judge knew that there was someone with Connors and if I hadn't called him it would have looked suspicious. Not that it was looking much better now and Brady not yet under cross-examination.

"And do tell us, Mr Brady, where was this hut?" I asked.

"Oh, the hut was in the park," said Mr Brady.

"I see. Well, were you able to see Ms Connolly from the hut?"

"We were."

"Tell the court what you saw happen to her," I commanded, hoping that Brady would become a little more amenable. In vain.

"Why are you asking me to repeat all of this? I told Mr O' Reilly. I wrote out a long statement and I went through it word for word with you ten times, if at all, just a short time ago. Now do I really have to say it all again? Wouldn't it be easier if you simply gave my statement to the judge?" Brady was clearly impressed by this idea of his for legal reform.

And what about the hut? What about the fact that there is no refer-ence to the hut in your long statement? I thought to myself. I was losing patience.

"I'm afraid the legal system hasn't advanced quite as far as you would wish, but perhaps it will have by the next time you visit us, Mr Brady. Now if you would just tell his Lordship what you saw happen to the plaintiff."

Unfortunately, what little coaching had taken place didn't avail Mr Brady at all. He proceeded to recite his three pages of evi-dence in much the same way as he might have a dreaded and little-understood poem for the Leaving Cert in years gone by. He hardly paused for breath.

I left him to Handy, who was very interested in the hut.

"Tell us about the hut, Mr Brady. Where exactly was it?"

"About fifty yards from the playground and opposite the gate."

"How very convenient. And what were you and Mr Connors doing in it?"

"Getting ready to go home."

"Is that all?"

"Well, we were having a cup of tea and playing a game of cards."

"In the hut?"

"Yes."

"About four o' clock?"

"Yes."

"It was getting dark?"

"Yes."

"And you saw Ms Connolly fall?"

"Yes."

"Why didn't you go to her assistance?"

"Because we didn't want to get involved."

"Why not?"

"Frankly, because that day we should have been on another job altogether and if the boss found out, we'd have been in right trouble. And anyway, someone else arrived."

"Her mother?"

"No. The woman looked much younger."

Not a word of all this in three pages of illegible A4. I hadn't anticipated that Brady would be this bad.

"How come we heard none of this from Mr Connors?"

"Ask him."

"Of course, if the accident happened where Ms Connolly says, then she fell in a hole of your making. Isn't that right? And you or at least your employer would be responsible. Isn't that right?"

"She was nowhere near the hole."

"That's what *you* say, Mr Brady."

"That's what I saw."

"I put it to you that your evidence is a total fabrication invented for the purpose of self-protection. I don't know whether you were in the hut or not. Indeed, in the park or not. But I suggest that you have no idea where Ms Connolly fell and that you did not see her fall."

"You're wrong there. I saw her fall all right and she fell just before she reached the gate, chasing her child. I looked up from the cards at just that moment."

"Quite a coincidence, Mr Brady."

"Call it what you like, Mr Handy. That's how it happened." Handy's cross-examination was finished.

That was my case. All that remained was the medical evidence the following day.

Arnold and Connors and Brady and I discussed the case outside in the corridor. Brady, who didn't quite appreciate that he had just landed a moderately strong case on the top floor of Liberty Hall, was on the attack. In particular, he had a few retrospective ideas for cross-examination.

My patience was exhausted at this stage. I intimated to him that I had had enough of his impertinence and added that, for future reference, it might be helpful to Counsel if, in going to the trouble of making a lengthy statement, he were to dabble, however briefly, in the truth. On that note, I exited, pleased that I had taken a stand.

My friend Mark was very anxious to know how things had gone in front of O'Brien. Over coffee and a slice of banoffi in the Barrister's Restaurant, I gave him a blow by blow account, beginning with Handy's performance in sending the devil in to have the case put back to two o'clock. I told him that we were going nicely until Brady gave his evidence, which was so bad that by now O'Brien would have probably forgotten any negative impression he might have had of the plaintiff. Obviously, the medical evidence wasn't going to change things on the liability front. Wilkinson was coming down for the finish.

I bumped into Arnold on my way back to the Library. By then, I had cooled down and had begun to worry if my departure from the post-mortem had been a trifle precipitate.

"Arnold, I hope you didn't mind me saying what I said to Brady upstairs and leaving as I did, but really I couldn't take any more of his rudeness."

"What are you talking about, Mac?" Arnold looked at me, puzzled.

"It's just that I might have been a bit rash in what I said after the case and a bit abrupt in my departure. I hope that I didn't embarrass you in any way."

"Not at all. Don't know what you are talking about, in fact. I thought you were fine."

"Oh, good," I replied. How did Arnold not know what I was talking about? Did he not notice me storming out?

I gave the case some thought overnight and even mentioned it to Rachel. Arnold had made it very clear that a win was important. Impress Wilkinson and all that. But what could I do? I thought the case had gone quite well until Brady decided to sink us. With only the medical evidence left there was nothing further to be done. I could make submissions, but that would surely antagonise O'Brien, who would tell me in no uncertain terms that he was quite capable of mastering the facts.

There was just one question that Rachel thought might be asked of the plaintiff's doctor.

I was still trying to make up my mind about that very question at the hearing the next morning as Mr McInerney, orthopedic surgeon, gave his evidence about Priscilla's severe ankle fracture.

The right answer might tilt the balance in my favour. *Might.* I couldn't be sure. On the other hand, if the judge was coming down on the defendant's side, then the wrong answer could rescue the case for the plaintiff.

I was in two minds, hardly listening to the medical evidence, which I did not notice ending.

"Mr McNamara, do I take it that you have no questions for Mr McInerney?" his Lordship inquired impatiently.

I rose slowly, tentatively, almost as if I was not rising at all. I wasn't committing myself to either rising or not rising.

"Just one question, my Lord," I heard myself say before I had finally made up my mind whether or not to ask it. *Nothing for it now but to ask the question.* "Mr McInerney, you saw the plaintiff immediately upon her admission to hospital, isn't that right?"

"That is so. Yes."

"Did she tell you how the accident happened?" All or nothing.

"Did she tell me how the accident happened? Let me see. I don't seem to have anything in my report about it. Just let me consult my notes."

There was a short delay while Mr McInerney located the relevant entry. It was customary for doctors to take a history of the accident. This was taking a little time. The courtroom was completely silent except for the shuffling of the doctor's cards. Tension heightened. The answer may or not matter in the long run. O'Brien may have his mind made up and this answer might not change him. But for the moment, you could sense the significance of this question and the delayed answer.

"Oh, yes. I have it now. Yes. She told me that she was running to catch her child who was heading for the gate when she fell. Yes. That is what I have written down here. Does that answer your question?"

"Thank you, Doctor. It most certainly does." I resumed my seat with a certain ceremony. I could be wrong, but I thought I caught a look of disappointment in his Lordship's eye.

I didn't bother calling my doctor. The case was over, except for the judgment.

I looked behind me. Wilkinson was sitting in the corner. If only now we could get the right result. The court was quite full, as all of the day's cases had yet to be heard. This was a moment in the sun.

Judge O'Brien delivered himself of what was for him quite a detailed judgment, in which he summarised the evidence witness by witness. It was impossible to know which way he was going to end up. Now he was with you, now he wasn't. He only had to decide the case on the balance of probabilities, he said. This was not a criminal case. He didn't have to be certain. Also, if he was wrong there was the comfort of a higher court. Yesterday afternoon, he felt that the plaintiff had discharged that onus, though not by much. He was inclined to find for the plaintiff – didn't he realise what this case meant for my career? – but he could not overlook the doctor's evidence this morning and accordingly, not without reservation, he was finding for the defendant. Without costs.

"May it please your Lordship," I said. *Your magnificent Lordship.*

I owe Rachel one, I thought to myself. However, then and there any credit that was going I gladly kept to myself.

We bowed most deeply and withdrew. Brady was anxious to tell me how the result was in the bag all the time and really was it necessary to go through all that mumbo-jumbo to arrive at a decision. He still thought his idea of written statements was a good one. I was in no mood to talk to Brady, whom I happily ignored. I was keen to shake the outstretched hand of Mr Wilkinson.

"Well done, Dermot. A brave question. And it worked." I positively glowed with pride. "What about an early lunch?" asked Mr Wilkinson.

"Thank you. I'd love to."

"The Lord Edward, perhaps?"

Where else?

Dermot's Posh Brief

There is no question – it is *the* most prestigious address in Dublin: *The Newman House Hotel, St Stephen's Green*. It sits on the southwest corner of the Green, risen from the ashes of its famous forebear, the Russell Hotel. More than a touch of class. Neither jeans nor mobiles here. "No riff-raff," as Basil Fawlty would say. In this age of inclusiveness, its policy of exclusivity was a little unexpected. It was as if the proprietor had not quite made up his mind whether or not he wanted guests at all. They tended to spoil the tranquillity of this elegant retreat from the hubbub of city life. Even such exclusive guests.

In his day, von Karajan. Today, Anne-Sophie Mutter. During a Pinter season at the Gate, Harold himself. Top-drawer performers and artists only. None of your pop stars from The Point. From the world of sport, the Aga Khan teams from the Royal Dublin Society. Not a chance of Ireland's soccer team getting up the steps, let alone in the door. At a push, the IRFU management. But without the team. No pre-match drinks here. Neither the fall-out from the Law Library on a Friday night nor queues on Christmas Eve. You could go across the Green for that. The Newman House Hotel was for the leaders of nations and multinationals.

It was a short walk from every conceivable facility and none. From your bedroom window you could make out the silhouettes of summer couples in the setting sun. In winter, every inch of your corner of the Green was covered with a tablecloth of frost.

In brief, a haven of excellence.

Complaints were rare in this legendary establishment, accidents rarer. The former were likely to be met with tearing up the bill and a request that the complainant not return, and the latter, complete denial. Accidents did not, *could* not happen in this harbour of health and safety. Certainly not accidents tainted with the negligence of the staff of the hotel. Which is precisely what was being alleged, albeit reluctantly, by Miss Penelope Jones.

Miss Jones insisted on the "Miss". She had no qualms about her status. She had never wanted to marry. Her passion in life was horses. Horses morning, noon and night. They fulfilled her every need, though she did not go quite as far as Catherine the Great. In that regard, she recognised and took on board that men had a certain usefulness and when the need arose, had no compunction about taking on board the man of the moment for as long or as short as was necessary. There was no shortage of men of the moment were she so inclined, but her passion for horses left her little time for such dalliances.

As a member of the British equestrian team, she had ridden for Great Britain in the four corners of the world. Not without distinction. She had never had any difficulty filling her saddle and indeed this aspect of her anatomy was the focus of universal attention and no little lust. In recent years, this had become impossible. Not the attention. Not the lust. These remained. She no longer fitted her saddle. After considerable innings, she decided to retire and become an alickadoo. Nowadays she was more likely to be gracing the commentary box than the arena.

Earlier, as a competitor, and now as an alickadoo, she enjoyed coming to Dublin once a year for the Horse Show. Relieved of the rider's responsibilities, she had more time to enjoy the après-ski. She liked the intimacy of Dublin, particularly if the rain stayed away which, through no provable fault on the part of Bord Fáilte, it tended not to do. From the Tuesday through to the Sunday, there was not a Horse Show Ball that she did not attend. Not a bottle of champagne that she did not open.

In recent years, she had taken to staying at the Newman House Hotel where, notwithstanding her forceful character and equestrian language or, if you prefer, her forceful language and equestrian character, she was a much-liked guest. She did not spend too much time in the hotel reading room, so she did not disturb the tranquillity too much. The staff was happily employed there so there was a certain continuity and many of them would have noticed that, since her retirement, her fondness for a tipple, like her size, was on the up and up. No one objected if occasionally, through a combination of consumption and weight, she encountered a little difficulty with the stairs and had to be assisted to her room. They would not do this for many of their guests, though in fairness not many of their guests would suffer the dual handicap.

The previous day, Great Britain had seen off, but only by a time fault, the zealous attentions of Paul Darragh and his Irish team-mates. Celebrations had been long and furious and just as close. The dawn of that Saturday had been well and truly consigned to history by the time Miss Jones, singing her triumphant head off, took herself, or more accurately, was taken up the long and winding stairs in the general direction of her bedroom. Only Miss Jones, and maybe not even she, knows what happened in the hours that followed. The receptionist would not disagree that when she next graced the foyer, sometime around afternoon tea, she more resembled someone who had single-handedly minded the entire All Blacks pack for eighty minutes than a Horse Show celebrant.

I am not sure how much of anything, if anything at all, I had learnt since coming to the Bar. Law? Advocacy? Even common sense, that great quality without which success at the Bar is an impossibility? I am not quite sure why, but I have often heard it offered as an explanation for the failure of the academically brilliant and the success, utterly beyond anticipation, of the academically inept. You would not have enough hands to count the number of double firsts in Classics who vanished without trace within months of their call to the Bar, nor enough hands to count the number of academically inept whose annual turnover makes tribunal fees seem like an impoverishment.

One thing I had learned was that briefs were few and far between. Victories were even fewer and farther. I was still celebrating *Connolly v. Park Beauticians Limited* of a month before and regaling anyone with an hour or two on their hands with my unexpurgated version of how success had been achieved. If, however briefly, I had entertained the notion that my overall performance in the case culminating in the favourable result might lead to a run up the alphabet of Arnold's estimation and onto his "A" team, four weeks since that red letter day when his Lordship delivered himself so wisely of his judgment had consigned that little fantasy to the places where fantasies go. Could it be, I wondered, that not having been in attendance on the second day, he had not apprised himself, or had not been apprised, of the result? Extremely unlikely, I thought, but in deference to Arnold, it may just be an outside chance. Perhaps I should phone him and casually drop something like, "You must have been pleased with the *Park Beauticians* case?" That should clear the matter up one way or another. Of course, it was always another possibility that he well knew the result, had forgotten it was me and was distributing the credit to someone else on the panel.

Like Frank, for example, who would not regard it as imperative, morally or otherwise, to disabuse Arnold of his error. Frank was a contemporary of mine, also on Arnold's panel, but higher up the rankings. He was a young man of undoubted ambition with no doubt about his ability and no qualms about marketing himself. He did not need Arnold's errors to advance his career.

One of the features of life in the Law Library is the "handover". In fact, the Library, indeed the legal system itself, could not survive without it. Come four o'clock the Library is full of agitated barristers caught in *flagrante delicto* as the saying goes or, in translation, on their feet in another court. Their case is unexpectedly still at hearing and will continue into the following day so that their other case, listed for the morrow and to which they had sworn an attention more intimate than exclusive, is crying out for a substitute. At least that is how I had observed the hand-over system in operation because I had not had personal experience of it. Not until then, that is.

Now Frank was not someone you readily associated with handing over cases. Quite the reverse. He was much more likely to be on the receiving end of the system. Not, unlike me, for any lack of work, but simply because he would add to his pile of briefs the very brief another colleague felt bound – in conscience you understand (perish the word) – to hand-over through being already overstretched. If challenged on the point, he was wont to invoke that long-established maxim of equity: "things will work out on the day". And invariably they did. For Frank. And if they didn't, you didn't hear about it from Frank. And if he had to pay the ultimate sacrifice of losing a solicitor, so what? Weren't there hundreds of them out there?

I had just returned to my seat from coffee when Frank came up to me, more than a little perturbed. "How are you fixed tomorrow, Mac?" The old question. No less treacherous because it comes from a colleague. Suffice to say that while I did not think Frank would do me any favours, I did not think he would dump me in it, either.

"I think I'm okay, but just let me see." I knew I was perfectly okay, having checked my diary earlier in the day and I knew precisely how I was fixed for each day of the week. F-R-E-E. I didn't have to pay too much attention to the entries for the following day or indeed any day that week. I had developed a little diary stratagem. First thing every Monday morning I would enter a few entirely fictitious cases for that week so that if anyone were to be looking over my shoulder, as Frank most definitely was now, the stark reality of my practice would not be immediately apparent.

Accordingly, I knew what Frank was not to know, namely that the entry for the following day owed more to that Monday morning creativity than any commitment of substance.

"As I thought. I can help you out. One or two short matters but they shouldn't take too long," I said, conveying something less than total availability, while at the same time satisfying Frank's requirements and my pride. But things are rarely that simple.

"Not good enough, I'm afraid. Solicitor insists on exclusive attention. Very important client. In fact, I am very reluctant to hand it over at all. I'll see if Reggie is free."

Sensing that I was about to lose this little game of bluff, I pretended to have another look at the lying page of my diary. "Em. They're only two motions. I'm sure I can get them adjourned," I said, affecting nonchalance and hoping to conceal what bordered on panic.

"I promised the solicitor I would get him someone who would give the case undivided attention. So much so that he wants an early morning consultation in his office. Load of nonsense if you ask me, but that's what he wants. In fact, he gave me other names but I thought you might be interested."

Of course I'm interested, I thought, *but how do I get out of all these monopoly cases I have on tomorrow?* "Look Frank, if it's that important I'll make arrangements for these two motions this afternoon. My solicitor will probably be a bit annoyed but that's my problem. I will make myself totally free for your case. Now what is it about?"

I didn't really mean him to spend the next hour and a half going over every paragraph of the brief. I could read it just as well as he could. Obviously, he was very reluctant to let it go. "Will you give the solicitor a ring just to let him know you are doing it?"

I called immediately. "Hello. Walsh, Hogan, Murray, Maguire, Phillips and Fitzsimons. Maeve speaking. May I help you?" Obviously an honours graduate from *The Irish Times* School of Secretarial Skills.

"I wonder if I could speak to Mr Phillips please?"

"I'll put you on to his secretary. May I say who is calling?"

"Dermot McNamara."

"I'll put you on hold, Dermot."

I didn't actually ask to speak to Mr Phillips' secretary, but refrained from pointing this out. There was a certain delay getting through to her. Presumably, Mr Phillips being a very busy solicitor, his secretary would be a very busy secretary. As I waited, listening to a little ditty from Pavorotti (a change from Arnold's "Three Blind Mice"), I perused the magnificent note paper of my newest instructing solicitor. There must have been forty names on the page if there was one. Apparently, in the seventies and before my time, amalgamations of smaller firms led to bigger firms and bigger names. More recently, these same bigger firms, while staying bigger, were tending to disentangle their names, presumably because the Maeves of this world were having difficulty getting their tongues around the elongated version when they were answering calls. The new fad had not yet reached Messrs. Walsh, Hogan, etc.

Time passed. Pav paved the way for Nige on Viv. Fingering the brief, I reflected. At last, a posh brief, even if it was a hand-me-down. Magnificently put together, even if it looked a trifle large for the sort of case Frank outlined to me. One proud folder after another, each boldly announcing its important contents: *AGENT'S INSTRUCTIONS, PLEADINGS, COUNSEL'S OPINIONS & ADVICE ON PROOFS* and many more until, finally, the biggest, *DISCOVERY*. It was certainly different from Arnold's briefs. I was glad Frank didn't leave it 'til the morning to hand it over. Although Frank had told me it was a personal injury case, it had all the appearances of a commercial brief likely to last the rest of the term in the High Court. Then, of course, Mr Phillips was the commercial partner.

Half an hour later and half the brief read, Mr Phillips' anxiety to speak to me was not immediately apparent when we finally spoke.

"Well, Dermot, Phillips speaking, what can I do for you?"

"Mr Phillips," I thought I should opt for the surname, for the moment at any rate, "Frank has handed me over a brief in *Jones versus Newman House Hotel.*"

"Yes, I know. Frank was on to me some time ago. I was expecting you to phone sooner. In fact, I gave Frank the names of a number of other Counsel with whom I am familiar."

"If there is any problem, Mr Phillips, I will return the brief to Frank and you can make other arrangements," I responded with great magnanimity, knowing full well that that was not an option at five o'clock the evening before the case. There was hardly anyone left in the Library at this stage.

"That won't be necessary," replied Mr Phillips, who I am sure knew well the logistical difficulty of obtaining alternative Counsel at this stage in the proceedings. "I'm sure you will do just as well. It's just that I haven't heard of you before. You do personal injuries, don't you?"

"Nothing else Mr Phillips," I replied, growing in confidence, borne of the knowledge that were I to have replied, "Well actually Mr Phillips this is my first personal injuries action" there was nothing in the world he could have done. Five o'clock in the evening. For better or worse he was stuck with me.

"It's just that this is a rather important client and I wouldn't like anything to go wrong," he continued, implying that from time to time there were clients who were not important and Mr Phillips wouldn't care less if anything, or indeed the entire thing, went hopelessly and irretrievably wrong. At least that was the inherent logic of the remark, but as Mr Phillips was not favoured with my reflection I never got to debate the issue with him.

"Mr Phillips, you can be sure that the case will have my fullest attention."

"That's another thing Dermot, I know you personal injury chappies. I may not be in that area myself, thanks be to God, but I have my ear to the ground. I know you take on several cases for the one day. Well I won't have any of it. None of that slipping off to another court. I want my client to be properly looked after. Is that clear?"

I didn't care for his attitude but I thought better of so enlightening him. The words that sprang to utterance were, "You need have no worries on that, or on any other count, Mr Phillips. In fact I have one or two other matters listed in my diary," I said, risking another lie, "but I have already made arrangements to have them attended to by other Counsel. Your client, indeed *our* client, will have my exclusive attention."

This must have convinced Mr Phillips because his final contribution to the late afternoon's discussion in relation to his very important case was, "Very well then. Meet in my office at eight thirty." He rang off without waiting for an answer.

I was half the night reading the brief. Had it been pared down to the strictly relevant facts, an hour or an hour and a half would have done it. But no. There wasn't a word that Miss Jones had uttered in the three years since her accident that wasn't recorded in triplicate in this brief. Not just in attendances on her, but copious statements. Not a doctor in this country or in hers who hadn't been seen over those three years and who hadn't furnished an unending report. God spare us from unending reports, be they medical or engineering. "Brevity is the soul of wit," as the bard said. Were there ever truer words? It should be written up in triplicate on the office wall of every commercial partner who dabbles in personal injury litigation.

As I climbed into bed at about one thirty, I suggested to Rachel that I might travel in with her in the morning as, for once, we were going to neighbouring city centre squares. Unfortunately, as luck would have it, it was the one morning that week that Rachel didn't have to be in that early. Otherwise, of course, we should have travelled together. DART as usual therefore. We were too long into our marriage for me to begin insisting at this stage on my entitlement to our sole conveyance, the convertible Golf. That was a battle long since lost. Rachel's father had bought it for her as a wedding present and it was not something Rachel was prepared to concede a 50 per cent interest in. She barely shared it with herself she was so possessive of it.

Such was my enthusiasm that I arrived a full half hour early for the consultation. This wouldn't have mattered too much on a dry day. Or even on a day when a raincoat or an umbrella might have offered some protection against the elements. I haven't any personal experience of a monsoon but insofar as I have seen such a downpour on the television, it is but the poor sister of what was falling on the centre of Dublin that early morning between eight and half past. I lapped the square. Countless times. What else could I do?

Mr Phillips wanted to know if I had any trouble parking my car. How Mr Phillips could think for even a moment that I had travelled by car when small ponds had formed in every crevice of my outer garments I will never know.

His indifference to my condition, or at the most charitable, his complete lack of observation, I will never forgive. "No trouble at all Mr Phillips," was my cowardly reply, preferring his assumption that my convertible BMW was parked outside his hall door to the stark and penurious truth.

We made our way through empty reception areas, down endless corridors, up umpteen floors until, at last, the library where the engineer, two doctors (the remainder on standby), Amy and Sophie, two beautiful apprentices and, of course, the plaintiff herself were gathered around the mahogany table. Not to mention the founding fathers who adorned the wall.

Mr Phillips introduced me to Miss Jones. "A bit on the young side, don't you think Phillips? Has he the experience?" she asked, not even bothering to whisper.

"No doubt about that, Penelope. I have chosen carefully," replied Mr Phillips, lying through that part of his anatomy which from time immemorial has been associated with the uttering of untruths. "A leading Counsel in the field, if you'll excuse the pun."

Miss Jones not only excused it, she enjoyed it. Whilst I recognised it for what it was, no more than a reassurance for the client, a mere empty formula of words, I still basked in the hollow compliment. My confidence soared at the thought of being regarded, no matter how insincerely, as leading Counsel. I was making my way to the top of the table to occupy the presiding chair when Mr Phillips, arriving there before me, pointed to a more anonymous seat at the side between one of the doctors and either Amy or Sophie – I hadn't caught which was which. Not a position of any advantage.

Not that it mattered. I wasn't intended to get a word in, nor did I. Mr Phillips ran the entire show. He was completely at home – his client, his office, his conference, his team. Even his apprentices asked a question or two. Insofar as he invited my participation it was to endorse his outline of how he expected me to run the case, finishing with, "Isn't that so, Dermot?"

On one occasion I tried to raise the particulars of contributory negligence, but to no avail. He simply dismissed them out of hand. "Nothing more than the usual generalisations that form part and parcel of every case. A figment of Counsel's imagination. No more, no less. And really we shouldn't waste time discussing them." Penelope agreed. And we moved on to the next topic of Phillips' choice.

A little after half past nine I had the temerity to suggest that we might interrupt this entirely one-sided and uncritical preparation of our case and resume as soon as the cross-city journey allowed outside Judge Bradley's court. Mr Phillips ordered a taxi for his equestrian client and her entourage and, as he ushered me as he thought to my convertible BMW outside his hall door, mentioned, more as an afterthought, that unfortunately he could not join us in the Four Courts due to the fact that Mr de Villiers was flying in from South Africa to close some multi-million deal with the IDA. I don't think he heard me say, "I quite understand" as he closed the door and I headed out for another soaking.

It wasn't a coincidence that the first person I met as I entered the Law Library was Frank. "Well, Dermot, how is my case going?"

"Fine, Frank. No time to talk now. Must get up quickly to Bradley." I darted down to the robing room and Frank, laden down with briefs, headed out into the Round Hall where the High Court personal injury cases are heard.

I robed quickly and made my way without delay to Bradley's court, Court 7 on the second floor of the building. You would be forgiven for thinking that the traffic on the quays was actually passing through the courtroom, such was the noise from outside. A careful balance had to be struck on an hourly basis between opening the window and allowing in the sound of bus and lorry on the one hand and closing the window and putting up with the stifling heat on the other. Control of this balance, like everything else in the building, was in the hands of his magnificent Lordship.

It hadn't occurred to me to arrange a rendezvous with Miss Jones *et al*. I had simply assumed that having crossed the city, they would have proceeded straight to Court 7. As I entered the courtroom, I looked in vain for evidence of my team. In truth it was difficult to be certain, because I doubt you could have fit more people into Landsdowne Road for the match against England. The court was packed. Plaintiffs, defendants, witnesses, doctors, engineers, all assembled for the call over at 10.30am. All, that is, except the visiting Miss Jones and her assembly.

The door of the chambers opened, the crier preceded the judge. "All rise." His Lordship emerged. Judge Bradley. For the next few hours our collective fates were in his hands. The most powerful man, if not in the land, then in the room. Judge Bradley was not a man to rush or be rushed. He made his most deliberate way to his bench. A serious judge who left no stone unturned. "Please call the list, Mr Bradley," he commanded the registrar of the same name but without relationship.

The registrar obliged. "*Jones v. Newman House Hotel*," he called.

In my rush I had forgotten to check the list and did not realise that my case was first and so was completely taken aback when my case was called so soon. After a pause I heard myself say, "My Lord, I think I am in that case."

"Mr McNamara, you are either in the case or you are not. Now which is it? I have a lot of work to get through."

"Of course, my Lord. I wasn't thinking. I am in it. I'm for the plaintiff."

"We are making progress, Mr McNamara. Now if you would be good enough to share with us how long the case is likely to take – in the time-honoured custom of the court."

"Of course, my Lord. Two hours, my Lord," I said and added without thinking, "well normally, my Lord. I mean, before any of your Lordship's colleagues the case would take two hours but before your Lordship I think it is more likely to take three to four hours, my Lord." To the delight of the well-paid audience. Coffee break gossip was secure and the court only a minute in session. "Your Lordship is so thorough," I added feebly.

"I see. Well thank you Mr McNamara for that little insight. A little feedback is always welcome. Now Mr Bradley, if we could get on with the list. I gather that Mr McNamara's case is not the only case listed this morning".

I resumed my seat with considerable fluster as the registrar, highly amused, proceeded to call the remainder of the list.

"*Murphy v. O'Sullivan*," announced the registrar, still struggling with his high amusement.

"Two hours," I heard my colleague say.

"Is that my two hours or Mr McNamara's?" the judge said to a wildly enthusiastic audience. Coffee just couldn't be missed this morning.

My colleague had the good sense to leave the humour to his Lordship. "I rather think your Lordship will complete the case comfortably within the estimated two hours," I heard the other side of the case offer obsequiously.

"Well that is certainly a relief. It looks as if we might get through some of the day's business at least," concluded his Lordship, who was as reluctant to let go of this little episode as the proverbial dog the bone.

I slipped further down the bench. Thank God Miss Jones wasn't in court. Not to mention Mr Phillips, who I was sure was having a better day. Nor his beautiful sidekicks, wherever they were at that moment. I attempted a furtive look over my shoulder just to confirm their absence. Oh, no. Right behind me. Big mouth himself. Jennings. With the broadest grin plastered all over his wicked face. No possibility now of any coffee table in the restaurant not being regaled with the maximum exaggeration, should that prove necessary. How did Jennings do it? His impeccable ability to be in precisely the wrong place at the wrong time. "Nice one, Mac. Right up his Lordship's alley."

Determined to ignore Jennings, I tried the other shoulder. Rows of grinning faces and winking colleagues. As the call over continued, I searched in vain for Miss Jones and her youthful advisors. By now my relief at their absence was giving way to panic as the moment for commencement of our case approached.

Inevitably, "I'll take *Jones v. Newman House Hotel* now. In view of Mr McNamara's estimate of how long it will take, it seems unlikely that any other case will be reached today. As matters stand there are no other judges available. However, in case we manage to get through Mr McNamara's case in less time than he anticipates, shall we say not before twelve o'clock for the remainder of the list?"

A quick dispersal and emptying of the court followed. Lots of "Good luck, Mac" from caring colleagues and no doubt at all about their destination and the subject of their conversation.

Time to discover my opponent. "I appear for the defendant, my Lord, instructed by O'Malley Simpson," intoned Robert Raymond, BL. Another square solicitor, if you know what I mean, but one who had reverted from the tongue-twisting name in which it had rejoiced until quite recently. If only I had known Robert was against me, I could have added another hour and cited him rather than his Lordship. No chance of another case being reached today. His Lordship could safely declare no cases before twelve o'clock tomorrow.

Robert was a formidable advocate. No doubt at all in his mind about that, and a painstaking one to boot. In the unlikely event of his Lordship leaving as much as a pebble unturned, Robert would be there, spade in hand, until the pebble yielded up its treasure or the lack of it. If there was one thing that was beyond certainty, Robert's client would have his case aired down to the very detail of his underwear. More accustomed to the chancery side of the court (something of an "affidavit-basher" as the personal injuries Bar might disrespectfully say, and with considerable underestimation), Robert owed his selection for this case to the identity of his instructing solicitors, a firm versed in areas of law more rarefied than the rough and tumble of personal injuries.

In all of this he was not unlike his Lordship. A chip off the old block as it were. In the halcyon days of his own career at the Bar, Francis Bradley, SC, as he then was, owed much of his practice which inclined more towards commerce and chancery to square or square-like firms that were today briefing Robert and me. To a reputation for lengthening cases far beyond their normal forensic life, a reputation which as I have hinted he guarded assiduously on the Bench, he had added an acerbic wit since his elevation.

"Well Mr McNamara, would you like to open your case now?"

"Of course, my Lord," I replied with my back to his Lordship as, in vain, I surveyed the scene seeking sight or sound of my equestrian team. There is a tendency on the part of the plaintiff and the defendant and his or her witnesses to line up on the same side of the courtroom as their Counsel. Much like the wedding guests in the church. To my right and rear as I faced the judge I could make out rows and rows of followers of Newman. Behind me as I faced the judge a void, an empty space. Like a modern work of art, an entirely blank canvass. Not a witness to be seen. Row upon empty row. I tried the door. Not a movement. No last minute dramatic entrance. I was on my own, like the groom at the altar whose bride has failed to show.

"Of course my Lord, I would be delighted to open my case. Indeed that is precisely what I am about to do. At least, was about to do."

"Mr McNamara, would you please stop speaking in riddles and get on with opening your case and stop wasting the court's time."

"My Lord, I am most dreadfully sorry but I am afraid I simply cannot open my case."

"What do you mean, you can't open your case?"

"I am afraid neither my solicitor nor my client nor any of her witnesses are in court."

"And whose fault is that, Mr McNamara?"

"Well certainly not mine, my Lord," I blurted out all too hurriedly and equally unthinkingly. Adding in a feeble attempt to tippex out that last response, "Not yours either my Lord, certainly not your fault."

"I should think not, Mr McNamara. I may be slow but at least I turn up," retorted his Lordship to the merriment of the biased audience who were beginning to think that this was vastly superior to anything they had seen in the Dublin Theatre Festival. And free as well. I could see some of them wondering if they could return the following day.

"What would you like me to do, Mr McNamara?"

"I have no alternative but to ask your Lordship for a few minutes. Would your Lordship rise for fifteen minutes and I have no doubt that my team will have arrived by then?"

"Something of a self-fulfilling prophesy, Mr McNamara. I see now why you said the case would take three to four hours. With this sort of punctuality, three to four days might be more accurate." His Lordship was in sparkling form. "What do you say, Mr Raymond?"

"Well my Lord, far be it from me to take my friend short."

Two lies in his opening line. Not bad, even for Robert. A gross insult to the concept of friendship on the one hand and as for not wishing to take me short...well, wait for it. "But I must tell your Lordship that I am here with all my witnesses and I am ready to go. It is really most inconvenient. It occurs to me that the true explanation for the non-appearance of my friend's entourage may well be that the plaintiff has had second thoughts about going on with her case, in which event, I am instructed to seek my costs."

Well if ever there was a definition of not wishing to take a colleague short, that was not it.

"Mr McNamara, what do you say about Mr Raymond's suggestion that perhaps Miss Jones has had second thoughts about proceeding with her case?"

"I can assure your Lordship that nothing could be further from the truth. Miss Jones is intent on prosecuting her case. If I could repeat my application to your Lordship to rise for fifteen minutes I am sure that my client will have turned up."

"What do you say to that, Mr Raymond?" his Lordship enquired.

"Has your Lordship ruled out dismissing the case?" Robert suggested helpfully, still clinging to the notion of not wishing to take me short.

"I am very tempted to. It is just not good enough to be wasting valuable court time like this, taxpayer's money and all that. Particularly when the lists are so crowded and there is such a backlog."

This was rich coming from Bradley, who had cost the taxpayer a fortune by the length of time he took to hear cases. Between that and the fact that he had the reputation of being the laziest judge in town, a position for which there was no shortage of candidates, Bradley would think nothing of spending the entire day sitting in his chambers to avoid having to hear a case. And if all came to all and there was no alternative to fulfilling his duty under the Constitution, then he would take so long to do it that there was every chance that the Constitution would be amended before he could manage to complete his task. And here he was now, pretending that it was a great inconvenience that he might have nothing to do.

"However, at the end of the day I must do justice between the parties and to dismiss Miss Jones without having heard her would not be justice. *Audi alteram partem* and all that. Reluctantly, I'll allow you the fifteen minutes you ask for. On second thought, half an hour may make more sense in the long run but Mr McNamara, your client had better be ready to go on then and better have a good explanation for not being in court when her case was called."

"I am extremely grateful to your Lordship."

"Your Lordship will strike out the case at that stage if my friend is not in a position to go on?" enquired Robert, utterly consistent in his anxiety not to take me short.

"Yes Mr Raymond, I'll strike it out." Bradley hurried off the Bench, not to waste any of the time allotted to wasting the tax-payer's money. For my part I fled, even more quickly, before Robert could sink his teeth into me.

I couldn't check every traffic jam between Fitzwilliam Square and the Four Courts so I did the next best thing and headed for the public restaurant.

Nearly right. Down a few storeys to the unfindable, undirectable to, yet always crowded, court brasserie. Not a sign. Neither Miss Jones nor her two apprentices nor any of her equestrian entourage.

"Case not take as long as you expected, Dermot?" enquired a colleague, tongue so deeply in his cheek that he appeared to be french kissing himself, who had obviously enjoyed the call over in front of Bradley and was now bringing some of his colleagues up to speed.

"Hasn't even started," I replied. "Can't find my client."

"Try next door," he suggested.

"There you are!" I shouted, shedding the last of my composure. Everyone looked up. Most were having tea or coffee and a biscuit or cake, but Miss Jones was just raising to her lips a companionable whiskey. Many flights below court level, this emporium to Bacchus stiffened the resolve early in the day and helped to unwind later on. I was somewhat taken aback to find my client consuming alcohol before her case had even got off the ground. I explained that the case had been called and as they had not been present had almost been struck out, but by a great feat of advocacy I had managed to persuade the wise judge to allow us half an hour.

"In that case, we can finish our elevenses in comfort," declared our Olympian, who had been through too many moments of real drama and tension to be fazed by a judge in Dublin who was ready to hear her case.

How was I going to explain their non-appearance to Bradley?

"Would you like a drink, Dermot?" Miss Jones invited. Nothing I would have liked better, but long gone were the days when it was acceptable for Counsel to start the day on the right note.

"A quick coffee would be fine Miss Jones, but really I am anxious to get back up to court."

"Call me Penelope. Miss Jones makes me feel rather staid and staid I am not."

"Very well, Penelope. While we are waiting there is something I need to know. How much are you looking for? When we go back up Robert, my opposite number, will be asking me about settlement terms. At least I expect that he will."

"No idea, you tell me. I know nothing about the law, first time in fact and of course your courts over here are even more of a mystery to me. I haven't a clue about values and will be guided entirely by you and your two friends here. What do you think my injuries are worth?"

"Well, this is not an exact science but in my opinion your injuries are worth between fifteen and twenty thousand pounds – that is on full value."

"Is that all? After all I have been through? Nonsense, Dermot. I'd have to get more. A good bit more."

Hadn't a clue about figures...would be guided entirely by my good self. "Well Penelope, what would you like me to ask for?"

"Ask them for fifty thousand."

"I can't."

"Why not?"

"Because the jurisdiction of the Circuit Court is thirty thousand."

"Well we'll go to the High Court then."

"We can't do that either."

"What do you mean we can't do that?"

"Strictly we can but it would mean another day in court and you would have to pay the defendant's costs of today. Anyway, you will never get more than thirty thousand."

"All right then, ask your opponent for thirty, but make it clear to him that you are not taking a penny less."

"I'll ask but please bear in mind that that is more than the full value of your case and if they offer something less than that, you would really have to consider it, especially having regard to the difficulties on liability."

"What difficulties on liability?"

"Well, the liability position is by no means clear-cut. I tried to raise this at our consultation but no one was listening. They have pleaded that it was your own fault because you were under the influence of alcohol at the time."

"But I hardly ever take a drink," replied Penelope, knocking back her second whiskey and it wasn't yet midday.

"I know that. I believe you but the judge may take another view, particularly when we can't really explain how you sustained your injuries."

"But the bar broke, didn't it? As I was getting out of the bath, the bar broke."

"But the hotel says that was due to a combination of your condition and the fact that you are overweight."

"Nonsense Dermot, you go out there and ask for thirty thousand."

I looked pleadingly at Amy and Sophie, seeking a shred of reality but in vain. The girls were absorbed in their Rombouts coffee and if there was any surplus attention it was in Miss Jones' favour. With my gown between my legs I exited and made my way back up the several flights of stairs to court.

There are barristers who want to settle at all costs. Maybe they want to get off for coffee. Maybe they want to get onto the next case. Make more money. Maybe, however, they have grasped, with experience, an inner truth. A forensic truth as it were. It is just possible – an outside chance – that they realise it might be in their client's interest to settle. If a plaintiff, the client will go away with more money in his pocket than a judge would be likely to give him. If a defendant, he might have to spend less money than a judge would order him. Either way the client wins.

There are barristers who will tell you that they want to settle cases and that they are doing all in their power – moving heaven and earth being part of that empowerment – to achieve a settlement. Beware such barristers. The chances are that their overtures of settlement to you are in inverse proportion to the tunes they are singing to their client. "I am trying to get you an offer but it is like pulling teeth" to you becomes "they know their case is weak – wouldn't offer them a bob – don't think they'll go on" to the client.

There is another breed of barrister – born to fight cases and doesn't pretend otherwise. Runs into the Round Hall of a Tuesday morning, claps his hands and says aloud, "Give me a plaintiff." His buzz is fighting, cross-examining, winning and, if necessary, losing. Settlement is not part of his vocabulary. He will not be suggesting it to his client and will not be saying to you, "I'm trying to get you money".

Robert fell into this third category.

The aggression started immediately. "Mac, where were you at ten thirty?"

"In court along with you, Robert. Don't you remember?"

"Not you, Mac. Your client. I was all set to go. We were first in the List. I couldn't see it lasting beyond lunchtime and so I held on to a chancery brief for two o'clock. What on earth am I to do now?"

"No problem, Robert. You can easily make it by two."

"How?"

"Settle. Make me an offer I can't refuse. Now don't get me wrong. I have a difficult client. Head in the clouds. Fortified by two little beauties down from the office. But I am not as convinced as they are. Make me an offer. I'll do the rest."

"How can I make you an offer in this of all cases Mac?"

"Every case has a settlement value, Robert."

"Not this one. After all, I have a reputation to think of."

"Whose?"

"Mine, of course."

"And what about the reputation of your hotel? Think of all the publicity."

"And what about you - 'British rider drunk as a lord' - how do you think Miss Jones will take that?" I was making about as much progress as the *Titanic*. "Mac, apart from everything else, I have done a long opinion saying that the hotel cannot lose. What do you want me to do? Tell them that my opinion is wrong?"

"That was foolish. No case can't be lost."

"This one. This one can't be lost."

"How are you so certain?"

"She was plastered. As she usually was in Horse Show Week since she retired. I have three witnesses."

"That is not her evidence. Says she was not feeling very well and came back early to go to bed. You won't find her easy meat Robert. That aside, what about the bar? Wasn't that defective?"

"No, frankly, it wasn't. My engineer will say that the combination of her obesity and inebriation is what dislodged the bar." My engineer was useless so there was little comeback. The *Titanic* was going backwards.

"Am I wasting my time?"

"I am afraid you are, Mac."

"Will you tell your client what I am looking for?"

"There is no point, but if you want me to I will."

"Very well then, my client is looking for the full jurisdiction, thirty thousand, but if you got me something in the region of twenty I'll do everything I can to get her to take it."

"I am sure you will, Mac. I'll pass on the message." Robert went off to his cheerless client and I returned to my plastered and obese one (all of which is denied, as the best defences say). I started to lay the ground for a cheaper settlement on the off chance that Robert might have a personality change.

He didn't. "They even want their costs," he muttered disinterestedly as we went through the door. Not that it would have mattered. Wild horses wouldn't have persuaded Penelope to take a penny less than thirty. "There is an opinion from the barrister in the case before you came on the scene, Dermot. He says twenty-five and there is no mention of liability. Even twenty-five is not enough." That was the first I had heard of Frank's opinion. So now we had the plaintiff's case being controlled by Frank's opinion. So much for the man on the ground. The coal face and all that.

Exactly thirty-six minutes since he left the Bench, his Lordship sat for the second time that morning. So far his Lordship's morning was going very well. Nearly twelve o' clock and he hadn't done a stroke of work. "Well, Mr McNamara, has your client bothered to turn up this time?" enquired his Lordship wittily.

"Oh yes, my Lord. My client is here with all her witnesses

and my solicitor. And they ask me to convey to your Lordship their sincerest apologies for not being here earlier and for inconveniencing the court," I replied with the utmost invention.

"Well they might Mr McNamara, and where may I ask were they? Not down having coffee I hope?"

"Oh no my Lord," I answered immediately (this was in part true as Penelope was having a whiskey), adding with some hesitation, "I eventually tracked them down in another court. They went to another court by mistake," I explained with considerable relief, pleased with my fabrication which I convinced myself was not so far from the truth as to constitute a breach of my duty to the court.

"Well in that case Mr McNamara, shall we get on with the case?" coaxed his Lordship, adding after a moment which gave him enough time to think out the full implications of this judicial suggestion, "or would the parties like a little time?" Bradley would go to any lengths to avoid hearing a case.

Robert, thinking of his chancery case at two o'clock, got in ahead of me. "We've been down the settlement avenue my Lord, but to no avail. I think your Lordship will have to hear the case."

"In that event, gentlemen, let's get on with the case. Nothing to be gained by wasting time," his Lordship advised in a frenzy of false enthusiasm and expedition.

"Twenty years show jumping for Great Britain, Miss Jones?"

"That's correct, Mr McNamara," she replied, without a hint of shyness from the confines of the witness box.

"Frequent visitor to the Horse Show?"

"Indeed, Mr McNamara."

"And participant in the Aga Khan?"

"On more occasions than I wish to remember, Mr McNamara."

The penny began to drop with his Lordship. A more interesting case than he had realised. "Excuse me interrupting you, Mr McNamara," (*quelle politesse* from his Lordship, quite a sea-change from what had gone before). "Miss Jones, could you be *the* Miss Jones, of Olympian fame, whom I have watched on television and indeed, if I may be so bold, in the flesh on so many occasions?"

"Unless there is another Penelope Jones, my Lord," replied

Miss Jones is a visitor to this country and apparently something of a sports celebrity to boot. What I am trying to say to your Lordship is that this admiration of Miss Jones must not be allowed to cloud your Lordship's judicial vision."

"You would agree, Mr Raymond, that Miss Jones is entitled to a fair crack of the whip." Bradley, pleased with his judicial witticism, looked down at me. Not to be found wanting or in any way disloyal, I beamed up at his Lordship. *Nice one, judge. Don't stop now, Robert.*

"Of course my Lord, but I submit that sympathy is not enough. The law requires that Miss Jones prove negligence. In this case this means that she must satisfy your Lordship that the bathroom bar was defective. If your Lordship keeps an open mind on the case until all the evidence is concluded, your Lordship will find that the bar in question was not defective and that it broke for reasons unconnected with the defendant."

"Did I hear you correctly, Mr Raymond? Were you advising me to keep an open mind on the case?"

"I don't think I quite said that, my Lord, and certainly I didn't mean it in that sense. I simply meant that –"

"Mr Raymond, I would remind you that I have an entirely open mind on all issues. I merely thought that it would be helpful to the parties if they knew what way my open mind was working. At least it might help to shorten matters, which of course this debate, whilst most interesting, is not doing. Shall we get on with the cross-examination Mr Raymond?"

"As long as your Lordship doesn't think that the result is a foregone conclusion?"

"As I said Mr Raymond, an open mind. The case isn't over until the fat lady sings." A titter went around the court. His Lordship enjoyed making witty remarks and was basking in the glory of this one for a moment or two, until its full implication dawned on him. "I am most dreadfully sorry, Miss Jones. It is an expression we have over here. I don't know if you are familiar with it. Of course it was not intended to refer to you."

"Thank you, my Lord," she replied.

Cross-examination at last. "Miss Jones, according to my instructions you have enjoyed a distinguished equestrian career?"

"Thank you Mr Raymond, I have."

"And you have many fans on this side of the water," continued Robert, looking up at his Lordship.

"I have always enjoyed coming to Ireland, Mr Raymond."

"For how many years have you been in retirement?"

"Almost seven. The time goes so quickly."

"But you are still heavily involved as a commentator I think?"

"That is so."

"Notwithstanding this considerable continuing involvement, I think you have been able to relax a bit more since your retirement?"

"I am not sure that I know what you mean, Mr Raymond."

"Nor I," chipped in his Lordship.

"Let me put it this way. No longer being an active participant, you have a little more time on your hands, your life is less disciplined and you can enjoy yourself more?"

"I am afraid I am still not with you, Mr Raymond."

"My Lord, I have no idea what the relevance of this line of cross-examination is. I think my friend should be required to come to the point," I interjected.

"I agree. Mr Raymond, this isn't an interview for *Hello* magazine. This is a court of law and I think if you have a point to make now is the time. Time to bite the bullet, Mr Raymond."

"I most certainly have a point to make my Lord, and I will have no hesitation in making it. However, I would ask your Lordship to refrain from interrupting me. Miss Jones, am I right in thinking that you enjoy a drink?"

"And what is wrong with that, Mr Raymond?" enquired his Lordship.

"*Please* my Lord. I simply can't conduct this cross-examination if your Lordship keeps interrupting me. I have a duty to my clients to put the defendant's case to Miss Jones. May I proceed?"

"I wish you would, Mr Raymond. We certainly aren't going anywhere very quickly."

"Well, Miss Jones, have you an answer to my question?"

"If I enjoy myself? Well I certainly do. I love horses and I love life."

"I think you know very well, Miss Jones, that that was not the question. What I was asking you before his Lordship's interruption was if you enjoyed a drink."

"I most certainly do. Is that a crime in Ireland, Mr Raymond?"

"If you don't mind Miss Jones, I'll ask the questions, you answer them."

"Well Mr Raymond, where does that get you? The witness enjoys a drink. So what? Don't most people? What about yourself? I think you've been known to imbibe a little, more than a little maybe, from time to time?"

"My Lord I protest. My drinking habits are not on trial here."

"Nor are Miss Jones', Mr Raymond. She is not charged with drunken driving."

"No my Lord, but if your Lordship would stop interrupting your Lordship would see the relevance of Miss Jones' drinking habits. Miss Jones, you enjoy a drink?"

"I've already said so."

"Have you been known to drink to excess on occasion?"

"Certainly not. Never. I know how to hold my drink. In fact, I am what you would call a social drinker. A glass of wine with my meal." *Not to mention elevenses*, I thought to myself. "That sort of thing."

"I suggest to you, Miss Jones, that you are being a little economical with the truth in that answer. Do you know Monsieur Mitanchet?"

"Very well."

"Monsieur Mitanchet will say, reluctantly, that on many evenings he has had to escort you to your room with the assistance of the night porter."

"I reject that completely."

"Why do you think that Monsieur Mitanchet would make that up?"

"I have no idea. As far as I am concerned, however, it is a load of rubbish."

"The night porter will give similar evidence."

"I am not responsible for what they say."

"My Lord, what has all of this got to do with the night of the fourth of August?" I inquired.

"Just coming to that, Mr McNamara. Miss Jones, I suggest to you that on the night of the fourth of August, Monsieur Mitanchet and the night porter helped you to your room. You attempted the stairs on your own but you fell. In short, Miss Jones, that you were drunk."

"Mr Raymond, I will not have it alleged in my court that a person was drunk. This is not a criminal case. It is a civil case. Someone may have had a bit too much to drink, fine. But drunk, no. Not in this sort of a case. I won't allow this sort of allegation to be bandied about especially about, such an illustrious visitor."

"Very well, my Lord. I'll rephrase my question. Miss Jones,

on the night in question you had had an excess of alcohol and required to be helped to your room?"

"Certainly not, Mr Raymond, I reject your suggestion out of hand and in fact I take exception to it."

"I'll go further, Miss Jones. The reason the bar broke was that you were so drunk -"

"My Lord, I object to my friend using the word drunk, particularly when your Lordship has already made a ruling."

"Absolutely, Mr Raymond. Another question to rephrase."

Robert impatiently continued, "Miss Jones, because you had consumed an excessive amount of alcohol, you applied too much force to the bar and it broke."

"Would you mind telling me how you can apply too much force to a bar that is provided to help you exit from the bath?"

"That is precisely it, Miss Jones. You bring me onto the second leg of our defence in this case. Miss Jones, would you agree with me that you are somewhat heavier now than in your competing days?"

"Mr Raymond, I don't like your attitude," Penelope huffed.

"Nor do I, Mr Raymond. Am I to take it that your client's defence to this action is going to include a personal attack on Miss Jones?"

"My Lord, I regret having to be personal but I must carry out my instructions and I can assure your Lordship that the line I am pursuing is extremely relevant to the question of causation."

"This is really going too far, Mr Raymond."

"The defendant is entitled to a hearing as well as Miss Jones, my Lord. May I proceed, my Lord?"

"Very well Mr Raymond, at your peril."

"Miss Jones, I have a report from an engineer which says that this bar was in perfect condition and the reason that it broke was due to a combination of your intox- I mean, your excessive intake of alcohol, on the one hand and your obesity on the other. What do you say to that?"

"You're someone to make that allegation, Mr Raymond," replied Miss Jones with a good deal of accuracy and her eyes firmly fixed on Robert's girth. It was hard now looking at Robert to spot the athlete who was once three times University sprint champion. *Chariots of Fire* and all that. Pounding the pebble-stones of College Park. All in the distant past, if it ever happened at all. Looking at him now, the evidence was weak, if there at all. All well and truly traded in. If Miss Jones was obese, then Robert, at twenty stones, gave the word new definition. Well might Miss Jones respond as she did.

She was well up to Robert and her retaliation had struck a chord. "I have to remind you again Miss Jones that it is for me to ask the questions, you to answer them," retorted Robert, not for a moment enjoying this parity of attack and counter-attack. Unlike the audience who were enjoying every moment. We were coming up to lunchtime and those associated with the remaining cases in the list had returned to court. Miss Jones was making new friends. Amy and Sophie were ecstatic. Even some in Robert's team were finding it hard to conceal their merriment.

"I don't like you referring to my weight, Mr Raymond. It is hardly chivalrous. Are you suggesting that in excess of a certain weight one should not have a bath in the most exclusive hotel in Dublin?"

"I am suggesting nothing of the sort, Miss Jones, simply that one must exercise care at all times, all the more so if one has a tendency to being overweight, and of course one simply should not be in the situation if one has had too much to drink."

"I do not accept that I had too much to drink and anyway, drink or no drink, the bar should not have broken."

Robert decided to leave it at that. Were he to cross-examine her for another three days he would make no progress. The more he persisted in his drink and weight line of enquiry, the more he was driving the judge and Miss Jones into an intractable alignment. The judge looked up at the clock at the back of the room and saw that it was five to one.

"Shall we say two o'clock gentlemen? Does that suit you Miss Jones? Hopefully we will get you away by four o'clock," he said.

"Thank you, my Lord." Penelope replied. Out in the corridor she said to me, "What a delightful judge, Dermot! I thought you said he was testy."

"Only if you don't turn up for your case, Penelope," I said, but she wasn't listening.

"It never ceases to amaze me how interested in sport you are in this country. That other chap, your opponent, he's a rather dour sort isn't he? Doesn't seem to get on too well with the judge, does he?"

"It's a bit like your horses, Penelope. It's a question of knowing your judge and how to handle him," I replied to her ample back as she strode off down the corridor flanked by Amy and Sophie, no doubt in the direction of more companionable whiskeys.

As I made my solo way to my lunch table I wondered if this could last. At some stage Bradley was going to have to face up to the fact that, as in the case of Robert's athletic past, the evidence was a little thin. I was looking forward to sharing my morning's work with my lunch table, but apparently Man United had had a very good win over AC Milan the night before so there wasn't much interest in how Miss Jones was doing against Raymond.

"All rise."

"Mr McNamara, Mr Raymond, I was just wondering over lunch if the parties would like to consider matters for a few moments. It may be that you could bring your considerable negotiating skills to bear on the impasse. We all now have a better idea of what the case is about and the attitude of the respective parties and it should be easier to resolve matters. What do you think? Will I give you ten minutes? Another factor is that I am sure you both have a number of witnesses and therefore it is unlikely to finish by four o'clock. Miss Jones will be detained here for another night and of course there will be a second day's costs." This seemed like an excellent idea to me. I looked at Robert. As I expected, he did not look very enthusiastic.

"I think that ten minutes could be very useful, my Lord," I said.

"I am not so optimistic," Robert muttered, more to himself than the court.

"Ten past two, then. No, let's say two fifteen and of course if progress is being made the time can be extended."

I made another attempt to settle the case. I tried to get Robert to offer twenty thousand or at least fifteen, but Penelope would only hear of twenty-five. Robert, on the other hand, only offered five thousand with a hint of ten thousand, so we were wasting our time.

"We are grateful to your Lordship for the time but I am afraid we have been unable to settle our differences," I informed Bradley when he sat at twenty past two.

"Well let's get on with it then, shall we? We still have a good bit to go."

I called my engineer. I was becoming more and more apprehensive. It wasn't that the case couldn't be won. It was more that there were inherent risks which hadn't been seen by Mr Phillips at our early morning consultation and were not being seen by Penelope or her confidantes from Fitzwilliam Square now. The case had a settlement value and Penelope was pitching it too high. The court was about to receive a more balanced insight into Miss Jones' case.

Mitchell was neither the brightest nor the most imaginative of consulting engineers who frequented the Four Courts. True to form he brought neither brightness nor imagination to Miss Jones' brief. He was a solid and pleasant performer and owed his practice more to efficiency and accessibility rather than any over-abundance of talent. In fairness it may be that no amount of talent could have come up with the engineering evidence Miss Jones needed. Mitchell explained that the bar had come away cleanly from its socket in the wall.

Bradley intervened, "Why was that?"

"Impossible to say, my Lord."

"There must be some explanation?"

"Oh yes my Lord, there are two explanations. Either there was something wrong with the installation or too much force was applied to it."

"And which was it, Mr Mitchell?"

"That is what I can't say, my Lord."

"Can you say on the balance of probabilities, Mr Mitchell? In other words, that one was more likely than the other? For example, was it more likely that there had been some defect in the installation of the bar?"

Your opening Mitchell, go for it, I silently begged. "I am afraid I can't, my Lord. I have thought about it a great deal and all I can say is that it is one or the other, but as to which it is I am at a loss." Honesty – what a terrible burden on top of a lack of brightness and imagination. His Lordship had done his best but Mitchell couldn't rise to it.

So much for the plaintiff's case. The doctors were unavailable in the afternoon so with everyone's permission it was agreed to deal with liability first and should Miss Jones win, to call the doctors in the morning.

Robert called his engineer. Nothing but the best for the Newman House. Garland. By coincidence I had been against him in my last (successful) outing, *Connolly v. Park Beauticians Ltd*, though in that case he was for the punter (rare) and I was for the establishment (rarer). If Mitchell's success was based on his popularity, Garland's emphatically was not. Were he to depend on a solicitor saying, "Let's engage Garland, he is very nice," it is unlikely that he would be engaged this side of the end of the next millennium. Garland didn't smile and didn't need to. He relied entirely on his competence. He enjoyed the respect, if not the friendship, of all. There was no ambivalence about his evidence. Neither the bar nor its installation was defective. There were not two ways about it.

His Lordship attempted to soften him up. "Mr Garland, I hear what you say and indeed even Mr Mitchell did not say that the installation was defective. He could not go that far. All he could say was that it was one of two equal possibilities. But may I put something to you Mr Garland? Your Counsel, Mr Raymond, suggested to Miss Jones that it was a combination of her weight and her intoxication...or rather, her inebriation that caused the bar to break. I have to say that this seems unlikely to my lay mind. While I accept that these factors could have a bearing, surely the bar would not break unless it was improperly installed?"

"I take your point my Lord, but I regret to say that from an engineering point of view, your Lordship is not correct. Your Lordship's is indeed a layman's view. Weight and inebriation could dislodge a perfectly installed bar. That is a matter of engineering fact." *Thank you, Mr Garland. Precisely what you are paid for and good value at the price, whether pounds or guineas.* There was no point in trying to dissuade Garland from his expert opinion. I tried but I didn't spend much time trying. And I was right. There was no point.

The case had shifted perceptibly in a matter of minutes. The two engineers in the box had altered matters seemingly beyond repair. I wondered if Miss Jones now saw the wisdom of my earlier advice. From the expression on the faces of Amy and Sophie they clearly did not. His Lordship was looking decidedly more wrinkled. It wasn't going to be quite as easy to find for Miss Jones as it had at first appeared. Robert had stood his ground and the wind was turning at last. I wondered if Bradley would express another encouragement towards settlement, but he didn't.

"Monsieur Mitanchet, please."

Monsieur Mitanchet was from Lyons. Magnificently choreographed, he resembled a more plausible version of Monsieur Poirot. He made his elegant way to the witness box every bit as comfortably as he would have crossed the foyer of his no less elegant hotel. In an English, perfect except insofar as it was broken, he swore to tell the whole truth. As he took the Oath I was aware that this was my last chance. Much as he wanted to, things were now so changed that as matters stood Bradley could not decide this case in Miss Jones' favour. By their unwelcome duet the engineers had altered all that. I didn't envy me my task.

He spoke eloquently of Miss Jones. A clever forensic ploy, but I think he meant it. How welcome a visitor she had been over many years and he hoped this would continue. How much a fan he was of hers and how he would always take off the Aga Khan Friday afternoon to join the other revellers in the RDS to watch her.

However, in recent years, or more precisely, since her retirement, she had become fond of a drop of wine. He did not object to this. In fact, he was delighted to see her relax. He had seen how seriously she had taken her chosen career while she was competing. She was single-minded and dedicated. He believed the modern word was "focused". In those years there was little time for enjoyment or relaxation and he felt that if she enjoyed a glass of wine now she had more than earned it.

He supposed that you could say that she began to approach her relaxation with the same dedication that she had once bestowed on her riding. So much so that from time to time she would return to the hotel of an evening, how do you say it in your country, "a little worse for wear". As a result, it was sometimes, perhaps often, necessary for him to escort her to her room. If she had relaxed more than was normal for her, he might have to recruit the assistance of Fred, the night porter. It wasn't that she would be difficult or aggressive, simply that she couldn't make it on her own. They didn't mind this little weakness on the part of their equestrian star. It was all part of their comprehensive service. He recalled that on the night in question, she was more "worse for wear" than usual. He definitely needed Fred and together they escorted her to her room, helped her onto her bed and discreetly left. They knew no more until she reappeared around afternoon tea the following day looking very cut up indeed. There had never been an accident in that room and of course the bar had been in place for many years without interference. He had checked the diary himself.

It was very difficult to see how this evidence in relation to assisting her to bed could be disturbed. I decided to leave it alone for the moment.

"Monsieur Mitanchet, you say you checked the diary yourself?"

"*Oui*. Yes. That is correct. I was extremely careful in my investigation of this case. When my solicitors – I mean the Newman House Hotel's solicitors – asked me if any repair work had been carried out to this bar I investigated the matter personally. I wanted to be absolutely sure that the correct answer was given. If no work had been done they would be told. If work had been done they would be told also. How do you say, I left no stone unturned."

"What diary are you referring to, Monsieur Mitanchet?"

"The repair diary, Mr McNamara."

"How does it work, Monsieur Mitanchet? Is there one repair diary for the whole hotel?"

"No. There is a repair diary for each floor."

"A separate diary for each year?"

"Yes."

"And you personally checked each diary for this floor for the past six years?"

"Yes."

"And what did you find?"

"Absolutely nothing of relevance to this bathroom."

"And what does that mean in repair terms?"

"That no work was done in this bathroom for at least six years prior to this accident."

"And are you sure of that?"

"Certain."

"Monsieur Mitanchet, do you know what discovery is?"

"I didn't until this case, but I do now."

"You know it means that you, on behalf of the Hotel, have to make available to the plaintiff all documents that are relevant to this case, even if they are against your interest?"

"As I say, I know that now. It was explained to me by my solicitors."

"And do you know that voluminous documentation was discovered by your side prior to this hearing?"

"I do. I was personally involved in its preparation."

"I have it here as part of my brief. Do you agree that this was the discovery that was made by your hotel in this case?" I asked, holding up the discovery part of my brief that was copiously flagged to show how diligently I had made up the brief the night before.

"Yes, I accept that that must be it. It took days to assemble."

"Well, Monsieur Mitanchet, would you mind explaining to the court how not one of these six diaries you refer to is included in this meticulous discovery?" We had been moving along very nicely. I was asking the questions and Monsieur Mitanchet was answering them. All very smooth. No raised tones. No clear indication of where all this was leading until this last question. Monsieur Mitanchet seemed to be completely taken aback. He paused. For the first time his composure seemed a little ruffled. He looked towards the judge, who looked back. He looked towards his Counsel seeking assistance and then his solicitor, but he was nakedly on his own. He was in the witness box now. He would have to deal with this himself.

The pause continued. I asked, "Well Monsieur Mitanchet, do you have an explanation? I am sure his Lordship would like to hear it." Only now was I confident that maybe I was getting somewhere with Monsieur Mitanchet. Up to that moment I was sure there would be a simple explanation. The diaries were destroyed or something of the sort. But it looked as if that was not the case. Perhaps there was something to hide. "Well, Monsieur Mitanchet?"

"I have to admit this comes as something of a surprise to me, Mr McNamara. I dealt with all of this myself and I was sure that all the documentation had been given to you. May I consult my briefcase?"

"Of course, Monsieur Mitanchet," said his interested Lordship obligingly. Monsieur Mitanchet made his way – slightly less elegantly this time – to his seat behind his Counsel, where he had an embarrassed consultation with his briefcase. After a few moments he returned to the witness box.

"Well Monsieur Mitanchet, can you explain now why these six diaries were not given to my solicitor?"

"I am afraid I can't. I have four of them here now. There should be six. The two most recent years are missing."

"Do you know where they are?"

"Off-hand I do not."

"Why didn't we get the four you have and of course the other two?"

"I am at a complete loss."

"Perhaps it was an oversight?" enquired his Lordship with I thought a hint of scepticism.

"Perhaps, my Lord."

Bradley turned towards me. "Mr McNamara, you tell me there was discovery in this case? On a previous application your client sought all relevant documents?"

"That is so, my Lord," I replied. Amy leant over to me. "If your Lordship would allow me a moment while I take instructions."

"Of course, Mr McNamara."

Amy gave me the benefit of her Obsession perfume while she filled me in. "My Lord, my solicitor reminds me that not once, but twice was discovery applied for. My solicitor was not happy with the first discovery, in that she felt there must be further documentation. She was proved right and more documentation was produced the second time around. However, on neither occasion did these diaries turn up."

Bradley was listening intently. He had grasped the point. "Discovery twice. No diaries," he summarised succinctly.

"In a nutshell, my Lord," I replied. He said nothing for a moment. I was wondering if I should.

"Do you have an application, Mr McNamara?" The green light.

"I most certainly do my Lord." And I did. "My Lord, let me get to the point immediately. I apply to your Lordship to strike out the defence of the Newman House Hotel for failure to comply properly with the court order for discovery and enter judgment for Miss Jones."

"On what grounds, Mr McNamara?"

"On the grounds, my Lord, that in failing to comply fully with the court orders, at the very least Monsieur Mitanchet – or rather, the defendant – is treating the court in a cavalier manner and, at worst, there may be a more sinister explanation."

"Mr Raymond, what do you say to that?"

"I say, my Lord, that my friend is becoming rather excited by what was manifestly an innocent oversight by Monsieur Mitanchet in the preparation of this case. It may well be, of course, that my friend's over-excitement reflects his concerns in relation to liability. He cannot meet the case on its merits so he makes the most of any little technical opening that presents itself. The fact is, my Lord, that my friend can have these diaries immediately and then any lacuna that may exist in relation to the preparatory work may be made good. I ask your Lordship to refuse my friend's application."

"I wonder, Mr Raymond, if we are addressing the same issue here, because certainly what you lightly dismiss as a mere lacuna in the preliminary work I regard more seriously. The affidavits grounding the discovery herein are sworn documents – the deponent is every bit as much on oath as Monsieur Mitanchet is here in the witness box – and the documents that have been held back are crucial diaries. It may be that these diaries will reveal precisely the evidence Mr McNamara is looking for, namely that repair work was carried out to this bar."

"I can assure your Lordship that they will do no such thing," interrupted the temporarily forgotten-about Monsieur Mitanchet.

"Be quiet please, Monsieur Mitanchet. This is a matter of legal argument," the judge reprimanded.

"If Monsieur Mitanchet is correct, then it would be a gross injustice to the defendant if you were to strike out the defence," Robert interposed.

"Even still, the whole matter of discovery is too important. I am inclined to accede to Mr McNamara's application." Amy and Sophie were getting very excited.

"I regret to have to tell your Lordship that you can't."

"Can't what, Mr Raymond?"

"Can't accede to my friend's application. Can't strike out the defence."

"What do you mean I can't, Mr Raymond? Who says so?"

"The Supreme Court, my Lord."

"Since when?"

"The *Fiat* case, my Lord."

His Lordship paused. "In what way does the *Fiat* case say I can't?"

"That case, as your Lordship will know, sets down certain

criteria that have to be met before a defence may be struck out on grounds of discovery. And those criteria are not met in this case."

"I see," replied Bradley, not very convincingly. Another pause. I hoped Bradley was going to be able to handle this. It was beginning to dawn on me that Bradley might not be exactly intimate with the profounder truths of the *Fiat* case. Which made two of us.

"What do you say to that, Mr McNamara?"

I looked up at the clock. Ten to four. "My Lord, notwithstanding what my friend says and more importantly notwithstanding the decision in the *Fiat* case, with which we are all familiar, I submit that this is an appropriate situation for your Lordship to exercise your discretion in favour of the plaintiff." This didn't altogether satisfy Bradley's thirst for legal knowledge. For such a late hour in the afternoon, he was in far too inquisitive a mood.

"But Mr McNamara, Mr Raymond says that the *Fiat* criteria are not met here. What do you say?" I looked again at the clock. Six minutes to four. There was quite a gap between what I wanted to say and what actually emerged. Ideally, I wanted to tell his Lordship to lay off and to suggest if he wanted more information on the *Fiat* case to look it up himself. After all, isn't that what the Judges' Library is for? I felt that I had done rather well to get Miss Jones' rather fragile case to this high point. And I didn't really want my somewhat scanty knowledge – indeed, in all honesty, total ignorance – of the *Fiat* case to be explored in the same minute detail that one might Ladies View in Killarney.

"My Lord, I submit that this case is distinguishable from the *Fiat* case for a number of reasons." Living on the forensic edge. "But more significantly my Lord, the plaintiff has been seriously prejudiced in this case by the defendant's omission and of course my Lord, there is also the point that the court has been misled. I see that it is coming up to four o'clock. My Lord, I have one or two other points to make and if it were convenient for your Lordship I will complete my submission in the morning?"

"That seems like a sensible idea. We can bring fresher minds to this serious issue when we reconvene." *And hopefully more informed ones*, I thought. "Eleven o'clock then."

Bradley fled the Bench, freed from the intricacies of *Jones v. Newman House Hotel* for the next nineteen hours.

"Dermot you know perfectly well that Bradley can't strike out,"

Robert moaned over at me.

"See you in the morning, Robert," came my non-committal reply.

"What was all that mumbo-jumbo about?" asked Penelope when we came out of the courtroom.

"A lot of hot air. A storm in a teacup, really," I replied. "It won't count for anything at the end of the day. Simply some documents that they should have shown us earlier, that they will show us now and that will be of no assistance to your case. Unless, of course, there is a reference to repair work. Which is most unlikely. That fellow Mitanchet with his broken English is a bit of a creep but he doesn't strike me as a fraud. Obviously it is a bit embarrassing for him at the moment but he'll get over that. Anyway we'll see in the morning."

"I like your judge, Dermot. Are they all like him?"

"No, thank God. Of course you like him. He adores you. Obviously a great fan and he is giving you a free run. I just hope it is not all in vain."

"Oh no, Dermot, he'll find for Penelope. He obviously can't stand Raymond," contributed Sophie, who was barely old enough to vote.

"Anyway, would you like a drink?"

"No thank you, Penelope, I have a few things to do." Thinking of the *Fiat* case. "And any drink you have should be as far away from this building as possible. Where are you staying tonight?"

"The Newman House."

"*Where?*"

"Where else?"

"See you at eleven. Watch the bar. Both bars," I chuckled as the three made off.

It was about seven as I stepped onto the quays. It was one of those rare evenings when mood and mellow nature meet. The sun, going down over Heuston Station, was busy with its last messages across the city before closing up for the day. Down the hill from Christchurch bounded the sound of evening bells, curling up in the last rays of sunlight and together making their symbiotic way along the Liffey towards O'Connell Bridge and beyond. The air was warm and scented, summer but a sunset away. There was a lightness in my stride.

It had been a good day. Early morning showers and a somewhat inclement judicial climate had at last cleared. All history now. Moods had changed. No thanks to me, really – mainly due to Bradley's love affair with sport and of course Penelope herself. Robert was on the receiving end now. Neither rhyme nor reason to it. Unfair really, but who said life was fair? Why should I shed any tears for Robert? He was well able to stand up for himself. Indeed, hadn't he stood up to Bradley and if he was taking some stick now hadn't he only himself to blame? Anyway, he was impossible to deal with. He hadn't made any serious efforts to settle the case. Not that he ever did. Good enough for him if he was getting it from Bradley. It could be my turn again tomorrow. With such thoughts I regaled myself as I made by way up the quays. In merry mood indeed.

"Ever heard of Penelope Jones?" I asked Rachel over tea.

"Oh yes. The famous show jumper. Many's the time I watched her in the RDS. Many's the time we lost the Aga Khan thanks to her." Rachel came from horsey stock. She had spent much of her formative years in Iris Kellett's Riding School in Mespil Road. "She's retired now though, isn't she?"

"Yes indeed. You've got her in one. The very person. She's my client today. I had never heard of her. Bradley had though, God bless his little heart. We are getting a great run."

"I'm not surprised, he's sport mad. I have a vague memory of him in Kellett's. He tried a bit of riding there but he had a bad fall one day and never came back. A friend of Mother's."

"Wish I'd known all that sooner."

"Taken to the gargle a bit since her retirement."

"Is that the word?"

"So I heard."

"Bit of an issue in the case, in fact. The other side says she was plastered when she had her fall."

"More than likely."

"Hold on a minute, Rach. Be fair. You don't know anything about the case. She denies it. Says she only takes a social drink. Though she was knocking back a few whiskeys before court, so

I'm not sure. Mitanchet, the French manager of the Newman, says she was footless. Doubt if he's made it up."

"I wouldn't trust him an inch. Something about him. Can't put my finger on it but I wouldn't trust him."

"How do you know him?"

"Oh, I've had the odd drink in there with one or two of my clients who were staying in the Newman." There was a small bit of a gap between Rachel's clientele and mine, with the exception of Penelope, of course.

"Are you in this evening Rach?" I asked hopefully.

"Unfortunately, no. I promised the girls I'd join them for a drink around ten. In fact, any chance you could put the kids to bed for me? I've some work to do before going out."

"Sure," I said a bit flatly, but Rachel didn't notice. Her nose was already well and truly stuck in tomorrow's brief. "I haven't much to do. Just want to have another look at that *Fiat* case, in fact."

"Is that the one about discovery?"

"Yes. The very one. How do you keep so on top of everything?"

"Oh I don't know that I do, really." Then, after a pause, "Discipline I suppose. It must be discipline." Then she was gone again. Total concentration, flicking through the pages. She had no idea of whether or not I was in the room or indeed the house. I got on with the duties that in the dark and distant past would have been regarded as woman's duties. Who was I to say that the kids would have been better off with their mother putting them to bed? Rachel finished her brief more quickly than she expected. At about half nine she was combing her hair in front of the mirror in the hall. I could see she was admiring what she saw. As indeed was I. Pity she had to go out.

"Curious decision, that *Fiat* case," she said out of the blue. Before I had time to give her the benefit of my up to date reflections on the matter she was gone. A quick goodnight kiss for her sleeping wonders, grabbed the keys of our convertible Golf and off into the late-May evening.

I settled own at our desk in front of the window. It really was a smashing view across the bay to Howth, especially at this time of the year. I took out the *Fiat* case. The more I read it the more I realised Robert was right – Bradley couldn't strike out, the Supreme Court said so. Bradley was unlikely to ignore the Supreme

Court. However, I prepared one or two points just in case. Then I looked at the four diaries. Clean. Nothing at all to suggest anything untoward about Miss Jones' bathroom or indeed her bath. Maybe the defence was right. Maybe she was plastered and overweight. She was certainly overweight. I guessed that even if the other two diaries were available they would draw a blank as well.

Thanks to Rachel's commitments I got to bed and to sleep early. I never heard her coming in. Even still she was up before me. Maybe she was right. Discipline.

"Mr McNamara, I have been considering the *Fiat* case overnight." *So have I,* I wanted to add. "And really it seems to me that Mr Raymond is right. I don't think I can strike out the defence. The diaries were not discovered but you have them now." Four of them. I wrote a large four in my barrister's notebook. "And no one is prejudiced. Of course it might be relevant in relation to costs." I scribbled COSTS in large letters. A consolation prize if all else fails.

His Lordship's tone was a trifle harsher, his delivery quicker. I hoped this was not ominous. On the question of discovery, I felt his mind was made up. *No point in flogging a dead horse,* I thought to myself, and turned my attention to Monsieur Mitanchet, who was returning to the witness box more like his old self.

One last throw of the dice. "Monsieur Mitanchet, to return for a moment to something we were discussing yesterday." Mitanchet shifted in his seat.

"Yes, Mr McNamara."

"The diaries, Monsieur Mitanchet."

"I thought we had dealt with those, Mr McNamara."

"In part, Monsieur Mitanchet. You gave me four diaries. Isn't that so?"

"Yes. Four."

"And of course these should have been discovered? Isn't that right?"

Bradley impatiently interrupted, "Mr McNamara I think we have had all that. No point really in revisiting old triumphs. I think you have got as much mileage out of the discovery as is forensically possible. Let's move on."

The judicial mood is as fickle as an Italian stud. "My Lord, with your Lordship's permission I have just a few more questions on this point."

"Very well, Mr McNamara, but at your peril. I have given you your fair share of indulgence."

"Thank you my Lord. Monsieur Mitanchet, what about the other two diaries?"

"Which two?"

"The diaries for the two years leading up to the accident, Monsieur Mitanchet." Clutching at straws perhaps. What else was there to clutch at?

"What about them, Mr McNamara?"

"Did you find them, Monsieur Mitanchet?"

"As you know, Mr McNamara, when this came up yesterday I was quite taken aback. I went to my briefcase where I discovered four diaries and I gave them to you. I told you that the other two had been mislaid."

"Yes Monsieur Mitanchet, I know all that. You told us all that yesterday." I was a little surprised at his prevarication. "The two most recent diaries Monsieur Mitanchet, do you have them?"

"Well actually I have. I carried out a thorough search last night and eventually at about two this morning I came across them in the wrong filing cabinet."

"Look Monsieur Mitanchet, I am not interested in where you found them or at what time. I simply want to know if you found them, and if so where they are now?"

"Yes I did find them, and here they are." The Holy Grail. The two precious diaries were produced at last.

"Now Monsieur Mitanchet, would you mind explaining to his Lordship how at three thirty yesterday afternoon you did not know where these diaries were and yet they mysteriously turn up overnight?"

"My Lord, I object to my friend's use of the word mysteriously. The witness has already explained that they were wrongly filed. Nothing mysterious about that." Robert was piping up again, perhaps realising the turn this line of questioning was taking.

"Perhaps so Mr Raymond, but leaving that aside for the moment, surely at the very least when Monsieur Mitanchet discovered the diaries overnight he should have made them available to the court this morning? I am not sure if he fully understands our procedures over here or if he is not sailing a little close to the wind. Carry on, Mr McNamara," said Bradley. The judicial breeze had changed again. I thought I should run with it.

"Monsieur Mitanchet, to ask you his Lordship's question, why didn't you proffer those diaries to the court this morning?"

"I didn't think they were that important."

"What? How can you say that Monsieur Mitanchet, after all the hullabaloo about them yesterday?"

"I just didn't."

"Why did you bother looking for them then?"

"They were missing, weren't they?"

"And yet once you discovered them you don't bother to hand them over?"

"No, there's nothing in them." At this stage Monsieur Mitanchet was beginning to demonstrate a lack of ease more suited to a prime minister at question time whose wife has been found in bed with the leader of the opposition. He was shifting from one buttock to another.

"Could I have them please?"

"Of course." Mitanchet handed them to Amy, who handed them to me. There was a tension in the arena. I leafed through the bulky diaries. There were countless entries. A little time was called for. "My Lord, could I ask your Lordship to rise for half an hour to give me an opportunity to go through these diaries?"

"That doesn't seem unreasonable, Mr McNamara. What do you say to that, Mr Raymond?"

"I have no objection my Lord." Bradley rose to leave the Bench. After all, at this stage he had had an hour of uninterrupted hearing. Had this opportunity not arisen, another would have to have been created.

I gave one of the diaries to Amy and Sophie and kept the other for myself. The entries were not exactly written in block capitals. It looked as if a team of foreign doctors had written them up. I turned the pages. An impossible task. Almost. All of a sudden there was a shriek of delight. Amy's make-up almost fell off.

"Look! Here," she said. "*Thirtieth November. 156.*" Penelope's room number. "*Repairs. Bathroom. Bar loose. Guest slipped.*" Too good to be true. Admittedly it did not specify the bar. Then again, neither did it go on to say that this was the bar that broke when Miss Jones was taking her bath. It was good enough for me, and I hoped for Bradley, who was at this moment relaxing in his chambers, blissfully unaware of this momentous development. Amy and Sophie could hardly contain themselves. Indeed, Amy couldn't. She disappeared to the loo, which is about the most unfindable place in the Four Courts and hadn't returned by the time his Lordship next sat at twenty to one.

"Well Mr McNamara, have you had enough time to trawl through the diaries?"

"Yes, my Lord."

"Was it worthwhile?"

"I think so, my Lord. I wonder if Monsieur Mitanchet could return to the witness box?"

The registrar informed Monsieur Mitanchet that he was already sworn, but at this stage I was beginning to have my doubts about whether or not the oath was all that it's cracked up to be where Monsieur Mitanchet comes from. It was not something that seemed to overburden our Gallic friend.

"Just one more thing, Monsieur Mitanchet." *It's all I've got*, I thought to myself, *but surely it's enough.* "Would you mind reading out the entry for the thirtieth November?"

Mitanchet put on his ridiculous little half-moons. He kept looking out over the top of them at intervals he deemed suitable. He made quite a meal of turning up the correct page. In an English that was becoming ever more fragile he read from the sacred text, "Repairs. Bathroom. Bar loose. Guest slipped."

"Well Monsieur Mitanchet, what do you say about that on this, the second day of the hearing?"

"What do you want me to say, Mr McNamara?"

"Well for a start, were you aware of this entry?"

"In fact I wasn't. I read the diary, but frankly that entry is so small and so illegible that I must have missed it."

"How convenient, Monsieur Mitanchet, you must have missed it. Just as you must have missed handing over the diary in the first place."

"It's easy for you to say that Mr McNamara, but there were hundreds of documents."

"Most of them irrelevant except for this one. Anyway, what about the entry? What do you say about that? Isn't it clear that the bar that was responsible for Miss Jones' accident had previously been repaired?"

"I don't think that is at all clear from the entry."

"And in fact, not only was this bar responsible for Miss Jones' accident, but it also caused a guest to fall on the thirtieth November, before Miss Jones fell?"

"I don't think that follows at all. I think Mr McNamara, if I may say so, you are reading too much into the entry. There are, after all, a number of bars in the bathroom," Mitanchet said, his imagination running away with him. Bradley in his wisdom interrupted. Very often a witness can explain away even the inexplicable in cross-examination, but it is not always as easy to hide from the judicial gaze.

"I am sorry to interrupt you in full flow Mr McNamara, but there is something I'd like to clarify with the witness."

"Of course, my Lord. That would be most helpful," I replied in a spirit of obsequious co-operation.

Bradley fixed Mitanchet with one of his specials. "Monsieur Mitanchet, I wonder if I understand you correctly? I think you accept that on the thirtieth of November a guest slipped in a bathroom due to a loose bar?"

"I do, my Lord."

"And the following August Miss Jones slipped in the same bathroom and the bar which she was holding onto came out of its socket?"

"I accept that also, my Lord."

"What you don't accept, I think, is the connection between the two incidents. Is that right?"

"Your Lordship understands my position perfectly." Which was not quite the same thing as saying that his Lordship accepted Mitanchet's position perfectly. The nuances were flying about a metre above Mitanchet's head.

"In other words, Monsieur Mitanchet, in the one year, in the one bathroom, in the best hotel in Ireland there are two accidents, each involving a bar, but you say different bars. Is that what you say?"

"That is it, my Lord."

"That would be quite a coincidence, would it not?"

"It would be, as your Lordship says, a coincidence."

"Thank you, Monsieur Mitanchet. Any more questions Mr McNamara?"

The case, I felt, was over. "No my Lord. I had just finished," I lied. In fact I had more questions but I made a quick decision to abandon them.

"Very well. Mr Raymond, have you anything to add?"

"I have my Lord but I don't think there is much point. Your Lordship's mind seems well and truly made up."

"Indeed it is, Mr Raymond, well and truly made up."

Bradley promptly delivered his judgment. "One of Great Britain's outstanding athletes has had to have recourse to our courts. I have had the pleasure and privilege of watching Miss Jones on countless occasions. She rode with great distinction for her country. Now of course in deciding this case I have had to put my admiration for Miss Jones entirely out of my mind. As Mr Raymond, learned in the law, put it, the mere fact that Miss Jones met with an accident in a bath in the Newman House Hotel does not entitle her to damages. This is not a court of sympathy. The law in this jurisdiction, and indeed in her own, requires her to prove negligence. That is the law. I was unhappy with the manner in which the defendant dealt with discovery, or perhaps more precisely, its failure to deal with it and I was inclined to strike out the defence. Once again, I am indebted to Mr Raymond who was most wise and most up to date with his law, when he told me that I could not penalise the defendant in that way. He drew my attention to the decision of the Supreme Court in the *Fiat* case. Twice Mr Raymond, with his profound knowledge of the law, kept me right.

"But Mr Raymond cannot alter the facts. And fact number one in this case is that Monsieur Mitanchet did his utmost to keep these diaries out of court for the very good reason that they were so damaging. Fact number two is that it is clear beyond even an unreasonable doubt that the bar on which Miss Jones came unstuck was the same bar that was repaired the previous November. The repair was clearly below par. I have no hesitation in finding for the distinguished Miss Jones. *En passant*, I must compliment Mr McNamara on his advocacy. Were it not for his tenacity, these diaries would never have come to light and Miss Jones would have lost her case.

"Which brings me to the question of damages. But before determining that issue, I would like to comment on the manner in which this case was defended, for which I attach no blame whatsoever to Mr Raymond, who was at all times acting on instructions. The twin defences that Miss Jones was overweight and under the influence of alcohol is nothing short of reprehensible. I reject both allegations and wish to assure Penelope – I mean, Miss Jones – that she leaves this court with both her reputation and her distinction intact.

"In arriving at the appropriate figure for damages I must do justice not only to the plaintiff but also to the defendant. I must eliminate from my mind any disapproval I may feel for the manner in which the case was run by the defendant. The plaintiff succeeds on liability and it is simply a question on assessing in money terms the pain and suffering which she has endured and will continue to endure. Having given the matter much consideration, I cannot see how the plaintiff could return to Great Britain with a feeling that she had received justice in this court if her damages were less than thirty thousand pounds. Accordingly, I award the plaintiff thirty thousand pounds."

"May it please your Lordship. And costs, my Lord?"

"That follows, Mr McNamara."

"My Lord, there were two discovery applications and I apply for the costs of those as well."

"What do you say, Mr Raymond?"

"I am in your Lordship's hands."

"A dangerous place to be, Mr Raymond."

"I know, my Lord."

"Very well, the costs of those applications Mr McNamara."

"Thank you, my Lord."

"Mr McNamara, one final thing. I wonder if Miss Jones would favour me with her autograph... for my daughter, who is a three-day eventer. I am sure Mr Raymond won't mind now that the case is over."

"Of course my Lord. I'll give it to your crier."

"Thank you, Mr McNamara. As for the rest of the list, I'll take it up at two o'clock."

Miss Jones was over the moon. "Wonderful judge," she kept repeating. I joined in the chorus. She showered me with kisses and in between told me over and over again what a great barrister I was and what a successful career I had ahead of me. Amy and Sophie were ecstatic. Happy campers one and all.

"To a great judge...with affectionate gratitude...Penelope Jones," she wrote on a sheet of scented notepaper for his Lordship's daughter and handed it to the judge's crier. I looked across at Robert. The contrast could not have been more marked. Mitanchet was looking at him over his silly glasses. A lot of the wind had gone out of him, and indeed out of Robert as well. For the moment at any rate. He'd be back. Nothing would satisfy Penelope but to

treat us all to lunch and a glass or two of wine. I didn't think the Newman House Hotel was the appropriate venue but I kept that reflection to myself.

Much later in the afternoon I bumped into Frank back in the Library. "How did it go, Mac?"

"Brilliantly," I replied, momentarily eschewing modesty.

"What did you get?"

"Thirty."

"As I'd expected," Frank replied. "Was Phillips there?"

"Of course," I lied, "wouldn't have missed it for the world, he said, and what's more two beauties from the office Amy and Sophie. Do you know them?"

"No I don't," Frank replied, a trifle exasperated.

"We're just back from lunch. Penelope invited us. The Newman," I added, driving home my advantage.

"I'd better give Phillips a ring," Frank said.

"No point," I replied. "He's taken the rest of the afternoon off. Thanks for the hand-over, Frank." I was heading off when I asked more as an afterthought, "By the way, how did your case go?"

"Adjourned," he responded sulkily.

"Oh, bad luck" I sympathised, and I continued on my way. Frank went his more than a little downcast. I felt sure that my next hand-over from Frank was likely to be delayed.

There is nothing quite like that first intake of fresh air as you leave the Four Courts of an evening, all the more so if you leave a good day behind you. And for once I did. The air was positively balmy, summer definitely on its way. It was a little too early for the Christchurch bells but no one could have convinced me that they were not ringing. Too bad if Robert couldn't hear them.

As I strode up the quays, the word 'vicissitudes' kept bouncing around in my head. Truly the vicissitudes of litigation. If a case (as opposed to the *dramatis personae*) were amenable to psychiatric examination, then surely the diagnosis would have been "suffers from mood swings". Certainly this case swung in all directions at different times. Each side at different times was certain of bringing home the bacon. The respective parties got their money's worth. Ah, the slings and arrows of outrageous fortune. Could old Will Shakespeare have been anticipating *Jones v. Newman House Hotel*?

I reflected with satisfaction on my performance, savoured again some of the key moments. Put again some of the key questions. Recalled how much the case was going against me at times only to be rolled back. What was it Bradley had said? *"Must compliment Mr McNamara on his advocacy...were it not for his tenacity..."*

My feet hardly touched the ground as I accompanied Anna Livia as far as the DART station. In one or two more insightful moments I gave credit – just a little – to Penelope herself and recognised that were it not for her sporting pedigree the result might have been different. However, I didn't allow the truth to come between me and my celebration. The moment had had a prolonged period of gestation and, in the end, twins as it were. Not just a win, but back-to-back wins. There would be no stopping me now. I couldn't wait to get home and tell Rachel.

I dismounted the DART at Monkstown, a stop too far. A short detour into the village where I purchased a bottle of chilled Chilean Chardonnay for us both and a bunch of freesia for Rachel.

Who, for once, was already in and in good form into the bargain. After a day that might not have reached the dizzy heights of mine, it had clearly given her an elegant sufficiency of satisfaction. I put the children to bed while Rachel prepared the dinner. I lit the candle on our dining room table. We chatted enthusiastically about our days – the emphasis I have to admit being on mine for a change – and the Bar and our hopes and ambitions. In truth, an evening out of heaven. Out in the bay, a lone surfer danced with the dying light of day.

About ten, we took the phone off the hook – not tonight, Arnold – and went to bed.

Wigs on the Green

Ever since I came to the Bar, Mark had urged me to join the Bar Golf Society. "It's the passport to success at the Bar," he had said on countless occasions. "Look at the membership. Judges, Seniors, fellow Juniors. What better way to get to know your colleagues and the Bench and to become known to them?"

On one famous occasion, an even more famous Senior Counsel had decried the male habit of handing over briefs in the loo. Nonsense, the male Bar had responded in unison. But of course, she was right. In the loo, in the robing room, in the club – anywhere we were gathered in our name. But nowhere as much as in the Bar Golf Society. The Masonic and Orange Orders were mere montessoris in comparison. "Think briefs," Mark had said whenever he talked about it.

And I was beginning to think about it. Notwithstanding an improvement in my practice in recent times, it wasn't easy getting off the ground at the Bar. Initially, my ambition was to do it all on my own. Hard work and ability would win through. In a word or two, I would succeed on merit alone. *But what was wrong with meeting your colleagues socially?* I began to think to myself. And if there were a judge or two thrown in, what of it? No man is an island, etc., etc. I was in the process of being persuaded.

What of the right of passage? Golf. I hated the game, not to mention those who played it. In fairness, it wasn't just golf I hated. All sports. This was nothing recent. It went back to my school days. All those Wednesday and Saturday afternoons in Rathmines. Under threat of what I never found out, to drag my unco-ordinated body onto a pitch drenched by the latest seasonal downpour and swept by the Mistral to pursue an ill-shaped ball as it was passed from one more ill-shaped opponent to another, in a match that was reserved for what in legal terms might be called the rugby residue. The favourite and favoured sons – a distinctly more co-ordinated corps – were busy pounding the pitches of St Jones' Road (not far from a hallowed ground in which this ill-shaped ball would receive much the same welcome as a member of the RUC) and the appropriately named Lakelands, because it was rare indeed that this latter ground was drier than the Irish sea. Not to mention the sheep – nourished pampas of Cabra if you were unfortunate enough to be drawn against a certain northside institution.

Those of us who, for obvious reasons, did not make it to St Jones' Road or Lakelands or Cabra were consigned to in-house leagues for the mobility challenged on the unsubstantiated evidence of the poet who, a few years earlier, uttered the words "Mens sana in corpore sano". In the vernacular since Vatican II, this might be translated loosely as "character formation". As I inched my way through life, I discovered that none of the things that had been impressed on me in my youth as character-forming had any benefit whatever.

How often at a party or school reunion later in life did one hear a person, more than likely fortified with much wine, declare how wise his teachers had been in imposing certain disciplines (compulsory sport springs to mind) and how now in mid or later life, he felt the benefit of it (when precisely the benefit was first felt and in what manner is never revealed) and with what enthusiasm he was now imposing the self-same discipline on that section of the next generation for which he had immediate responsibility. Invariably, this mid-life philosopher is the adult version of the school boy who, years earlier, rarely darkened a pitch with his presence.

Not so I. Without the benefit of a Pauline conversion, seemingly experienced by so many, I remained utterly consistent in my condemnation of these early-life abuses which, far from being salutary, were often in my experience (here adopting the language of the top psychiatrists) "life-threatening".

Mark was very persuasive, however, and you didn't take his little pearls of wisdom lightly. This one became my New Year resolution. Hand-in-hand with this resolution went another one, namely to acquire a handicap because as the song says, "You can't have one without the other". The golf world is a strange one and full of contradictions. For example, the handicap. Most people in life, if saddled with a handicap, devote their time and their money to unsaddling it. Not so in golf, where aspiring golf-ers actively seek a handicap, devoting much time and money to acquiring one. In life, people tend to be shy about talking about any handicap with which they have been burdened. Not so in golf, where much of the conversation is taken up with talk about one another's handicaps. There are degrees of handicap. High ones and low ones. There are even travelling handicaps. They go in and they go out. If you have no handicap (you would think this is a cause of celebration), you are in the very uncom-fortable position of having to play off scratch. Apparently, there is no cure for this condition. Not surprisingly this is a lonely position and scratch golfers tend to play by themselves a lot.

One of the advantages of the handicap is the fact that a use-less golfer (and Mark reassured me there were many of these in the Bar Golf Society) can play competitively with the likes of Seve Ballesteros. For example, you can have a handicap of twenty-one (which really means that you shouldn't be playing the game at all) and you can grace the same course and competition as Seve. And if you manage to beat him – it would be hard not to playing off twenty-one – you will be fêted right down to a men-tion in your obituary and maybe even his. Imagine the handicap system transported to the Olympic one-hundred metre final. On the start line, Carl Lewis is going for his fifteenth gold medal. At fifty metres Mr Justice Fleming and at seventy five, Arnold.

No wonder golf is the only drug-free sport left. Who would need drugs when you can have a handicap?

I was one of those conscientious people who took New Year resolutions seriously, not to mention Lent. Whereas nowadays not even priests could tell you what was in and what was out on a day of fast and abstinence, time was that you weighed your food to make sure you weren't over the limit, like with your lug-gage at the airport. And if you were over, you paid the peniten-tial price. In those days before political correctness, it was called "the black fast". A bit before my time, but it still cast its shadow. Time was also when one gave up things: sweets, cigarettes, drink, romance. Serious sacrifice. Nowadays one receives a Protestant-type suggestion (no insistence, no persuasion, it's entirely up to you) to try to love everyone more. Whatever that means. How do you weigh that? Lent is not what it used to be. No wonder the Muslims are gaining ground.

New Year resolutions are a more secular affair. I used to make loads of them. Having nothing to do to pass those lost days between Christmas and New Year I would fill my new diary with pages of new resolutions, many of them identical to the entries in the previous year's diary. No matter. Undaunted, I would throw myself into the task again. Get up early. Work harder. Work out. Go to the gym. Jog. Do the Dublin Marathon in October. Lose weight. See a film, see a show once a month. Try to be punctual. Now there's a hardy annual. On and on without end, like lines for your teacher. If ever God showed his wisdom, it was in restricting the Commandments to ten and then reducing them to two.

When I eventually saw the light – after many years when not a single resolution made it to February – I went one better and reduced them to one. And this year, it was golf. For many this would be a resolution of love, not a chore, but given my antipathy for sport, love did not come into it. I even went so far as to place an each way bet. If golf went the way of all previous resolutions then I would renew it for Lent and play golf for God if not for love. One way or another this was to be the year of the golf ball and come hell or high water my aim was to be on the first tee for the President's Prize on the first day of the Whit Vacation.

According to Mark, my mentor in all things pertaining to golf, the first thing to do was to have a lesson and he knew the very person. On the appointed day at the appointed hour I presented myself at the feet of my golf guru, John. It wasn't until very early on in the lesson that he realised what a challenge I was to offer to his teaching skills.

"Just hit a few balls to begin with and that will give me an opportunity to assess your swing and generally to see where to start," the guru cheerily recommended in a tone that suggested that this would be another typical Monday morning lesson. It occurred to me to reply that the beginning might be an appropriate place to start but then I thought it might be better if he discovered certain things for himself. Like a new definition of "the beginning". He made the unfortunate error of assuming a certain degree of eye-to-ball co-ordination on my part. However, his mistake dawned on him when, after ten minutes shivering in the January cold my ball remained glued to the tee. The head of my club whizzed by the ball at great speeds and with great force at least ten times, but to no avail. The white thing remained there, impassive, unimpressed, motionless without even a hint of co-operation. Like an egg in an egg-cup and with about as much intention of scooting up the fairway.

"I can see that we have a bit to go," remarked John, revealing in a flash why he was a golf pro and not a philosopher. The thought of philosophy reminded me, as I attempted to improve my relationship with the golf ball, of the only pearl of wisdom that I retained from one year's study of philosophy in UCD as part of my first year legal studies. I think we were discussing the existence of God at the time and my distinguished lecturer attempted to illustrate a point by taking the game of golf as an example.

"Take golf," he said. "Millions of people around the world spending valuable time walking around golf courses with clubs trying to get a little white ball into a small hole." He paused theatrically. At least he had our attention, which for the previous ten minutes had drifted to the far side of Earlsfort Terrace where it settled on a horde of over-developed Alexandra girls as they made their uniformed way down to St Stephen's Green where they would while away some time smoking cigarettes and discussing Plato with their student boyfriends. "Why not make the hole bigger?" the professor asked, to the intense puzzlement of the crowded lecture theatre. What this graphic illustration had to do with the meaning of God, no one knew, not even the clerical students among us. As to what it meant we were none the wiser either, except that it seemed to undermine, in a few words, the vast sums of money that the State was ploughing in annually to golf tourism.

Anyway, as I endeavoured to cut the umbilical cord that bound my ball to its tee, it occurred to me that if the Royal and Ancient were to make the balls bigger this would have a more beneficial effect than even television in attracting people to the game.

Much of the remainder of the lesson was lost on me as I wondered why my efforts were referred to as "fresh airs". Was it something to do with a walk in the country? I kept these unhelpful reflections to myself as I strove to concentrate on the "Vs" my thumbs and index fingers should be forming with my shoulders, the breaking of my wrists and the arc of my swing. Really, if striking a golf ball was so complicated, should one even bother? At the end of the lesson, the fifty or so balls that I eventually hit, more by accident than design, ranged out in front of us like a highly localised snowfall, none more than fifty metres from the tee. A child of three could have sent them further with a plastic putter.

With the best will in the world, my instructor could not have described what had gone on in the previous half hour of our shared existence as progress. I must have left him wondering if he should not give up all this idealistic nonsense about teaching people a valuable life skill and instead get a job in a bank or insurance company while such jobs were still going. For my part, I was a little overwhelmed, not just mentally but also physically, as I departed the golf club laden down with golf tomes (*Golf in 80 Days; Golf: The Inner Struggle; The Simplicity of Golf*), videos and even photographs of myself that more resembled Francis Bacon's studies than what I was used to seeing in the mirror. Perhaps the inner torment shone through.

Over the next twenty-four hours as I tried to come to terms with my first lesson, I counted one hundred and fifty-six different steps that it was vital to have in mind between the moment of conception and the moment of delivery. While one was required to have these steps in mind, one must not be conscious of them. Apparently in time, no time mentioned, it would all become second nature to me and I would step up on the tee and dispatch the little white enemy with that absence of complication that one has come to associate with those golfing greats who daily dominate our screens. I had my doubts.

"How did it go?" Mark inquired enthusiastically on Tuesday morning. I didn't want to let him down.

"Not too bad. I think the pro was quite impressed," I lied convincingly. "But it's not as easy as it looks."

"Nonsense, Dermot. Nothing to it really. You'll master it in no time. All it takes is practice. You'll have a handicap before you know it." I felt I had that already. Easy for Mark to talk. He's played since he was four, when he was first presented with a golf club by his encouraging father. "The next thing for you is the driving range. There you can put into practise all the little nuggets your man taught you."

"Well?" Mark enquired again later in the week. "How's it going? Did you get out to Leopardstown yet?" Mark was full of enthusiasm. I think that he had pushed me so hard into golf that he felt a certain responsibility. He wanted me to enjoy it, wanted me to be good at it. I couldn't tell him the whole truth. One rarely can.

"We're getting there," I lied in a non-specific sort of way. "A good bit to go yet, but we're making progress." It was certainly true that there was a good bit to go, "we're getting there" was on the optimistic side and "we're making progress" was a downright lie. But what else could I say? Mark would have been very hurt if I had given him an action replay of every mortifying moment of my morning at the driving range in Leopardstown.

"I find the more I practise the luckier I get," the four handicapper confided. "Just keep at it. Practise, practise, practise." I didn't think I had enough time and wondered about putting back my debut for another year.

The weeks and months passed and I practised and practised and despite my protestations that I was not ready, Mark insisted on putting my name down for the President's Prize. According to him, he had fixed me up in a good fourball and I wouldn't have a bother.

It was the last day of term and the day before the President's Prize. I was lounging by the pillar in the Library, contemplating with pleasure the thought of the short Whit Vacation and with some terror the prospect of my golfing debut on the morrow. I hardly noticed Donal sidle up to me.

"Playing tomorrow, Dermot?" he asked.

"In fact I am, Donal. My first outing with the society. I'm dreading it. Not the society. The golf. Nervous as a kitten."

"Nothing to worry about, Dermot. You won't have any problem."

"I'm not so sure about that. To be honest, I can't get the hang of it at all."

"What do you mean?"

"Everything. At least almost everything. Chipping and putting not too bad. At least I'm not too much of a danger when I'm on the green. But tees and fairway, awful. The ball goes anywhere and everywhere. I am going to kill someone." I was getting into quite a state even as I lounged around the pillar. "Any tips?"

My first mistake. Donal must have been well into his seventies by then. Notwithstanding his age he still had a substantial practice. Mainly criminal, mainly prosecution. His twin passions in life were prosecuting and playing golf, which was no coincidence. They had much in common, prosecution and golf. Preparation was half the battle – painstaking preparation. Step by studied step until the conviction is secured and the little white ball discharged. Donal was unusual in that he took his work every bit as seriously as his golf. In truth, he was a bit of a bore, both at work and at golf, and if I had thought for a moment that my request for a tip might be regarded as rhetorical, Donal quickly disabused me of the notion.

He had read widely on the subject (golf, that is), and over the next three quarters of an hour or so he shared with me the benefit of his extensive reading. Not surprisingly we were given a wide berth during that tutorial by anyone who ventured into the vicinity of the pillar, a recognised place of congregation for those members of the Library who had a few minutes or a few hours to spare. Donal was to be avoided at all costs. Colleagues who typically spent most of their day up against the pillar were suddenly nowhere to be seen. Donal was always very polite and well meaning, it had to be said, but these characteristics apart it had also to be said that he was mind-blowingly tedious and long-winded. He cornered you and once he did there was no escape.

After about forty minutes, Donal moved from the theoretical to the practical. He examined my grip and my swing and demonstrated his.

"At the end of the day, Dermot, golf is a simple, straightforward game. In essence, what are you trying to do?" I realised by now that Donal didn't expect me to answer his questions. "Get that ball from tee to hole in as few shots as possible." I nodded. Difficult to refute that. "Specialising in the bleedin' obvious", as Fawlty would say.

"And take the drive. What are you trying to do there?" Once again, I left it to Donal. Who obliged. "Get the ball off the tee, as far down the fairway as possible." Golf lessons for the retarded. "See what I mean, Dermot? What could be simpler? Keep the ball on the fairway. That's all you have to think about when you're standing on the tee tomorrow."

I was beginning to think that Donal should be a psychiatrist. I owe a deep debt of gratitude to another colleague who every year runs Donal very close for the title of Biggest Bore in the Library and who appeared at that very moment.

"Could I tear you away for a moment, Donal?" the good Samaritan inquired.

"Please do," I had to prevent myself from saying. It's funny how they seek one another out and find one another. The bores, I mean. Indeed any subculture. Frequently you will find them huddled together. Bores. Eccentrics. Loons. Anyway, off they went, happy as could be. Donal and he who comes second for a riveting hour or two.

I went looking for Mark to clear my head. "I've just had an hour of Donal."

"How did you manage that?"

"Couldn't help it. Just standing at the pillar. Didn't see him coming."

"What were you talking about? His latest conviction?"

"Oh no. Nothing like that. Golf, of all things. I made the mistake of telling him that I was a little anxious about tomorrow. Well if he didn't see that as his opportunity of sharing with me everything he had ever learnt about the game. My head is reeling. I take it he is a bit of a crack shot?"

"Good God, no. He's useless. Or worse. Can't get the ball off the tee. Handicap of twenty-six."

"I don't believe you. I would have sworn he was single figures from the way he was talking."

"Not Donal. It is always the same with golfers. Their ability is in inverse proportion to the seriousness with which they take their game and the extent to which they rabbit on about it. You'll find out all about it tomorrow. See you at two."

At last the great day dawned, Friday the second of June, the first day of the Whit Vacation. The country basked in early summer sunshine. And when it came to basking, nowhere could do it as well as Milltown. From the balcony where we were enjoying the president's coffee and biscuits, we surveyed the course. Everyone agreed that it looked resplendent. The sun was high in its heaven and the fairways were fairly shimmering in its rays. Everyone was delighted for our popular president. Colin deserved no less. He had put a lot of work into the Society during his two years as president, which couldn't be said of all his predecessors. The year before him the president failed to turn up to his own prize. He was sailing in the Med. Got the dates wrong. Another year, the competition didn't take place because the incumbent failed to book the course in time. No such hiccups with Colin, who enjoyed the honour and ran the Society with friendly efficiency.

The locker room was buzzing. Mark had been right – where else would you get Bench and Bar, Seniors and Juniors assembled so cosily together? The Bar and Bench at play. There was a lighthearted tension in the air, and as we togged out you could almost feel how much everyone was looking forward to their round. For the moment at any rate, everyone was in with a chance. The prize was within reach. Everyone was at ease with their game. Maybe today would be the day.

The atmosphere was friendly. Colleagues you didn't normally associate with one another – in fact, who you knew positively disliked one another – wished one another well or if one had just completed his round, enquired with sincerity how the other had done. It was like Christmas Eve, as if each had made a mental resolution upon waking that morning to love his fellow member of the Bar Golfing Society.

For a beginner like myself, there was much useful information to pick up – whether the course was playing long or short, the greens fast or slow, the pin positions. I wasn't sure what a lot of this vocabulary meant and felt sure that it was for those taking the honours course. My single ambition at that moment was to get off the first tee.

In deference to the conditions, suncream was being applied to every conceivable part of the body. As we looked after our vulnerable flesh, the chat and banter was flying. I noticed that of those who had completed their round, most were wondering why they played the game at all, felt certain that there had to be a better way of spending a Friday morning and had already decided to give up the game. They had never putted so badly, had no idea what the fairways were like because they were never on them and could tell you the name of every tree on the park. Apparently this was all rather surprising, because only the previous week they had been hitting the ball immaculately. Funny old game, golf. Most of this information was quite gratuitous. No one asked for it and no one seemed particularly interested in it. Indeed, I doubt if it mattered much to those who were furnishing the information if there was anyone there to receive it at all. The same monologue would likely have taken place even if the locker room had been empty. It was all part of the ritual, part of the winding-down process.

On the other hand, those who were about to embark on the day's business were in lighter, less fatalistic moods. They were on their game, the omens were good and they were about to crack the course. Blessed be the innocent and those with hope in their hearts.

The time for curtain up was fast approaching. I changed into my golf gear, which included a brand new gleaming white glove. If sartorial sense converted into stableford points, I was on my way to a glorious round. Time to be on the first tee, to which I went via the loo as the last part of my preparations. Or so I thought. I hadn't counted on bumping into Donal over the urinal. All I asked him was "How did you do?" I assumed the answer would be "Well/not bad/poorly" and I could continue on my way to the first. But no. Apparently Donal bogeyed the first, having been in the sand, went into the car park on the second, behind the trees on the right on the third and played to the wrong green on the fourth and so on for eighteen holes and eighteen minutes.

So much for what an easy game it is and keeping to the fairways. I hadn't the heart or the time to remind him. The last thing I wanted to do was to keep this conversation alive. A few "oh dears," "really?" and "that was bad luck" was the extent of my contribution. And even still this conversation didn't seem like it was ending. Notwithstanding my flashbacks to yesterday in the Library, beads of perspiration forming on my brow and my regular reference to my watch – "Gosh, I'm due on the first." Undaunted, Donal was determined to talk me through it, no shot omitted.

In the end I was forced to abandon him in mid-sentence. As far as I can recall he was reliving his nightmare at the seventeenth. He put his second and third onto the road – which apparently was unlike him and indeed he hadn't done that for some years now – when I simply had to leave him or my playing partners would have left me. I am not sure how long it was before Donal noticed my absence, because when I returned to the locker room after completing my round, he was still there.

My debut could be delayed no longer.

I arrived on the tee to be greeted by an apologetic Mark, who was full of explanations as to why the fourball be had put together so carefully for my benefit had had to be disassembled just as carefully at the last moment. Paul had been called away urgently to look for an injunction and David's wife had gone into Holles Street overnight to have a premature baby. Mark himself had been invited to join the president's fourball, which had also suffered a last minute casualty. I was on my own, which would have suited me perfectly, particularly having regard to the identity of my new partners.

Judge Rogers I knew only too well, even though he did not remember me. "Brendan Rogers," he said to me, shaking my hand, "I don't think we've met." I wasn't sure whether or not to say anything about Letterkenny and the coconuts (a sure winner of a case in front of him that I had contrived to lose) and before I made up my mind he had moved on to the second member of our quartet. I knew from my disappointment in Letterkenny that he was an efficient, no-nonsense judge who didn't use two words if one would do. A ten handicapper according to Ronald Browning, my opponent in Letterkenny, so he obviously didn't use two shots if one would do. Like all good golfers he eschewed caddy and caddycar and carried his bag on his back.

"I haven't played for two weeks," Kevin O'Sullivan, SC informed me in a manner that suggested that this was a fact of some importance as we introduced ourselves. Kevin played off eighteen. He didn't play very well off eighteen, it had to be said. Not that I was one to talk. Golf and himself were O'Sullivan's great interests in life – in reverse order. He was a cheerless Chancery Silk who, despite his success, smiled little. Golf, like life, was a constant source of irritation to him, constantly letting him down. From the moment he hit the ball it was doomed, accompanied by his effing and blinding to whatever bunker or obstacle reared its ugly head. In his entire round, there was not a shot that he was pleased with. Even the lengthy putts that occasionally dropped did not do so in the manner intended by their maker. He had an all-consuming interest in his own game and played under the misapprehension that this focus was shared by everyone else. When he was not treating his playing partners to the *mens rea* behind his last drive or chip, he was regaling them with the intimacies of his last Chancery outing. Heavy jelly indeed.

The last of our group was Afric, who I'd had an unrequited crush on since our days in King's Inns. And when I say "our days" I do not wish to suggest that there was anything even remotely shared about our time in that institution, because there wasn't. Many was the night I had spent hoping for an opportunity to talk or dance with her, and many was the night I made my lonely way home back to my bachelor's pad. But all that was history.

On the first tee at Milltown on the occasion of the President's Prize, the president himself was in fine fettle. He spent the day on the tee wishing everyone well and informing them that if they survived to the tenth there would be a drink waiting for them there. Our hellos and, where necessary, introductions over, we got down to business.

The judge was first to go. Not a moment wasted. Muttering something about this 230 metre par four first really being a par three, he duly dispatched his ball to within a few metres of the pin. All within a matter of seconds. "Well done, Judge. Great drive," could be heard from all sides. The judge took it all in his stride with more than a hint that there was nothing out of the ordinary about what he had just done. Par for the course, as it were.

Kevin wasn't quite as efficient. He placed his ball on his bright pink tee and then stood over it for a while. He looked up at the flag several times and then at his ball. Repeatedly he brought the face of his club to within a centimetre or two of the ball, swinging his club lightly. Then just as we all thought he was about to settle into the actual drive, he would break away from the driving position entirely and take a few practice swings. All the time saying to himself that he hadn't played for two weeks. Then back to square one, where he resumed standing over the ball. Motionless, as if in some erect yoga position.

Then all of a sudden at a moment when we had decided he was unlikely to come out of whatever it was he was in, he unleashed a big one. Out, out into that great space between the tee and the searing sun. His ball rose and rose for a long time, making a nonsense of the laws of gravity until eventually it remembered its limitations and fell to ground far up the fairway, not far from the green. By anyone's standards (the judge excepted of course) a corker of a drive and a great start to Kevin's round. But was Kevin happy? Not by a long shot. We may not have noticed it but his club had hit the ground just before impact with the ball and were it not for that he would be effing well up there with the judge. "I meant to get out during the week but I was just too busy."

The culmination of six months of preparation or thereabouts. The fulfilment of my New Year's resolution. I am not sure if at that moment I was all that grateful to Mark for his conviction that the Bar Golf Society was the passport to success at the Bar. I was a bundle of nerves. It occurred to me as I planted my tee that my life seemed to be made up of a series of nervous occasions: college debates, Bar finals, first case, second case, wedding day, first case in the High Court and now this. If Prufrock measured out his life with coffee spoons, perhaps I measured mine in nervous occasions. The meaning of life – passing from one nervous occasion to the next.

I tried to focus on what I was doing. I was even having difficulty getting the tee into the parched earth. It was fair to say that by now a number of interested onlookers had assembled in the vicinity of the tee. Not to mention the overhanging balcony. Hadn't Kevin given them plenty of time? There is always interest in what a judge does – why is not altogether clear – particularly among the more junior members of the Bar, and so many of the assembled multitude were there to watch the judge, all the time entertaining the secret hope that he might knock down his ball. When he didn't do that, there was always the possibility of a bit of unseemly language from Kevin. The crowd certainly wasn't going to disperse when there was a chance of seeing Afric's swing, along with her legs, which were deemed the best in the Law Library, and so I was flattered by the attendance. How I wished then that I had been more sporty at school and that I could take my place on the tee and calmly send this ball to land somewhere between the judge's and Kevin's and so impress not only the crowd but also Afric.

I took my place. The sun shone down relentlessly. The ball resting on the tee cried out to be struck. Cries of "Good luck,

Dermot" from friends who knew what I was going through – I had mentioned to a few people (half the Library) over the previous days that I was not exactly looking forward to this moment – died down. A deafening silence ensued. I was on my own.

Again. I addressed the ball. One last look in the direction of the green. One last twitch of the club to within a blade of grass of the ball. One last (pious) ejaculation – who on earth is the patron saint of golfers? For a moment I felt the centre of the universe. It was time. Keep the head down. Don't bend the elbows. Slow backswing. Everything according to the book. All I had to do now was reverse the process. All of which I did, exactly as I had been taught. To unleash a big ball down the first fairway of my first President's Prize.

I am not quite sure where things went wrong.

Just in front of the tee and to the left there is a thick bush about three feet high. It is not an obstacle as such. Its purpose is solely cosmetic. It looks nice there. Colin was sure he knew the exact point of entry, which explained why he was down on his presidential knees examining the multitudinous leaves and twigs that were no match for the assault that had just taken place. It was like a treasure hunt. Everyone assembled around the bush looking for the reluctant prize. Everyone except the judge and Kevin, that is. Afric rose to the occasion. In her trousers and top, which were both about two sizes too small for her, she bent and knelt and stretched and reached to the delight of those who were more interested in watching her than looking for my ball. The judge said that he had never seen anyone put their drive into that bush before and Kevin was scanning the fairway to make sure that no one made off with his ball. No ball was ever looked for with more enthusiasm.

Eventually, the judge's patience got the better of him and he suggested that I hit another. This seemed a good idea and I reassembled myself on the tee. There was nothing for it. I had to go through the entire routine again. This time I had no recollection. At least the ball left the tee, barely missing a few ascending seagulls as it made its low trajectory towards the trees on the right. I was launched at last.

Afric's swing was studied with great intent. Had Seve Ballasteros turned up at that moment no one would have paid him the slightest attention. Afric had the floor. It could have been a master class, such was the attention given to her every movement. The demonstration would be stored in the memory bank to be invoked of a winter's evening when summer and Afric were far away and a brief had to be read. It didn't matter where Afric put the ball, but as luck would have it hers, too, headed down the fairway towards the judge and Kevin who were already on their way to their balls.

I took a few more shots to get to the green and eventually secured an eight. As the judge had said it was really a par three and he performed accordingly. Kevin three putted, which apparently he hadn't done for some time – two weeks anyway, because as we well knew at that stage he hadn't played for two weeks – so he was down in five. Afric sank a long one for a four and so we proceeded to the second with the judge calculating that if we spent as long on each of the remaining seventeen holes, the round would take six hours. I wasn't sure where time could be saved.

The second was uneventful and so we proceeded to the third, another high-profile tee, where the judge drove – another corker – and only just stopped himself heading off to play a second before the rest of us took our shots. Kevin went where no one should ever go on this hole, and that is to the right and into the trees. At this stage I wasn't certain if the crowd had gathered for Afric's lesson or my discomfiture. The balcony was packed with my good-humoured colleagues who were enjoying their day off. A sprinkling of judges and a smattering of Silks and you get the picture. Even the president himself had momentarily abandoned his post on the first, presumably in case there might be another treasure hunt at which he could be of assistance.

I could hardly hold the club. Even my mind was shaking. I had no recollection whatever of what my guru had taught me. I just wanted to get off this tee. Indeed, off this course and go back to Rachel and the twins. That was not an option. The audience would have demanded its money back. There was nothing for it. I had to play. And soon. I took the club back, wrapped it half a mile around my neck and let loose. If ever a ball was going to reach a green, this was it. But which green? I knew myself that I had struck it well. If I needed confirmation it was there in the immediate response of the audience, who began to say "Good shot, Dermot."

I am not sure if it was known until that moment that there was a design flaw in the construction of the clubhouse – it was built too close to the third tee. This defect was not helped by the presence of a small sign just off the front left edge of the tee. In retrospect I felt that the sign should not have been there but I was told afterwards by the secretary of the club that it had been in that position for fifteen years and upwards and no complaints. My ball, which everyone agreed had been well hit, ricocheted off the sign, turned in a right angle, or more accurately a left angle, and made its way up onto the roof of the clubhouse where, to the surprise of those having a late lunch, it bounced a number of times before dropping off onto the putting green where some serious-minded members of Milltown were putting in a little bit of practise while they waited for their turn to tee off.

The audience was cracking up. There wasn't even an attempt to restrain themselves. The merriment was out in the open. The only people who were not joining in were the judge and Kevin. The judge saw no fun in it at all and kept looking at his watch, wondering if he should revise his original estimate of six hours while Kevin was scanning the horizon for any sign of his ball. And Afric of course, who was turning out to be a real sweetheart. I had no idea why, after all those years of unrequited attendance on her, years when she wouldn't pay me the slightest attention. And now here we were in my six hours of great need and Afric playing a blinder.

She immediately came over to me and told me not to worry. "Things can only get better," she said, striking an optimistic note. I think that if it hadn't been for her sympathy I would have run off the tee and tried to drown myself in the hand basin in the men's. I was hoping that while Afric was taking her drive those on the putting green might have cleared off or died or something. Anything to spare me the ignominy of having to go over and ask for my ball back.

"Excuse me. Would you have any idea where I should drop?" I enquired of the putters in an obvious reference to my ball. Afric didn't know and there was no one else to ask. The judge was some hundreds of metres away preparing his wedge to the green. I could just about make out Kevin's shadow in the trees. At least Afric was showing some interest in my misfortune. One of the putters looked at me in a manner reserved for visitors from another club. The other putter at least engaged in dialogue. "I'm afraid I have no idea. I have never seen anyone do that before," he said, and he putted on.

The game settled into a certain pattern. The judge usually had the honour of going first, which was something of a euphemism in this less than exalted company. Then Kevin. Then me. Then we would converge on the ladies' tee where we would retreat into our individual and very different reveries as Afric drove. Needless to say, invariably I was all over the place. This didn't bother the judge or Kevin in the sense that they didn't waste any time looking for my ball or escorting me from one shot to the next. Exhortation wasn't one of their talents either. No golf-side manner, as it were. Their drives taken, they would stride separately from the tee. The judge normally had a straight walk, as he seldom left the fairway, which in a curious way I felt deprived him of some of the adventure of golf. He was the living exponent of Donal's theory that golf was a game of eighteen fairways, which certainly took a lot of the problems out of the game. It also tended to shorten things considerably. Invariably, Kevin was in the trees.

The eighth was another difficult hole for me. In truth they were all difficult in their own individual way, but the eighth was especially difficult. The eighth runs parallel to Orwell Road. Another design defect. As you play the hole, the road is on your left. Now it doesn't really matter whether the road is on your left or your right. Obviously it matters to those travelling on it. To those in buses and cars for example. To cyclists and pedestrians. Little old ladies. To all of these people it matters quite a deal.

It matters, too, to most golfers. When I say it doesn't matter which side the road is on I am really thinking of golfers like me, because whichever side it is on I am going to be on it. Stand by your road. If the road is on the left I will go left. If the road is on the right I will go right. Fatal attraction. If God came down in the middle of the night and switched the road from left to right I would follow with unswerving loyalty. Accordingly it is really for the sake of geographic accuracy that I record the fact that the road is to the left.

And so it came to pass. The judge, Kevin and Afric were down the fairway while I was still playing my third off the tee. And it isn't as if that is the end of the road. The road, like Afric's legs, goes the whole distance so that I was playing my sixth from where the others were taking their second.

As we walked down the ninth, an unforgiving sun on our backs, we relaxed a little and thought of the beverage on the tenth.

In the distance I could see a crowd assembled on the balcony looking in our direction. My second had landed just short of the bunker. This was my best play so far. Could it last? I approached the chip. I couldn't tell whether I was more nervous about the bunker or the clubhouse roof. I tried to put these bad thoughts out of my mind. Total concentration. Short backswing. Head down. Follow through. *Mirabile dictu.* My ball rose with grace and pace. I knew from the moment I struck it. Comfortably over the sand in the direction of the green. A perfect landing and roll. The ball rolled and rolled. I couldn't believe my eyes. On and on until finally it struck the pin and dropped, to thunderous applause from the sceptics on the balcony. My first birdie.

"See, I told you it would come right. And how!" said Afric as we high-fived. Even the judge permitted himself a smile as he enquired, "A three, Dermot?"

As we sipped the president's minerals, the judge gave us our scores. The judge himself had twenty points, Kevin had fifteen, Afric nineteen and I had five, four of which were achieved on the ninth. Kevin was calculating how he really should have had nineteen were it not for some bad luck on the sixth and eighth.

If the judge spent little time over the first nine looking for my ball or paying attention to how his golfing partners were getting on, he spent even less for the remainder of the round. At twenty points he was in reach of the President's Prize, so he began to give his focused approach to the game new definition. As his was, by and large, a fairway game, he didn't spend any time escorting me to the more scenic corners of the course, so he didn't waste any energy. The only conversation in the entire round that he allowed himself, apart from enquiring our score on each hole, was to ask Kevin as we walked up the tenth what he thought it would take to win.

"I'd say forty-three, forty-four points. Not much less. Conditions are too good. If it hadn't been for my disasters on the sixth and eighth I might have been in with a chance. Still, nothing is impossible." By this stage the judge wasn't listening. He had walked ahead, mentally calculating what he needed on every hole for a forty-four.

Notwithstanding Kevin's uncharacteristic flash of optimism, there was no way that he could feature now. Fifteen after nine simply could not become forty-four after eighteen, particularly after his drive on the tenth.

"That wasn't what I meant to do at all. I lost concentration in the middle of my backswing. Started thinking about my case yesterday. Before McCormack. Do you know what he asked me on the second day of the hearing? You'd be interested in this..." I think that Kevin secretly knew he was out of contention, as the chat about his cases was beginning to get the upper hand on the commentary on his game.

What neither of them realised – they were so consumed with their own games – was that Afric on nineteen was still in the frame, particularly after her pars on the tenth and eleventh. "What do you think, Dermot? Do you think I could do it?"

"Of course you could," I replied. I would have said that anyway, even if I didn't believe it, but in this instance, truth and diplomacy coincided. "But you must put winning out of your mind now. Bit of mental discipline. Just play each shot as it comes and enjoy yourself."

I was certainly doing what I could to keep her mind off winning. Not that I meant to go to such extremes to do so. We were back to the road on the short twelfth. On the right this time (not that it mattered). I thought a seven was the right club. And it was. Direction was the problem.

From the moment I struck the ball there was only one destination. I cringed, terrified of the possibility of causing an accident. I made to go out after the ball to reassure myself but was stopped in my tracks by the judge. In one of his rare excursions into communication, he said, "You'll never find it, Dermot."

"I wasn't thinking of that, judge. I just wanted to make sure that I didn't hit anyone."

"If you hit anyone you'll know all about it. Don't be bringing trouble on yourself." I deferred to judicial wisdom and played another, all the time terrified that perhaps some unfortunate pedestrian was lying on the footpath with a third eye in the middle of her head. As we made our way from the green to the next tee, I heard a roar. Looking back I could just make out a silver-haired gentleman with a bicycle. He seemed angry. He was holding up a golf ball with one hand and shaking a fist with the other. I thought I heard him roar something about an apology. The judge suggested that we play on quickly, that obviously your man wasn't the full shilling.

The fourteenth is a 434 metre par five. As far as I was concerned it was really two holes in one. When you eventually come within view of the green, you become aware of an elegant modern house just to the right of the green, but off the course.

Unfortunately, as I took my approach shot my concentration was divided. I was just thinking how pleasant it must be on a Saturday evening to be having your dinner in the dining room and watching the last of the summer golfers head down the fairway in the setting sun. A moment later, the silence of the afternoon was broken by the sound of an alarm. In my broken concentration, instead of sending my ball onto the green, I sent it onto the roof of this course-side villa where it activated the security system. Happily, no one was in so I was spared further embarrassment. But as we walked down the seventeenth, some twenty minutes later, I could still hear the alarm.

Word had got out that we might be bringing in the winner. Not only that, but it wasn't clear who that might be. The judge and Afric were neck and neck as we stood up on the eighteenth tee surrounded by a number of excited colleagues. They were both on forty-two points. There was a forty-three in the clubhouse. Kevin was out of it. I needed a bogey five to get into double figures. The judge had no shot, so he needed a par four for two points and forty-four. Afric had two shots, so if she could get down in five she would win. The judge had the honour. As ever, faultless. Giving the trees on the right a wide berth and sitting pretty for a wood to the green. "Great shot Judge" rang around the tee from a number of junior colleagues who had joined us to walk up the eighteenth. Kevin went next and he found the trees.

Despite the crowd, I was no longer nervous. I knew nothing was expected of me so I just played the shot. Right up there, just short of the judge. I bowed to those who showed their appreciation. We moved up to the ladies' tee. This was what the crowd had come for. Afric's drive. There was a certain uncertainty as to whether the superior viewing point was from the front or the back. Some couldn't make up their minds and so kept changing places, trying to have the best of all possible worlds. She took more practice swings than usual. Probably a little nervous. Playing to the gallery, perhaps. She could have stayed there in the sunlight for the rest of the evening and no one would have moved. The judge and Kevin would probably have played on but no one else would have left their post. Afric jigged and jerked to the heart's content of her fans. Eventually she struck the ball. No one had the slightest idea of where it went because they were all still looking at Afric. No one except the judge, that is. He knew. Just short of his. Neck and neck.

"Nice and easy, Afric. Nothing fancy," I said to her as we headed for our balls. Kevin was wandering through the trees trying to get out. Afric's second and mine, miraculously in my case, continued up the fairway. The judge was on the green. Two putts for a four seemed a certainty. Afric had to get a five. She faltered on her third and knocked it down. How could she get down in two from there? I put my third on the green. Kevin was on as well.

Afric hit a sweet chip that ended up ten feet from the pin. Kevin two putted for a six. I was delighted to finish on a high note with a five. Maybe I should just play the ninth and the eighteenth in future. The judge duly got his four, which was never really in doubt. More "great putt Judge" from all around. Up to Afric now. A ten foot putt for the President's Prize. It could have been the Ryder Cup for all the excitement and tension. At this stage there was quite a crowd around the green and more up on the balcony. A fitting climax. The president himself was on the edge of the green.

If Kevin took more than a little time with his putts during the afternoon, it was nothing to the time Afric spent on this one. And no one minded. Except the judge, who I could see was edgy. Afric paced the green, looked at the putt from every conceivable angle and was herself looked at from every conceivable angle. She stood up, bent her back, got down on her hunkers. The crowd accompanied her through these gymnastics. Eventually she stood over the ball and made the last measurements. Not a sound. There was only one person present who didn't want to see this putt sink. For a moment I felt sorry for him. No. For less than a moment. The fifty or so onlookers held their breath. Surely she would soon strike the ball. She drew back the putter and nice and gently brought it forward again. She struck the ball well. The line seemed right. It was a question of length. Had she given it enough pace?

The ball was making its way along its ten-foot journey but it was definitely slowing. It would certainly go very close but maybe it would stop at the edge. The crowd willed it on. Just when it seemed to give up it got an extra wind as it were and carried on up to the lip, where it dropped into the hole for a five.

A great roar went up. Afric leapt up in the air. She had done it. The judge was very gracious. He immediately came over and congratulated her. Kevin too, who told her it was a great win. Afric gave me an almighty hug and lifted me off the ground. It had been a long afternoon.

Immediately Afric was surrounded by her colleagues, whisked off to the bar for a celebratory champagne before changing for dinner. Her hour in the sun was just beginning. I wondered if mine had come to an end.

"Well Dermot, how did you play?" Mark enquired when we met in the bar.

"Very slowly," the judge, who was passing at that moment, answered for me.

"Bad luck Judge," Mark said. "Couldn't have been closer. Still, it's not as if you haven't been there before." The judge moved on. I could see Kevin trying to avoid him.

"Bloody awful if you really want to know, Mark. I was in a terrible state on the first and put the ball into a bush. Never done before. On the third I put it on the roof of the clubhouse. Never done before. However, I did have a good ninth and eighteenth. On the ninth, on the green in two..."

"Dermot, you're getting as bad as Donal," Mark interrupted.

"You're right. Or Kevin there."

"Anyway, did you enjoy it? That's the main thing."

"Can't say I did. Too embarrassing. If it hadn't been for Afric, I don't know what I would have done."

"Oh yes, of course. Afric. I had forgotten. You had the hots for her a few years ago. Hadn't you?"

"That's not how I'd have described it. Anyway that was years ago. It's different now. Purely platonic."

"Sure, Dermot. Sure. I'll be keeping an eye on you tonight. Maybe I should give Rachel a ring."

"Lay off, Mark. I'm still trying to recover from my first round with the Bar Golf Society."

Half an hour later I was back in the bar. As was Afric, looking stunning. Success and the afternoon in the sun lent another dimension to her legendary beauty, not to mention the backless dress. Seated on a barstool she was regaling those around her with a blow-by-blow account of her round. Funny, no one seemed to mind Afric talking about her golf. Those around her comprised a Who's Who of anyone who is anyone in the Library. Juniors didn't get a look in. The gong went for dinner. I saw my chance. As she left the bar I told her that I had a table for the four of us. After all, the tradition was that you dined with your playing partners as Mark had told me with a big wink.

"Oh Dermot, that's awfully nice of you. But I can't. You see, the president has asked me as the winner to join the top table. I'd much prefer to be on your table. Really I would, but I can't. You do understand, don't you?" What could I say? Nothing. And if I could, she was gone. Swept up to the presidential table to join the likes of Kevin and the judge, who were there for other reasons. At least they were gone, too. Could you imagine dinner with those two without Afric? It would have been worse than playing golf with them.

I sought out Mark. "Oh. No Afric? Little romance over?"

"I told you it was nothing of the sort. And anyway, she... em...they have been co-opted onto the top table. Any room for me?"

"Of course, come and drown your sorrows with your friends."

After dinner, the president tapped on his glass and introduced the winner to rapturous applause. At this stage I could hardly make out what was being said. The sun had gone to my head. Afric was becoming more beautiful by the glass. I wasn't sure if it was a backless dress or a dressless back.

"And I would like to thank my playing partners. Judge Rogers for being such a sporting loser. Kevin was great company and regaled us with action replays of his shots. A lot of the time it wasn't clear from where the ball ended up what precisely he had been intending to do with it and so it was very helpful when he explained it to us." Kevin was delighted with the accolade. Presumably he didn't get the precise nuance that had the rest of us hooting with laughter.

"A special word of thanks to Dermot. This was Dermot's first outing and while there is undoubtedly potential there, I am sure he would be the first to agree that this was not a memorable round. Notwithstanding his woes, he was able to give me time." Loud banging of table from Mark. "It was he who spotted that I was doing well and might be in with a chance. He helped me to stay relaxed and to keep my eye on the ball. Thank you Dermot. Thank you everyone. This has been a wonderful day."

Crowned by a standing ovation for Afric. I was barely able to stand. At this stage the sun and the alcohol were vying to destroy my remaining brain cells. I couldn't believe my ears, and wouldn't have were it not for the slagging I was getting which confirmed what I thought I had heard. "So you helped Afric to relax, Dermot? No wonder the round took so long." "Where are we off to tonight Dermot? Home early I suppose?"

"Lay off, Mark. She's only being polite."

This back and forth was interrupted by the president. "And now brothers and sisters, we have decided this year to introduce a new prize. *Pour encourager les autres,* as it were. It is hoped that this will encourage the weaker members of the Society. I put a lot of thought into what the prize should be and eventually I decided that every year the president of the Society will present a putter. The prize therefore will be called the President's Putter and will go to the person with the worst round. And this year, out on his own, no challenger in sight, the President's Putter goes to Dermot McNamara."

The table banging was now accompanied by stamping of feet. I struggled to mine and headed off vaguely in the direction of the president to collect my prize. I could hear someone say, "Over here." As I shook hands with Colin and thanked him more than profusely, cries of "speech, speech" went up. *Oh, no. Wait 'til I get Mark and the rest of them,* I thought to myself.

I heard the president say, "Dermot says he would like to say a few words." I could barely stand there, let alone open my mouth, and certainly the two things together seemed unachievable. Like most of the time, there was no way out.

"Colin...I mean President...brothers...and sisters," I began rather slowly, having difficulty first of all in thinking up each word and then in articulating it. "I am quite overcome." This was true. "I didn't expect to come away today with a prize." Also true. "It's a beautiful president Putter...I mean presidential putter...no...putter President and I would like to thank you for your magnificence." My early flow was slowing up. To the delight of my table, who got noisier and noisier with each missing word. Forgetting that my prize was for the worst round and not the best, I set about sharing the credit for my splendid victory with my playing partners. "I couldn't have done this without the help of Afric." My table went wild. "Judge Rogers, too, was of an enormous assistance." Not true. "As was..." I was having difficulty in recalling who our fourth was. "Em..." A number of names were tossed up to me, none of which I recognised. "Em...I would like to thank also the fourth member of our fourball who is well known to you. Finally...Afric did a lot for me. I mean for my game."

"How many Africs were you playing with?" someone from the table wanted to know. This brought the house down. Unfortunately I had no idea what he meant or even less what everyone was laughing at.

Delving into my reservoir of ideas – which turned out to be as dry as the drains of this sun-baked course – for a parting line, I could only manage, "With a little practice, I hope to defend my title next year. Thank you Mr President, thank you everyone." My table was on its feet, clapping and cheering. The remaining tables, no more than myself, were unclear as to the reason for the great excitement.

On my way back to my seat I spotted Afric – or more accurately, as I was staring at Afric I spotted the way back to my seat – and throwing caution to the wind made a mini-detour for the purpose of planting an alcoholic kiss on her fickle cheek. Confusing the occasion with the Ball after Wimbledon, I asked her to dance. Radiant was too dull a word to describe how Afric looked at that moment. "Shall I compare thee to a summer's day" but a weak accolade, a line that, needless to say, did not occur to me until hours later. She was Beauty itself. Surpassing with ease the great goddesses of myth and legend. I couldn't be certain but I was sure that she squeezed my hand as I held hers.

"Let me know if you are going on anywhere afterwards," she whispered in my ear. Somehow or other I conveyed my stumbling body back to my table. I was given a royal reception. A few said, "Great speech, Dermot."

"Did you show Afric your putter?" one wanted to know. I could scarcely believe what was happening. I ordered a round for the table. I was pleasantly surprised at how informal the proceedings were. The speeches were not too long and not too many and the summer evening moved on to the next phase of light entertainment. Music for middlebrows. With the exception of an aria from an elderly colleague who, had he chosen to sing professionally, would undoubtedly have eclipsed Pavarotti, and an eccentric interpretation of John McCormack the music was a little like the golf – strictly high handicap. However, everyone was quite relaxed now. Whatever tension the golf might have induced had now disappeared. We were at the commencement of a short vacation and members were not too exacting in their expectation.

It was about three when I hit the bedroom. In the end we didn't go on anywhere else. We were too comfortable in Milltown and we decided to stay there. Apart from catching her eye a few times, there were no further developments with Afric. I couldn't get near her and even had she wanted to disengage, she wouldn't have been able to break up the concentration of Seniors and judges around her.

I was in high spirits by the time I got home, singing to myself, quietly as I thought, as I undressed a little clumsily. "Shhh. You'll wake the children," was Rachel's idea of welcoming me home. "How did the golf go?"

"Great. I won a prize."

"What for? The worst round?"

"Well actually, yes. A beautiful putter."

"Who did you play with? Mark and the others?" Rachel was full of enquiries.

"No, that fell through. Judge Rogers and Kevin O'Sullivan."

"Oh, just a three ball?"

"No, in fact it was a fourball. Now let me see, who was the fourth? Oh yes. Afric."

"Afric? Oh, I see. Is she the one you had a crush on before you met me?"

"No, I never had a crush on Afric."

"Well, did you take her out?"

"I don't think so. No wait. Maybe we went out once or twice. But it never came to anything. I wasn't interested."

"Well, this is all very entertaining, but it is three in the morning and some of us had to work today and even though it is holidays, I have an early morning consultation. Will you give the kids breakfast?" So much for my hopes for now and a lie-on in the morning.

I went through the day again in my mind before going to sleep. Replayed some of the holes. More successfully this time. Conjured up images of Afric. Her swing. Her walk. Her talk. Her backless black dress. Her squeeze of my hand. Her whisper.

Wasn't Mark right after all? What better way to get to know your colleagues?

The Court Below

It felt as if I hadn't heard from Arnold for some time. There had been the *Park Beauticians* case of course, a famous victory, though I still had a nagging suspicion that Arnold didn't realise or didn't remember that I was his counsel in that case. Even if he did, securing victory for Arnold did not secure my practice. If I thought that winning a case for Arnold would mean that I would be briefed by him on a regular basis, I was wrong. Like Kipling, he treated triumph as an impostor. On my behalf anyway. It wasn't that he didn't want to win his cases. He did, just as much, maybe more, than others. It was just that he didn't give you, me I mean, the credit. He tended to reserve the credit for himself even if he wasn't there, like he wasn't for the second day of *Park Beauticians*.

In the meantime, I had had another famous victory: Miss Jones' case. I was anxious to tell him all about it – the fact that I was acting for one of the posh firms, the win, the judge's praise. I would drop these titbits subtly. Not too subtly of course, because then Arnold might miss them. And of course his sporting background gave him a special interest in the facts of the case and the *dramatis personae*. I was proud of my back-to-back wins and wanted to share them with as many people as might be prepared to listen, Arnold in particular. There had been enough defeats in the course of the learning curve. Now that the tide had turned and I was on the winning trail, I intended to keep it that way. McNamara the winning barrister.

I was clear as to what I wanted from Arnold: his practice. Maybe not permanently, because I didn't see myself servicing Arnold or the likes of Arnold for the rest of my life. But at least in the short to medium-term while I struggled up the ladder of success. He would provide me with experience and exposure, and case by humbling case, I would establish that most sought after of things, a reputation. For the moment, modest and even hopeless cases, then in time on to catastrophic injury cases. That was where the money was. Diversifying also. You couldn't spend your life doing personal injuries. In time, reputation established, spread my wings. So many areas out there and expanding all the time – chancery, commercial, constitutional.

I could see myself addressing the Supreme Court for days on end. The great issues of our time. Referring the Court to Articles this and that of the Constitution. Vindicating the rights of citizens. Delving deep into the well of the Constitution in search of authority for a proposition that would advance the well being of the Irish section of mankind. The Court packed with Bar and public alike to witness a great forensic moment. In years to come, young devils would ask their masters if they were in the Supreme Court the day McNamara persuaded the Court that, for example, everyone had a right to a job. A landmark decision. Not just in this country, but in Europe and around the world. A veritable forensic beacon of international proportions.

For the moment, however, Arnold. My ambition as far as Arnold was concerned was to get onto his "A" team. Promotion to the "A" team would hopefully eliminate the last-minute call-up because Robert and Frank were unavailable. Not that a last-minute call-up should matter. A case was a case after all, however and whenever you got it. But it would be nice to think that you were someone's first choice, not that you were always on the bench waiting for injuries to the first and second teams. In addition, while it may not be guaranteed, you might be more likely on the "A" team to receive the brief earlier than twenty minutes before the case is due to start, thereby improving your chances of showing yourself in the best light. Not to mention increasing the possibility of winning the case for your client, albeit a less pressing consideration.

My immediate future, therefore, was very much tied into Gardiner Street even if it wasn't always clear that this commitment was reciprocated. It was difficult to perceive a plan in

Arnold's way of doing things, save that he seemed determined not to promote me to a position that was permanent, if not pensionable. I had that uncomfortable feeling of being entirely dispensable. So many fish in the sea. Were I to die in the morning, would Arnold even notice? How I envied those more established colleagues who were sought after by their solicitors. It seemed to me that even some of my contemporaries enjoyed this status. It wasn't a question of being tenth on the list. The solicitor woke up of a morning and the only thing on his mind was to make contact with McNamara and confirm his availability for this very substantial commercial case in two weeks time. He didn't want Robert or Frank or James. He wanted McNamara. *Needed* McNamara. Better still, the client himself was *insisting* on McNamara. Had heard of him by reputation and wanted him to head up his team. Solicitor's neck on the line. Get McNamara or else.

How often had I heard a colleague boast, "I didn't want to do the case, but my solicitor insisted. Said I could name my fee. The client was too important to him and he had to have me on board."

Dream on, Mac.

Wednesday morning. Trinity term if you went to Trinity, summer term otherwise. Nothing on. Nothing unusual about that. Happily I was over the stage of having weeks on end of having nothing on, but I could still get a run of quiet days. Like now. Nothing Wednesday or Thursday, a consultation on Friday. I didn't like having nothing on any more than a prostitute likes standing on the side of the road. One prefers to be busy. All the old insecurities invade the idle mind. Would I ever be briefed again?

Rachel rarely had a day when she would not be in court. But that was the nature of the matrimonial side of things, she told me whenever I asked. I didn't admit this to myself very often, but what would we have done without Rachel's matrimonial practice? It wasn't something I reflected on too frequently, and certainly not to be raised in front of Rachel, but the fact was that she was bringing in more money than me. Of course this was only in the short-term. Once my personal injury practice was up and running – already it was heading in the right direction, receiving a timely boost from my recent victories – there would be no stopping me and then Rachel could have the option of giving up practice and staying at home to rear the kids in the grand tradition. The vice versa was too unbearable to imagine.

I breakfasted as usual with those of my colleagues who were prepared to talk at that hour of the morning. A leisurely breakfast. I was in no hurry. Colleagues came and went, dashing to meet their solicitors and clients in preparation for the fray. I sat on through a wide range of conversations, the day's headlines, the latest political scandals, tips for the impending Circuit Court appointment and already there was mention of the Autumn Silks and how their promotion might impinge on our lives. From time to time, a colleague, hurriedly sipping a coffee, shared his problem with us, desperately seeking some last-minute assistance. Any law on this or that? The value of such and such? How many years would he be likely to get? When it was no longer decent for me to remain at the breakfast table, I took myself off to my empty desk where I resumed waiting for Arnold or other legal luminaries. I was in the middle of the crossword when I heard my name called.

"Dermot, by any chance are you free? I am frightfully sorry. It's such dreadfully short notice but I have been badly let down at the last-minute by one of your colleagues. I sent him the brief and asked him to confirm his availability. I have just been told at the reception desk that he is in Sligo today. I would be extremely grateful if you could take the brief and of course this will mean immediate and irreversible promotion to the firsts."

This was what I thought I heard Arnold say to me, but he put it a little differently.

"Mac. You're in luck. A brief for half ten." It was then ten o'clock. "Tried all day yesterday to get Ronald," *of all people* "and when he didn't get back to me I tried all last night to get Frank but without success. Anyway you're here and you'll have to do. Beggars can't be choosers, as they say." And with that he handed me what I assumed to be Counsel's brief. Never for a moment doubting or even enquiring as to my availability. Which was in part confirmed by the fact that I was not robed at that hour of the morning.

"Unfortunately, Ronald has the brief and we didn't have enough time to make up another one," Arnold said, looking at what he had just handed me. A single letter. Addressed to Ronald. It gave the name of the case and the date and time of the hearing. In twenty-nine minutes time. No, twenty-eight to be exact. It stated that it was proposed to hold a "detailed" consultation at nine twenty-five. It mentioned that a brief was enclosed but this information was of course incorrect. Arnold kept his cards close to his chest. Not a great subscriber to the Age of Information in which we lived. "Why don't you go off and change and I'll bring the client down for a cup of coffee?" Obviously, at one point it was felt necessary to have a "detailed consultation", and suddenly there was going to be no consultation at all.

It wasn't immediately clear to me how I could hold Arnold's single letter, now my brief for the day, to the best advantage. There was one benefit to receiving a single letter as a brief and it was that you didn't have to read anything. It cut down the preliminary work. In particular, you didn't have to trawl through a large bundle of papers, many if not most of which were irrelevant. Though of course where Arnold was concerned, you never got a large bundle of papers in any event. The disadvantage was that you knew nothing about the case at the consultation, so the client might wonder what was going on.

What *should* happen, of course, is that you sail into the consultation announcing, "Good morning, Mr Ryan. Now there is good news and bad news. The good news is that you are on in ten minutes and the bad news is that I know nothing about your case. Absolutely nothing. All I have is this one letter which tells me your name. Unfortunately, Mr O'Reilly, presumably because he was so tied up with other cases, left it until this morning to brief me and further the brief itself has gone astray in his office – which is not at all surprising if you have ever had the pleasure of visiting him there. Now, if you would kindly tell me what the whole thing is about I can set about representing you to the best of my compromised ability. It would be preferable if you could keep your account short and simple."

That would be the honest thing to do and also it would be the easiest way of belatedly getting to grips with the case. But of course you can't do that. If you did, it would be your last case from Arnold. Instead, you go to the consultation pretending you know everything there is to know about your client's case. Say as little as possible. Get the client to elucidate. "Mr Ryan, Mr O'Reilly has sent me a very full brief" (hopefully Mr Ryan won't have the courage to ask you where it is) "and I have read it with interest, but of course when you get into the witness box you will be on your own and you will have to tell the judge all about your case in your own words. You will not be allowed to refer to the voluminous notes and letters that you have so helpfully sent in to your solicitor. I think it would be a good idea, therefore, if you were to tell me now the whole story in your own words. Start at the beginning as if I knew nothing about your case."

Hopefully, Mr Ryan is so nervous and keyed up about his case that he will blabber out the entire history and not notice you taking down every word so that you will be able to repeat the whole thing verbatim to the judge when it comes to opening the case. Hopefully he won't notice or ask why you have in front of you no more than a single letter, after all the times he was in to see Mr O'Reilly and all the attendances that were taken, not to mention the other documents that must have been generated by the case.

All you have to do then is avoid obvious pitfalls, like asking some question that gives the whole game away, such as, "Now tell me, Mr Ryan, how do you feel now?", not realising that there was nothing at all wrong with Mr Ryan, who is simply doing his familial duty in taking an action on behalf of his great aunt who was killed in a car crash.

If something does arise and Mr Ryan rises above his station sufficiently to remark, "But Mr McNamara, I told Mr O'Reilly that on umpteen occasions," no matter what Oscar says, you must resist the temptation to reply, "How can I be expected to know that, Mr Ryan, when all I have is this piece of paper and that for all of ten minutes?"

Instead, you say, "You're quite right, Mr Ryan. Completely slipped my mind. Up very late reading the brief. Momentary lapse. Entirely my fault. Anyway, I have the information now and that is what is important." Who said lying doesn't pay?

The client isn't the only potential source of danger in this situation. Arnold himself cannot be ruled out. Arnold, with his obsession with "detailed" consultations and his passion for taking copious notes even now on the morning of the case, when his familiarity with the facts must be such that he could give the evidence himself without a single prompt, is even more likely than the client to make an embarrassing entry. Embarrassing to me, that is. With his highly personalised version of amnesia, he intervenes, "I have to agree with Mr Ryan, Mac. That information is dealt with at many different places in the brief. I really don't understand how you could have missed it." *Thank you, Arnold.*

Arnold was up to high doh about the case. "Mac, this is one you've got to win," he said, leaving me in no doubt as to what the goal was in this case.

"Well, Arnold, you've come to the right man. I'm on a roll. Two wins in a row. This will be the hat trick." I was expecting Arnold to ask me about the second of the two wins, Miss Jones' case. But no. Arnold was higher up to doh than I thought.

"Don't be facetious Mac. This is important." *Obviously. Otherwise why would you brief me as early as ten minutes ago? Could have waited 'til the case started.* "The client is Stephanie, Samantha's sister." *Oh, that important.* Sure enough, there was Samantha, Arnold's secretary, in the corner of the Square Hall outside the Law Library, chewing away. No sign of a walkman on this occasion, but presumably that was a concession to the presence of her sister rather than any waning of her interest in popular music.

The Square Hall where the reception desk for the Law Library is situated was beginning to fill up. It was ten fifteen and people were assembling for their cases. I would have expected Arnold to book a consultation room for such an important case, but it seemed that this thought did not occur to him. There are a few cubicles flanking the Square Hall, where a modicum of privacy can be achieved. These were already taken, so I led our team to a little nook beside a private entrance to the Chief Justice's chambers. Perhaps the proximity to the Lord of the Law might rub off and enlighten our consultation which, of necessity, had to be of short duration and if we couldn't have privacy at least I could have a wall to lie up against as I took notes on Arnold's letter.

At this stage, I was beginning to get a little anxious. We were on in fifteen minutes and I didn't know the first thing about the case except that my client was Stephanie, Samantha's sister. I would need a little more than that to open the case.

"Stephanie, I would like you to meet Dermot, who will be running your case for you. I've just been discussing it with him and he thinks it is quite straightforward and he doesn't anticipate any problems. Isn't that so, Dermot?"

"Well, I'm not –" I was about to enter a caveat but Stephanie didn't give me a chance.

"But Arnold, you told me that Ronald Browning was doing my case and that he was the best barrister in the Law Library."

"Unfortunately, Ronald had to go out on Circuit somewhat urgently. I'm afraid these things happen. The law is very unpredictable," announced Arnold in a rare moment of jurisprudence. "However, Dermot is the next best barrister in the Library" (this was news to me) "and he has read the brief, is fully *au fait* with the facts and has had the benefit of a discussion with Ronald. So you've nothing to worry about. You're in a safe pair of hands. Isn't that so, Dermot?"

"Well, I'm not –" I was about to enter a second caveat, and was beginning to wonder was there a category of caveats known as near-caveats or almost-caveats, but again Stephanie didn't give me a chance. Clearly not one to linger too long on any one point, and while obviously disappointed by Ronald's lack of fidelity, she seemed to accept Arnold's explanation.

She moved on, a little over-familiarly I thought. "Dermot, do you always wear your wig at an angle?" she asked as she leaned over to adjust my wig. The angle of my wig was not something that was uppermost in my mind at that moment, as I was anxious to start learning about the case. I recoiled slightly but not sufficiently to avoid Stephanie's interference with the administration of justice. I felt like someone at a fancy dress whose mask was about to be removed or how I imagined a falling woman might feel as her legs went up in the air and more than she wished to reveal was revealed.

There really wasn't a suitable answer to Stephanie's maternal interest in my appearance, short of telling her to keep her sticky hands off my wig and get on with telling me about her case. "Thank you Stephanie. Now if you wouldn't mind, I would like to hear your version of how this accident happened." I thought I was safe in assuming that there must have been some sort of an accident.

"But Mr O'Reilly told me that you knew all about the case, Dermot."

"And I do. There are just a few matters on which I need clarification and perhaps the best approach would be for you to tell me in your own words what happened."

"Well, where would you like me to begin? At the beginning?"

"Certainly not. There isn't time. Just come right to the point. What were you doing and what happened? Tell me as you will have to tell the judge in a few moments and remember, the judge knows nothing about your case."

Stephanie was dressed – if that be the appropriate verb – in a tracksuit. A bright pink thing. It did nothing for her. Now this surprised me. Not that it did nothing for her, because if there was any dress code that did less for women than jeans, it was a tracksuit, whether of the bright pink flecky variety or not. What surprised me was that she was here in the Four Courts for her case in this ghastly outfit. Never before had I seen anyone in this hallowed building in a tracksuit, apart perhaps from a few eccentric barristers about to run home. Tracksuit apart, Stephanie had no difficulty in catching the eye. Coal-dark hair, stretching further down her back than modest hands dared to reach, her nut-brown eyes parenthesised by bushy eyebrows and lashes long as matchsticks, the overall impression was South American. Hard as it tried, even the tracksuit could not conceal her upper body strength.

The mystery about her dress code was about to be solved. She told me that her passion in life was jogging. *What a waste of passion*, I thought to myself.

"I've run in marathons all around the country and even abroad," she told me before I interrupted her to tell her that we would have to leave the colourful detail of her strange hobby until after the case.

"What about your accident? The judge is about to sit," I said, panic creeping into my voice.

"I was coming to that when you interrupted me, Dermot. You see, I was in training for the Dublin Marathon at the time of my accident."

"Look, could we ever move on from the jogging and the marathons and get on to your accident?"

"But that's how the accident happened. I was out jogging at

the time, as you know." *No, I didn't know. How could I know? No one told me*, I thought to myself.

"Of course, Stephanie, I know all that. And what happened?" I added with a mixture of increasing curiosity and creeping panic.

"It was a February evening, about six o'clock, pitch dark, piercing cold and driving rain. I was jogging along the Bray Road between Foxrock Church and White's Cross, heading in the direction of town. At this stage I had run fifteen or so miles and was tiring. The rush-hour traffic was coming against me."

Normally I liked to allow the client to complete his or her version of events before interrupting, but because of the time constraints I thought it might be more efficient if I cleared certain things up as we jogged along.

"Were you on the path or the road?"

"The road."

"Why?"

"The path at that stretch was very uneven and the public lighting was poor and as I didn't want to break an ankle I thought it wiser to jog on the road."

"And what happened?"

"Well I hardly know. There I was jogging along –"

"I know Stephanie, I have that. What *happened*?"

"Well this car, a Jaguar, hit me. Just before it did, I noticed a break in the traffic. The lights must have changed back at White's Cross. This car must have been the first away when the lights changed to green and it was travelling at a great speed."

"What were you wearing? A tracksuit, like the one you're wearing now?"

"Except for the colour, yes."

"What colour was it?"

"Black." Just as I thought.

"Any chance of a luminous belt?"

"Afraid not. I had one all right but I forgot to put it on that evening. I was in a terrible hurry when I left home." So much for the circumstances of the accident.

"Your injury, Stephanie?"

"Broke my leg. It was bad at the time but I made a good recovery. Unfortunately I wasn't able to run in the Dublin Marathon the following October. I was bitterly disappointed about that. So what do you think?" I was on the point of giving

Stephanie my opinion on her case when she continued, "Samantha knows a lot about these cases and she thinks it is quite straightforward. It's simply a question of how much." *Thank you, Samantha, for such clear thinking.* "Isn't that so, Samantha?" Samantha chewed and nodded. "So what do you think?" For the second time.

"Well it mightn't be –" I didn't get a chance to complete my pessimistic opinion.

"Samantha says that I was doing the right thing in running against the traffic so that they would be the better able to see me." *And what about the footpath? On your side of the road and the other side?* "Also, she says that there is a law, a statutory instrument she called it, which says that a driver must drive at a speed which will enable him to stop in the distance he sees to be clear. Don't understand it myself, but apparently it means he was going too fast, which he was. He was flying. What do you think, Arnold?" she enquired, giving up on me.

It was a curiosity about Arnold that whenever one asked him a question, no matter what the question, no matter how simple, there was always a long delay, like you get on long-distance telephone calls, only longer. It was as if the question was asked in some remote African language and Arnold was struggling to see if he could identify any word that would give him a clue as to the nature of the question. Physically motionless, and to all external appearances intellectually motionless too, though I realised that this could be unfair. There could well be certain mental processes taking place unbeknownst to those present, indeed to Arnold himself. Eventually it became apparent that the question had got through at some level of consciousness because Arnold replied, "What do I think?" followed by more delay. "I'm inclined to agree with you Stephanie," he finally said, after all that.

"Dermot, you haven't told us what you think." *Not for want of trying, I haven't.* Looking into her South American eyes, it would have been much the easier option to go along with the prevailing view. But in the long run wouldn't it be better if I squared with her? I would have appreciated a moment or two to gather my own thoughts. I don't mean as long as Arnold, just a moment or two, but time didn't permit. It was ten twenty eight and time to get up to court. In particular I drew attention to the footpath. "If you had been on the path there would have been no accident."

"Yes, but if he had seen me, there would have been no accident, either."

"I'm not going to argue with you. You've asked me for my view and I am giving it to you. Maybe I'm wrong, but I have considerable reservations about the case and I think that if you were to get an offer of fifty per cent you would have to take it." I was in a minority of one and this was made very clear to me. Indeed I was looked at as if I was some kind of extraterrestrial. In truth I didn't even fancy our chances at fifty per cent, but I hadn't the courage to be that outspoken.

No time for further debate. No time for coffee. Indeed the question was, was I on time at all for the call over at ten thirty when the judge sits and each case listed for hearing that day is called and the judge is informed if it is settled or going on and how long it is likely to take.

In a hierarchy of what is important in the conduct of one's practice, the requirement to be in court on time is right up there at the top. The consequences of unpunctuality where court is concerned are draconian. Your case will be struck out and your client made to bear his opponent's costs, a result enormously embarrassing and expensive. So no matter what happens, Counsel must be in the correct court at the correct time. The fact that I had only received the brief thirty minutes ago would not be an excuse. The fact was that I was in the case for that thirty minutes and knew that my first duty as Counsel was to be in court on behalf of my client when the case was mentioned at the call over. Which explains the speed at which I mounted those stairs on my way to the top of the building.

I had only just realised that it was half ten. Since Mr Gandon placed the final brick, I doubt if those stairs were ever mounted so quickly. I was quite out of breath as I entered the packed courtroom. My heart sank. The judge was already sitting. We were first in the List so I had certainly missed the case on first calling. The only margin for error was that if you were not there on the first calling over of the List, you had another chance when the List was called over for a second time, seconds or at most minutes later. This was my only hope.

For once, thank God for Reilly, who was on his feet. He had been in practice for fifteen or more years and I had overlapped with him for six of those. I cannot speak for his earlier years, but for those six I had never seen him do a case. In court often enough, of course, but never actually doing a case. Always applying to adjourn it and always for great length for a constellation of complicated reasons.

"I regret, my Lord, to have to apply for an adjournment at this late stage. I'm afraid the case just can't go on." Unlike Reilly himself, who was quite capable of going on and on.

"Is it on consent, Mr Reilly?" Some judges were pathologically opposed to adjournments and would break out in spots at the mere mention of the word. This was not one of those judges. If the parties were agreed he saw his function was to implement that agreement.

"In fact it is, my Lord."

"Very well then. Adjourn next term on consent." The judge knew Reilly well and that if he wasn't quick and decisive he would still be listening to this unopposed application in half an hour. But Reilly was well up to him.

"It's not quite as simple as that, my Lord."

"What could be simpler? An adjournment on consent. Would you prefer if I refused your application, Mr Reilly?" his Lordship asked impatiently.

"My Lord, it is just that there is some background information that I think your Lordship should be aware of. Will your Lordship permit me?" With that, Reilly, for reasons only known to himself, launched into the background to the application. His Lordship, along with everyone else in the courtroom, switched off. Eventually Reilly must have satisfied himself that he had imparted sufficient information to his patient Lordship because he resumed his seat. I, for one, was grateful to Reilly.

"Thank you Mr Reilly. Now Mr Donnelly, if we could resume the List while there is still some daylight left," the judge directed the court registrar with some relief.

The registrar announced second calling and then immediately said, "*Harmon v. Nicholson.*"

"Going on, my Lord. One hour," I announced, Reilly's application having given me time to recover my breath, not to mention saving my case from being struck out.

"A close thing, Mr McNamara."

"Indeed, my Lord." His Lordship finished calling over the List for a second time and assigned our case to Judge Doherty. Judge Siobhán Doherty. With that, his Lordship was gone off the Bench as fast as his fat little legs would carry him for fear of being held up further by Reilly or his ilk. Enough work onto the hour and we wouldn't see him again until eleven o'clock, by which time he might have recovered his normal equilibrium. How his equilibrium got on between then and eleven o'clock mattered not at all to Stephanie's team as we were now in the jurisdiction of Judge Doherty at the far end of the building. I decided to head there immediately to avoid any further unseemly rushing.

Stephanie, who had never heard of Judge Doherty until a few moments earlier, was delighted with the draw. The sisterhood and all that. If her rating of her chances had been a trifle optimistic a few moments ago, then they had shot right up to gung-ho now. What chance did a cigar-smoking, Jaguar-driving, fat-cat have against her, an innocent jogger, in front of a female judge, she thought to herself. I wondered. Stephanie asked me what I knew about Siobhán Doherty. I told them two things.

While at the Bar she had been stridently feminist on the one hand and intellectual rather than sporty on the other. In the days before Fitzwilliam Lawn Tennis Club opened its sexist floodgates to the women of the world (something of a catastrophe according to Rachel's father), its secretary would have received more correspondence in that vein from Siobhán Doherty (who it had to be said had never played a game of tennis in her life) than any other individual. Needless to say, once membership was opened to her, she had no intention of joining. She moved on immediately to the golf clubs of Ireland. All of this was grist to Stephanie's mill, who wondered aloud if we could establish that the fat-cat was a member of both Fitzwilliam and the golf clubs of Ireland. In an attempt to counteract this information and reintroduce some balance to Stephanie's view of her case, I could only add that, as Judge Doherty was a recent appointment, her form was not yet known. I drew attention to the fact that in my experience, when members of the Bar with ideological tendencies were appointed to the Bench, very often they left their ideologies behind them, but no one was listening to this little gem of enlightenment.

In Stephanie's case there could be very little dispute about the quantum. If she won she was unlikely to get less than the full jurisdiction of the Circuit Court, namely thirty thousand pounds. That was the easy part of the case. The question was liability. Would she win in full? Lose in full? Would there be an apportionment? There was no doubt at all about what Stephanie, Samantha and Arnold thought. For my part, I thought we would either lose or, if things went well, bear the greater share of an apportionment. I felt that Stephanie was likely to get a better result in a settlement than in court. As we huddled in the window frame opposite the entrance to Court 5, I wondered how best to approach my opposite number. I didn't have long to wonder.

I emerged from my corner and signalled to my opponent who, with her team, was occupying the neighbouring window frame. Miriam was a complete pet, a delight to be with and a delight to be against. Not the best looking girl in the Library perhaps – not that that mattered. Neither had she the best figure – again, something of neither consequence nor relevance. But from the point of view of personality, she was way ahead of most of those who featured prominently in the charts. She was a member of the Bar Golf Society, played Bar tennis, was a jogger herself and had no hang-ups about the Fitzwilliam Lawn Tennis Club or the male-dominated golf clubs of Ireland.

Professionally she was easy to deal with. Not a pushover by any means. Relaxed and confident, she was well able to assess her cases. Neither asked too much money if she was for the plaintiff, nor offering too little if for the defendant. She had the confidence of her clients. If she told you she was trying to get some money for your client, it was true, and if she was trying to get you some money she probably would succeed. You would ignore her offer at your peril, pitched as it was at the Marks and Spencer level of the market. It may not keep you in designer clothing for the rest of your life, but you would not go naked and where liability was in issue, it might represent a very good result indeed. Of course, there was the possibility of the judge awarding you more, but if he could award you more, he could also award you less. And of course he could also send you home with your proverbial tail between your legs. With some colleagues you could be confident of doing better in court because their offer was not even in the ballpark, but not with Miriam. Her offer always merited serious consideration.

Accordingly, I was pleased when Miriam told me that there was ten thousand pounds there and maybe a little more. Not much more, but a sweetener nonetheless. And costs, of course. Sure, none of us would be here at all were it not for the costs. I told Miriam that seemed eminently reasonable and I would do what I could but that I had a difficult team led by my solicitor's secretary who was calling all the shots.

"What do you think, Stephanie?" I asked, having conveyed Miriam's message. We had gone through the upside, the downside, even touching on the sea-side of the offer and its implications.

Samantha answered for her, "Wouldn't touch it, not with a barge-pole. Not enough. They've no idea what you went through. And as for liability," Samantha continued with all the authority of someone who had no experience, "I can't see any judge throwing you out – especially not a female judge." So much for my comprehensive exposé.

"What do you think, Arnold?" Samantha enquired, finally assuming my role completely.

In fairness, Arnold was not the best person to deal with inquiries suddenly thrown at him like this. Even though his business was giving advice and he had been purporting to do just that for more than half of his fifty or so years, actually asking his advice always seemed to take him by surprise. The enquirer, in this case Samantha, and anyone listening, in this case Stephanie and I, were invariably left with the feeling that somehow it was unfair to have popped the question quite at that moment. Any other moment perhaps except that one, as if that was the very moment that he had chosen to take an intellectual – or whatever the appropriate word was in Arnold's case – time-out.

Maybe the enquiry should have been signalled. For example, "Arnold, I would like your advice on this point and perhaps if I come back to you in, say, fifteen minutes?" Or maybe like the Ministers in the Dáil, the questions would be written out days in advance. None of this is very practical when you have all of a few minutes before going into court.

Arnold had a tendency to agree with the client, which meant that very often my job of advising the client as to his or her best interests was made more difficult. "I agree with Samantha," Arnold finally offered, certainly not to my surprise. Arnold wasn't finished, though, and this did surprise me. "It is worth remembering that if, which I think is unlikely, we fail here, there is always the option of appealing. Second bite of the cherry and all that." I didn't think that this was very good advice.

"Well said, Arnold," Samantha interposed. "That's a very

sound piece of advice. I had forgotten all about the right of appeal. That could be very useful indeed. Now Stephanie, have you got all that?"

"I certainly have. It's all quite clear," Stephanie replied. There wasn't exactly an over-anxiety for my advice, but nonetheless I thought that Stephanie should have the benefit of it. After all, that was another part of the service she wasn't paying for. I was quite clear that Miriam's reasonable offer should be accepted and anyway I had indicated to Miriam that I would recommend it to my client.

"I suppose you would like to know what I think about the offer," I said.

"Not really," Samantha answered on behalf of her sister. At this stage, Samantha was exhibiting her piece of chewing gum, which on her protruding tongue resembled some abstract work of art. "Stephanie's mind is made up. I agree with her and so does Arnold. There is nothing more to be said."

I see. Well that's pretty clear. Notwithstanding the lucidity of my instructions I thought I would have one more go. "If there was a little more there, say another one or two thousand, would that make a difference? Now I'm not saying it is there, but they have offered ten thousand and they might be prepared to increase it just a little. What would you say to twelve thousand if I could get it for you?" One of Stephanie's advantages was that she was not alone. Two for the price of one. I'll never know if Stephanie intended answering this or indeed any other enquiry, such was the rapidity of Samantha's intervention.

"She will have to come to twenty, Dermot. You couldn't reasonably expect Stephanie to take less than twenty, now could you? In all honesty?" *Well actually I could,* I thought, but I was never going to persuade Samantha and as for Stephanie, I was never going to get to talk to her without the presence of her guardian angel. "What do you say, Stephanie?" Samantha asked.

"Absolutely," Stephanie replied.

I went back to Miriam. "Sorry Miriam. Ten won't do it, not even twelve. That is, if you could have got twelve. It would have to be twenty. I might be able to get the real client to take twelve, but I can't get anywhere near her. Her sister is calling the shots and she has her own mind. Didn't even ask me what I thought. And Arnold of course is useless. He is completely said by the sister, all the more so that she is his secretary. I suppose he doesn't want her bitching about the result for the rest of their office-shared days."

"I suppose we'll just have to get on with it then. I would be struggling to get you twelve. Think they'd do it at the end of the day but that would be the height of it. Sorry."

"Thanks for trying, Miriam. Will we go in?"

No sooner were we in the courtroom than our case was called. Stephanie had no difficulty settling into the witness box. Unfortunately, her considerable natural beauty was undermined by the pink and baggy tracksuit. First of all, Stephanie needed her very own Henry Higgins to teach her to "speak proper", and secondly to dress her and in particular to show her how to dress for court. He would also have had the prescience to advise against the bottle of water, or at least to leave it behind when she took the stand. The witness box was no place for Stephanie, pink and baggy-suited, to be slugging bottles of water.

She was too softly spoken and kitten-like for a strident feminist like Judge Doherty, and with her elbows resting on the edge of the witness box, a trifle too relaxed in the presence of one so recently called to a position of such eminence. Stephanie's demeanour might be confused with over-familiarity and a certain lack of respect for the dignity of her surroundings, and in particular, the dignity of her Lordship. All of this might have been meant to do an injustice to the new judge, who, in any event, did not take long to indicate where she was coming from.

"Ms Harmon, I'm afraid you will have to speak up. I'm the judge and if I don't hear your evidence it is as if you haven't given it. If you take your elbows off the witness box and speak into the microphone you might give your case some chance."

I thought this was a bit ominous, and so early on in the case. Even before any evidence was given. Usually one didn't get the benefit of his or her Lordship's insights until at least some evidence had been adduced. Judge Doherty was bringing judicial efficiency to new heights. I wondered what Samantha and Arnold were thinking about this. I couldn't see Samantha because she was sitting behind me. It wasn't difficult to speculate as to what Arnold was thinking. He wasn't. He was writing furiously, like a student at a law of property lecture, desperate to catch every word. No time for thought. Understanding, should it come at all, would come later, much later, in the student's case as well as Arnold's. It wasn't immediately clear to me why Arnold should be writing down what her Lordship was saying in relation to the necessity for Stephanie to speak up. It seemed unlikely that the case was going to turn on this. Down it went anyway, every word. Perhaps it was Arnold's thirst for thoroughness.

After that poor start, it was time for some evidence. Time for her Lordship to learn from Stephanie herself what it was that made Stephanie determined to take up the time of the court. She had read the pleadings, of course, which would have told her that the case was virtually indistinguishable from thousands of other personal injury cases she had heard or would hear. Traditionally, the purpose of pleadings was to make sure that each party informed the other as to what his case was so that neither party would be taken by surprise when the case came on for hearing. That was the theory. The reality was that these pleading documents had become so standardised, the only certainty when the case came on for hearing was that the one thing each party would be taken by was surprise.

Hopefully, when I opened the case, I shed a bit more light on the issues that Judge Doherty would have to determine over the following hour or two.

Stephanie wasn't far along the Bray Road when her Lordship was in again. Usually it is a few months at least before a new appointment becomes interventionist. For a few months she will let the barristers and the witnesses get on with what they are expert at while she finds her feet. In this regard Judge Doherty was clearly a departure from the norm. At this rate the case would either take two weeks because she wouldn't stop interrupting or two minutes because she would have decided it in the absence of evidence.

"Ms Harmon, have you ever driven a car?" Judge Doherty enquired.

"No Lord, I haven't," Stephanie replied with an unintentional excess of deference. I had told Stephanie to address the judge as "my Lord". This is the form of address laid down in the rules and hallowed by centuries of use. In recent times, the advent of female judges has led to a degree of uncertainty as to how they should be addressed in view of the fact that they are female and "my Lord" is more closely identified with the male of the species. As far as I was aware, Judge Doherty had not yet made it clear how she would like to be addressed and accordingly, I opted for the traditional "my Lord" and so informed Stephanie, who like many witnesses became confused when confronted by the situation. Usually American television took over and the witness addressed the judge as "Worship" or "your Honour." "Lord" simpliciter was novel.

Judge Doherty decided to make her views known. "This is your first time before me Ms Harmon so I couldn't have expected you to know what mode of address to employ. But Mr McNamara, I thought that by now you and your colleagues" until very recently hers, too, she seemed to have forgotten "would have been aware of the fact that I had made my wishes known in this regard. I have said on a number of occasions that I wished to be addressed as Judge. Perhaps you would let this be known in the Library."

"Of course, my Lord, I mean Judge. I apologise. I meant to enquire before the case started, but in fact my Lord...I mean Judge...I only came into the case at the last moment."

"That's perfectly all right Mr McNamara, but if you would just pass the word around in the Library, maybe we could avoid this unnecessary distraction in every case. Now Ms Harmon, you were telling me that you don't drive a car yourself, isn't that right?"

Stephanie was beginning to think that this might be material to the outcome of her case. "Well Judge, I don't drive regularly. I have had a few lessons from my boyfriend...I hope to be able to drive by the end of the year." Stephanie had a brainwave. "In fact Judge, I intend to buy a car with my winnings." Stephanie was pleased with herself.

"Your winnings, Ms Harmon?"

"I mean my damages, Judge." Doherty wasn't impressed.

"I hope you haven't bought it yet, Ms Harmon."

"No my Judge," Stephanie replied, realising that her pleasure at her little insight might have been premature.

"What I was getting at, Ms Harmon, was this. Have you ever been in a car in rush-hour traffic on a wet winter's evening and been confronted by an almost invisible jogger on the road in front of you?" Stephanie had no idea what Judge Doherty was getting at.

"Eh...no Judge, I haven't."

"Well I have, Ms Harmon."

"I see," said Stephanie, not seeing at all. Arnold was taking down every word. I doubt if he saw, either.

"And what were you wearing, Ms Harmon?"

"A tracksuit, Judge."

"Like the one you have on now?"

"No, Judge. This is my casual tracksuit. I have another one for jogging."

"And what colour was that?"

"Black."

"And what about a belt? Were you wearing one of those luminous belts, Ms Harmon?"

"No Judge, they're too uncomfortable," Stephanie said, pointing to that area of her body between her ribs and her neck. "You know what I mean, Judge." Doherty, who was not as well endowed in this department as Stephanie and who had never jogged in her life, had no practical knowledge of the discomfort Stephanie was alluding to but knew what she meant nonetheless. Some of the spirit of this part of the evidence was going to be missing from Arnold's note.

"So, Ms Harmon, you were jogging along in the wet night. Rush-hour traffic coming against you. In a black tracksuit. No luminous belt. Do I have the picture?" *Only too well*, I thought to myself.

"Perfectly, Judge."

"There's a footpath there, Ms Harmon. Isn't there?"

"There is, Judge."

"Why weren't you jogging on it?"

"Too dark, Judge, and the footpath was in poor condition. I was worried about going over on my ankle."

"And I suppose the road wasn't dark?"

"No, Judge. The lights of the cars lit up the road. I could see the surface quite clearly."

"And what about the car drivers? Do you think they could see you?"

"I didn't think of that, Judge."

"Sorry, Mr McNamara," said Doherty handing back the witness to me. "I shouldn't have interrupted you."

"Not at all, Judge. Your Lordship's questions – I mean your Judge's questions – I mean your questions, Judge, have been most helpful," I said without a hint of sincerity. It was already very easy to see what kind of a judge Doherty was going to be.

"It's just that I had an accident myself once with a jogger. Very similar circumstances, not far from where your client was jogging. Bad weather. Dark. Impossible to see the jogger. He was lucky not to sustain more severe injuries."

"I could see there was something troubling you, Judge. Happily, from my client's point of view, you will be able to put your own unfortunate experience out of your mind," I said a little dangerously. Doherty looked down at me. She wasn't sure how I meant the remark. She let it pass.

It was about time we moved on to the fat-cat.

"Ms Harmon, you were about to tell the judge what happened as you jogged along the road."

"Well there I was, jogging along. Drenched. The conditions very bad."

"You've told us that, Ms Harmon. Tell us what happened." I was anxious to get to the point.

"Well what happened was this." Stephanie paused to dramatise the moment. "This car hit me."

"What sort of a car was it?"

"A Jaguar."

"And where did it come from?"

"Out of nowhere." *Oh God no. Not out of nowhere.* Judges just cannot handle that expression.

"What do you mean 'out of nowhere' Ms Harmon?" Doherty was in faster than the Jaguar, cat or car. "A car, not even a Jaguar, cannot come out of nowhere. It had to come from somewhere." Her Lordship was full of insight this morning. *Please Stephanie, stop now. Please get away from that expression,* I silently begged her. *Explain what you mean, that there had been a break in the traffic – presumably stopped at lights back up the road – suddenly this Jaguar appeared way ahead of the car behind it – must have accelerated at great speed from the lights.*

"That's what happened. I can only tell you what happened. The car came out of nowhere." Stephanie obviously thought that the judge hadn't got the point.

I had a minor brainwave myself. "Ms Harmon, I think there is a bend in the road at this point and perhaps that is why you had the impression of the Jaguar coming out of nowhere?"

"No, Dermot. I mean Mr McNamara. No bend. Perfectly straight. Came out of nowhere," Stephanie replied.

Doherty, who had obviously made up her mind that my earlier remark was mischievous rather than innocent, decided to add to my discomfiture. "Poor Mr McNamara, the first rule of advocacy, we learnt it in first year – never ask a question you don't know the answer to. Bad luck, Mr McNamara."

"May it please your Lordship...Judge." I ate humble pie. *Why do they appoint women anyway?* I asked myself in a moment of political incorrectness.

"Ms Harmon, if, as you say, the road was dead straight at this point, isn't that all the more reason for you to see the car?" Doherty wanted to know.

"And the car me, Judge." *Good for you, Stephanie.* She had begun to realise that things were not exactly going her way and she had obviously decided that she was not going down without a fight.

"Did the driver take any evasive action?" I enquired a trifle pompously.

"Any wha?" Stephanie wanted to know in return.

"Did he swerve or sound his horn or do anything?"

"No. Nothing."

"And why, Ms Harmon, do you think he hit you?"

"It was two things. First of all he mustn't have seen me and secondly he was driving at a hell of a lick." It was Doherty's turn to seek clarification.

"A 'hell of a lick', Ms Harmon?"

"Yes, Judge."

"What does that mean?"

"Oh, very fast."

"I see. Thank you, Ms Harmon." Stephanie went to leave the witness box, whether because she thought she was finished or because she was trying to avoid cross-examination or whether because she intuitively realised that there was no need for Miriam to ask her anything, such was the gale force wind that was blowing in her direction, I didn't know.

"Before you go, Ms Harmon, would you mind answering one or two questions from me?" Miriam asked. Stephanie returned to the box. She wasn't stretching her arms on the ledge of the box now. I was actually surprised that Miriam was bothering to cross-examine. It was going so well for her that the only possible outcome of cross-examination was an improvement in Stephanie's fortunes. Or so I thought.

"Ms Harmon, my client Mr Nicholson will say that when he first saw you, you were looking down at the ground. Is that correct?"

"I don't remember. But if he says so, I may well have been. It was sleeting rain at the time and also I had to look where I was stepping. So he is probably right. But why didn't he see me? Can he tell you that?"

"If you don't mind Ms Harmon, I'll ask the questions," Miriam reprimanded, gently but firmly. "He will also say that he bipped his horn and you didn't look up. First of all, do you agree that he bipped his horn?"

"I can't agree or disagree. All I can say is that I didn't hear any horn."

"Is there any reason why you may not have heard the horn, Ms Harmon?"

"I was listening to my walkman."

"Your walkman, Ms Harmon?" interrupted Judge Doherty, incredulous.

"Yes, Judge."

"I don't believe it. Are you seriously telling me that as you were jogging along the road in the dark rain in a black tracksuit without a luminous belt, you were listening to your walkman?" the outraged judge inquired.

"I am, Judge. It's a long run and the walkman is company."

"I see. Thank you Ms Harmon."

I was wrong in my prediction about Miriam's cross-examination. It was possible to cross-examine Stephanie without her case improving. The picture was complete. Miriam's ten thousand pounds was looking very generous now. I was debating whether or not to call my only other witness, Gordon Somers, the Consulting Engineer. As he was already making his expert way to the witness box before I had an opportunity to announce him, the decision was rather taken out of my hands. Somers was of the old school of expert witnesses. He regarded himself as independent of the person who employed him. A sort of *amicus curii*. There to assist the court, a bit like the judge herself, without fear or favour. Which explained his diminishing practice. He was something of a loose cannon and one called him with a certain trepidation. For some reason, of which I was not aware, Arnold always used him "in this sort of case". He should be accompanied by a health warning.

Arnold was writing again as Somers brought the judge through his map and photographs, somewhat superfluously as everyone in court knew this stretch of roadway like their back garden. He gave measurements and sight lines by day and by night. For what distance the jogger should have seen the fat-cat and vice versa. He was able to measure the lighting at the location. Eventually he opined that if the defendant had been keeping a proper lookout he had ample time to see the plaintiff and take avoiding action. So far, so good.

Miriam rose to her pleasant, if plain, feet but before she had a chance to trouble Somers, her Lordship was testing him. It was quite clear from Somers' demeanour that the oath was something he took extremely seriously. Doherty had spotted this.

"Mr Somers, what is your opinion of joggers jogging on the road?" Long pause. "Mr Somers?"

"Do I have to answer that, Judge?"

"I'm afraid you do, Mr Somers. It would be of an enormous assistance to the court." The magic words.

"If I must, Judge. They are a menace. A perfect menace."

"As I thought, Mr Somers. Thank you."

Miriam resumed her seat. "No questions, Judge." She was having an easy ride.

Somers returned to his place in the well of the court, unable to look at Samantha, Stephanie or even Arnold, who had briefly abandoned his writing, who were looking at him in that order of ferocity. I had a feeling that Arnold might be reviewing his policy of always using Somers in "this sort of case".

"That's my case, Judge."

"Well, Ms Reddy, I suppose you'd better call your evidence."

"If you say so, Judge."

Mr Conor Nicholson made his way to the witness box with great ceremony, pausing at the last bench as if to extinguish his cigar. He was wearing a Hugo Boss suit and an Armani tie. Altogether his gear must have cost as much as the car. He wore an air of lofty resignation. It was clearly a terrible waste of his valuable time. Court was for criminals and for people less fortunate than him who, in the pursuit of filthy lucre which he earned by honest toil, were obliged to resort to spurious claims like the one in hand. He was big into civic duty and moralising and accordingly saw it as his duty to attend for the purpose of exposing the plaintiff as the opportunist she clearly was. Now if there was to be an audit done on Mr Nicholson's business he might find himself in the Four Courts for another reason altogether. Offshore accounts and all that. But that's another day's work.

I wasn't quite sure, but as he reached the witness box he seemed to bow and the judge seemed to bow back. He took *The Bible* in his right hand and swore to tell the whole truth. He even seemed to find this ceremony distasteful. It was as if someone of his standing in the community shouldn't be required to take an oath. He wiped the seat lightly with his handkerchief before sitting down. Once seated, somewhat less than comfortably, he drew delicately on his shirt-cuffs, revealing a magnificent pair of gold cuff-links.

Miriam allowed him to complete his warm-up before asking, "Mr Nicholson, I think you are the defendant in this action?"

"Unfortunately," Mr Nicholson replied without any attempt to disguise his ennui.

"This won't take very long," Doherty interjected. If at that moment I still entertained even a particle of an allusion that maybe the judge still had an open mind on matters and that perhaps I might by cross-examination have some small bearing on the proceedings, such hopes were well and truly shattered by this interjection. It was clear, even beyond certainty, how her Lordship felt on the issue between the jogger and the fat-cat. The rest was for the fans. Nothing now would affect the result.

"I am extremely grateful, Judge. I do have one or two other matters to attend to today," he replied in a tone that suggested that the rest of us were off home to bed.

Miriam took the judge's hint and kept Nicholson's evidence to the bare minimum. Even as he gave his abridged version he became increasingly bored with each answer. My task was impossible.

Behind me sat two unhappy campers. Not just unhappy but disillusioned also. Let down by the sisterhood. At regular intervals I would receive a tap on my shoulder urging me to "for God's sake do something". They were consistently strong on the injunction but pitiably weak on what precisely it was that I should do.

In front, Arnold was still writing tirelessly. He was on to his second notebook. He hardly ever looked up except to hand me the latest in a succession of notes on which he had written, illegibly, some remarkably obvious question. Occasionally he would look up with an expression similar to that which he wore when asked a question at a moment when he was not expecting to be consulted: dropped jaw, opened mouth, eyebrows visiting forehead and eyes receding into skull where there may or may not be an impact with the brain. I assumed this to be the physical manifestation of some temporary intellectual deficit brought about by the evidence. In the unlikely event of an impact between eyes and brain this expression relaxes much like that of a child in a classroom who, suddenly filled with enlightenment, understands for the first time and forever what her teacher has been explaining. In default of such impact, the expression lingers lastingly until eventually, with the efflux of time, what gave rise to the expression originally is entirely forgotten by Arnold, who happily resumes his note-taking, the lack of understanding just as effectively resolved by memory failure as by sudden comprehension.

My own team may not have made things any easier, but it was the other two protagonists, Nicholson and Judge, who made my task impossible.

In the witness box, fat-cat Nicholson. Whether by accident or design, he had stumbled on a highly effective way of dealing with my attempt at cross-examination – a combination of superiority and boredom, which mightn't have been quite as insurmountable were it not for the unequivocal support he was getting from her recently appointed Lordship.

"You're boring me, McNamara. Your questions are boring. Irrelevant, too. You've already asked me that. Why do you repeat yourself? Why don't you get to the point? I am a busy and important person with busy and important things to do. Why don't you sit down and let me get on with my life?" He may not have said so in as many words, but that was the gist both of what he did say and of his body language.

Nicholson had a point. What was the purpose of going on? I was getting nowhere. Fighting a lost battle. Doherty had made it quite clear even as I outlined my case to her that she was against me, hated joggers, favoured fat-cats. Any inroad I might think I was making was quickly sealed off, a no-entry sign speedily erected by the judge who was untroubled by her inexperience.

I was tempted to announce "no questions" when my turn came to cross-examine Nicholson. But if such a course would bring pleasure to the lips of Nicholson and Doherty, what would it have done to Stephanie and Samantha? Not to mention Arnold?

"Just one or two questions Mr Nicholson...if you don't mind." We were all very anxious to facilitate fat-cat's early departure to his heavy schedule. Very often, "just a few questions" is the precursor to a day-long cross-examination. But not in this instance. Though that might have been what Samantha *et al.* would have liked. Even if I had enough questions in me I knew this would not be politic. After all, I would have to appear before Judge Doherty again, probably for the remainder of my life.

I had often heard it said that the first question of cross-examination was the most important and perhaps even the most important of the case. Accordingly I usually tried to put some effort into formulating it.

"Mr Nicholson, you heard the plaintiff say that you came out of nowhere?" was my unenlightened opener, in which I broke the cardinal rule of giving the judge an opportunity of revisiting an earlier attack of exasperation brought about by my client's evidence. So low was my morale at that point that the question was out before I realised the potential for horror.

"And Mr McNamara, you heard what I thought of that piece of evidence?" she promptly asked.

"I did Judge," *I just forgot for a moment...but perhaps it could be turned to advantage...give me an opportunity to clear up what exactly Ms Harmon had meant...*"but of course what the plaintiff meant when she said the defendant came out of nowhere"...*oh, no, the cock crows...third time...* "I mean that what the plaintiff meant when she said those words –"

"Mr McNamara, it is for the plaintiff to give the evidence in whatever words she chooses. It is no part of your function as her barrister to explain or translate them."

"But Judge, with respect, these words are but a formula, a figure of speech, which when heard intelligently –"

"Intelligently, Mr McNamara?"

"Sorry Judge, I am getting a little confused myself. I mean intelligibly," I explained, hurrying up a little so that I could get my point across before another interruption, "a figure of speech which means going too fast. Everyone," *even you, Judge* "knows that."

"That may be so, Mr McNamara, but the words the plaintiff chooses to give her evidence are of paramount importance and we all know that the defendant can't have come out of nowhere. Nowhere doesn't exist." *Perhaps we are about to embark on some philosophical argument about the existence of nowhere?* "The defendant has to have been there. As I understand the plaintiff, this is her way of saying that she didn't see the defendant." As we weren't going anywhere ourselves at this moment, I felt that we might actually be close to nowhere.

"Judge, may I proceed or would you prefer if I resumed my

seat?"

"Oh no, Mr McNamara, please proceed. I am merely trying to be helpful. When I was at the Bar," *yesterday, have you forgotten so soon?* "I always thought it was very helpful when the judge gave you some idea of her thinking and I resolved that when I became a judge I would assist Counsel by giving them some hints as to how the judicial mind was working. Please don't take it to mean that my mind is made up. Far from it. Do ask any questions you like and as many of them as you like and as often as you like. It is very important that each of the parties walks from this court believing that the judge has listened carefully and patiently to their respective cases. Very important indeed. That is what the court is for. That is what the parties are entitled to. Indeed, this is what our forefathers fought for." She could have fooled Samantha, who was thumping my shoulder blades at this stage with suggestions for suitable replies.

"May it please you, Judge," was my craven response. I was tired and despondent and wondering what was the point when I got a sudden flash. The offer of ten thousand pounds, maybe twelve thousand pounds. Was it still there?

"If you would bear with me for a moment?" I scribbled a note to Miriam. If the money was still there I would ask Doherty to rise for a few moments and try to get Stephanie to take the offer. Maybe if I got her on her own, away from Samantha, I could persuade her to take it. Miriam whispered that she would take instructions. I carried on.

"Mr Nicholson, there is a thirty mile per hour speed limit along that stretch of road where the accident happened, and my client's case is that you were travelling far too fast." Judge Doherty's anxiety to see that each party left court feeling that his and her case had been fully aired was short-lived.

"But Mr McNamara, Mr Nicholson was driving a Jaguar. He didn't spend all that money on a car like that to drive at a snail's pace. Now did he?" Not a wet day on the Bench and already inventing a new jurisprudence. One speed limit for the drivers of Jags, another speed limit for everyone else. Now that the special position of the Catholic Church had been removed from the Constitution, perhaps it could be replaced by the drivers of Jaguar motorcars.

If Doherty was going to ignore the speed limit, I was going to ignore the tolerance limit. I had had enough.

"Do I understand you correctly, Judge? Are you saying that the speed limit does not apply to the defendant?"

"Of course I'm not, Mr McNamara, as you well know. It is just that the law cannot always be applied strictly. It must be tinged with flexibility if justice is to be done between the parties. Which is another way of saying that common sense must prevail." *Or that you can do whatever you want to do*, I thought to myself.

So far, Nicholson hadn't had to answer a single one of my questions. I looked over at Miriam. She was nodding all right, but in the wrong direction.

"Sorry Mac, the bastard has withdrawn the offer," she whispered.

There were not many cards left. "One final question, Mr Nicholson. What if the plaintiff had been a child crossing the road?" The old reliable. I could see Nicholson becoming a little uncomfortable, which was surprising and, in the circumstances, quite unnecessary.

"But she wasn't, Mr McNamara, was she? Entirely hypothetical. You may as well ask Mr Nicholson why he wasn't driving on the footpath." I couldn't for the life of me see the logic in this. "Facts, Mr McNamara, facts. Let's stick to the facts. There is enough to deal with without straying into the murky world of the hypothetical," Judge Doherty interrupted for the last time.

Game, set and match. There is only so much a brain can take.

"May it please you, Judge," I concluded, investing as much venom into those five words as I could manage. I resumed my seat.

Miriam looked over at me and apologised again. She was such a star, the only one in this particular galaxy.

Very often one waits for the judge's deliberation with a certain sense of excitement and anticipation. Occasionally one doesn't. This was one of those occasions. There was no one in court who had any doubt about how the judge was going to decide this case and there were no surprises.

"I do not have any sympathy for joggers," *as I say, no surprises*, "and as I intimated during the case I have had my own run-in with one. But of course it is my duty under the Constitution to put extraneous matters, such as my own experiences, completely out of my mind. And this I did." Samantha was thumping me again. "I listened carefully to what Ms Harmon had to say and of course she blew it, to use a colloquialism, when she said that Mr Nicholson's car came 'out of nowhere'. We all know that a car cannot come out of nowhere," *and in case we were all severely retarded,* "it has to come from somewhere." *Brilliant.* "Now where did it come from? This is a long, straight stretch of road and obviously this is the 'nowhere' from which it emerged. This, of course, begs the question as to why Ms Harmon hadn't seen it." But not, of course, the corresponding question as to why the fat-cat hadn't seen Stephanie, Samantha wanted me to interrupt. "And then there was Mr Nicholson's evidence. I found him to be a most impressive witness. His evidence was at all times consistent. He stood up well to Mr McNamara's forceful cross-examination." There was no cross-examination for him to stand up to. It was her Lordship who stood up well to cross-examination. "I agree with Mr Somers, the engineer. Joggers are a menace. I have no hesitation in dismissing Ms Harmon's claim and awarding costs to the defendant." *May it please your prejudiced Lordship and every good wish for a long and biased career on the Bench.*

The registrar called the next case. Another Counsel jumped to his feet. Already Stephanie's case was history as the court and justice moved on. We bowed our humbled heads and withdrew. In a matter of moments we were in the corridor licking our wounds. Not surprisingly, the engineer had disappeared, probably to close up shop and to think about a career change. I was waiting for the allocation of blame, in which event I would remind one and all of the offer of ten thousand pounds, maybe more, that I had strongly recommended. To be fair, blame was not allocated, not in front of me anyway, and I kept the reminder of the offer to myself.

When each of us had said what had to be said about Judge Doherty, Stephanie asked Arnold, "What were you saying beforehand about an appeal?" Arnold explained to Stephanie her right to appeal Judge Doherty's decision to the High Court.

"And what do you think I should do, Arnold?" Arnold was in full flight now, working on all cylinders, so the customary interval between question and answer was mercifully missing.

"I've no doubt at all as to what you should do. You should appeal. The offer was not enough. Judge Doherty did not give you a proper hearing. You should appeal." Arnold's advice had the advantage for once of being clear. Wrong maybe, but clear.

"And you, Samantha?"

"I agree wholeheartedly with Arnold, who has shown great foresight all along. Even before the case started he was talking about an appeal. I think you should take Arnold's advice." Stephanie seemed to be replete with advice, for she didn't bother to ask me. She did have one or two other questions, however, which she addressed to Samantha, presumably because she recognised that Arnold must be exhausted at this stage after dispensing so much advice.

"But Samantha, who hears this appeal?" Stephanie wanted to know, not unreasonably. "Judge Doherty again?"

"Oh no. You're finished with her. She is what the lawyers call *functus officio*." Not just a short skirt our Samantha, who blew a little bubble to celebrate this outpouring of erudition. I thought that I should intervene – not that anyone else had the same thought. It was just that if we were going to discuss law I felt that we may as well get it right, no matter how informed Samantha might be.

"You see, Stephanie, what happens is Arnold lodges what is called a Notice of Appeal and this is processed and, in a matter of months, the appeal will be listed on a Monday morning before a High Court judge. As Stephanie says, you are finished with Judge Doherty."

"Thank you, Dermot. You certainly seem to know a lot about all of this." *What did she expect?*

"But Dermot, one thing puzzles me. Surely when the case comes before the High Court judge the result will be the same?"

"Not necessarily. That's the whole point of an appeal."

"You mean two judges hearing the exact same case could come to different conclusions?"

"That's exactly right."

"And what happens if the decision of the lower court is the right decision all along?" she asked, her thirst for legal knowledge unquenched. I was on the point of suggesting that she pursue a career in law herself when I thought better of it. In fact, she had a point.

"That's a good question, and I think the answer is that the higher court is right even if it's wrong, if you know what I mean." Which she didn't, but she decided to abandon this line of enquiry nonetheless. Much to my relief.

Samantha's turn. "Who does the appeal, Arnold? Is it Dermot again?"

"No. Usually a Senior does the appeal."

"Excellent. Well then, you should brief that new Silk Margaret Thompson for the appeal. I was very impressed by her in that case about the horse in the park which she did against Dermot shortly before she took Silk. No offence, Dermot. It wasn't your fault today. Doherty didn't give you a chance." *Thanks, Samantha.* "It's just that I think Thompson is tougher. Horses for courses, as it were. If you remember, Arnold, I suggested her to do the case in the first instance but you said she had just taken Silk and therefore couldn't do it. Well, now is our chance. What do you think, Stephanie?"

"I agree entirely."

"Dermot?" Mustering as much cowardice as I was capable of at that moment and for which I was well-known, I agreed wholeheartedly with the plan of action, notwithstanding that I regarded the whole exercise as futile. When you stood back from the facts of the case it became crystal clear that it couldn't be won. Sure enough, Doherty had given it an awful hearing and Stephanie was entitled to feel hard done by, which is often why cases are appealed, but the fact was that I could not put my heart on my breast and say that Judge Doherty had got it wrong.

On that appellate note we went our separate ways. As I made my separate way down the quays that evening in the rain to get my DART, the city's colours bouncing off the Liffey, I reflected upon the day's proceedings. Really, I hadn't done a bad job, all things considered. Briefed at the very last moment in a case which, whatever the optimism of those around me, really didn't have a leg to stand on, I had given it as good a run as was feasible having regard to the hostility of Doherty. What more could I have done? Nothing, I assured myself, which was reinforced as I stepped off the Ha'penny Bridge and almost collided with a jogger, duly walkmanned and with head down against the driving rain, as she made her mindless way home from her city office. When I recovered my balance I resumed my reflections for the way home. Arnold's cases – where did he get them? Was there any other solicitor who had so many dud cases? How did he survive? Not to mention myself.

Another free day – for the client that is. Unfortunately my roll had come to an end and the hat-trick wasn't to be. Not for now, anyhow. The vicissitudes of life at the Bar, as I had reflected often enough on this well-worn route – one day riding high, the next as low as the leading river when the tide is out. *And what of the appeal?* I thought, as Tara Street Station loomed and I sought to bring my reflections to an end. Another service that Stephanie wouldn't pay for? Are we mad or what? Not to mention being led by Margaret. Of all the Silks in the Library, why Margaret? As I stepped into my sardined DART I remembered that it was Rachel's night in the kitchen so I hoped her day had gone better.

There were few things that Rachel didn't do well. Cooking was one of them. On her night on it tended to be a take-away from Marks and Spencer or if she had had a particularly good day something from Butler's Pantry in Mount Merrion. I didn't complain about either. Unfortunately there was nothing at all to complain about this particular evening because Rachel wasn't there. As I dried out in our empty and cold flat opposite a hostile bay, the phone rang. Six twenty five exactly.

Rachel? No. Arnold. Who else? To discuss the case. He had been re-reading his notebooks and had come up with a few more unanswered questions. Unasked ones, too. Perhaps I should have asked Nicholson if he had been drinking. I wondered if Arnold had been. Maybe we shouldn't have called the engineer. Maybe we should have taken the offer. Maybe this. Maybe that. On the whole, Arnold was really ringing me to talk to himself. I tried to remain calm. He thought that Margaret would probably manage to put things back on the rails. He was very anxious to do the best for Stephanie. For obvious reasons. I suggested to Arnold that he give Margaret the brief sometime, anytime, before the hearing of the case. There were certain advantages. And wished him a pleasant evening. As I put the phone down I heard Rachel at the dark door.

"Would you mind terribly collecting the children?" she asked. "I had an awful day." *And my day, Rachel? What about my day?* I thought to myself. "My case and my consultation afterwards" *uptown and upmarket, both of them* "ran over. I didn't have time to buy dinner and I'm late for the girls." Tuesday was her night out.

Which did my night in. Obviously.

The Court Above

Stephanie didn't have to wait too long for the next stage in her pursuit of justice and damages. A matter of weeks. Arnold thought that we should have a consultation the Friday before the Monday. Not many solicitors arrange consultations for four twenty-five on a Friday afternoon. In fact, consultations are rarely arranged for Friday afternoon at all. From lunchtime on, the Law Library celebrates the imminence of the weekend and many adjourn to culinary haunts within the vicinity for a liquid lunch. Which is certainly what I would have done had it not been for this totally unnecessary meeting. Any Senior of any standing would not have agreed to the arrangement and would have settled as usual for the consultation on the morning. But of course Ms Margaret Thompson, SC was in the first flush of her Silkhood and was keen to please. Not only did Arnold brief Margaret in time but he fitted her out with a consultation room. No lying up against walls for Margaret. Needless to say I wasn't even favoured with the single letter Arnold had given me instead of a brief in the Circuit Court.

Even if I hadn't been deprived of my Friday lunch, I would still have been convinced that the whole tedious exercise was doomed to failure. I thought of telling Arnold that I couldn't make the consultation because I was committed to another one, but thought better of it. There is never much fun in an appeal. You have been through it all before and when a Silk is brought in, your contribution is more like a walk-on part in a play. There is even less chance than previously of anyone asking you your opinion and yet you have to put up with the endless churning over of facts you have off by heart, and of course there is the posing and posturing of your Silk. Altogether a forgettable experience.

I had come up against Margaret before. Indeed, it turned out to be her last case as a Junior. There was no denying either her good looks or her ability. When God gaveth, He gaveth in abundance. To Margaret anyway, including an overdose of self-confidence. I couldn't get a handle on her when I was against her and felt that I was equally unlikely to get a handle on her now that we were together.

No one was particularly concerned, least of all Margaret, as to what sort of a handle I felt I was getting or not getting on her. The important thing was how she was getting on with the others and, in truth, Arnold and the girls were delighted with her. She was completely on top of her brief, which was less difficult when (a) you have one and (b) you are given it in time, otherwise known as sour grapes on my part. She hit the right note on every topic. Even when she suggested that the offer which I had so painstakingly secured in the Circuit Court and which Stephanie, or more accurately, Samantha had so painstakingly rejected, if reinstated, might be accepted this time around, they were eating out of her Silken hand and agreed enthusiastically. When I think of the reaction I received. Of course, she added diplomatically, they were right to reject the offer when it was originally made but things had moved on and in the light of developments since the offer was made (the dismissal of Stephanie's case with costs awarded against her was, I think, the development Margaret had in mind) different circumstances prevailed and prudence then dictated that the offer should be taken up. Samantha said she couldn't have put it better herself.

Margaret had no doubt that on Monday morning the defendant, and more particularly his insurers, would be seeing things in a different light (the introduction of a Silk into a case very often effected quite unexpected and beneficial results, Margaret modestly confided to her team) and she was quite confident that the offer would be reinstated. Stephanie and Samantha agreed with this analysis and apparently had at all times been quite sure that the offer would become available again. Arnold was well pleased with Margaret, so much so that he announced that he would bring all his cases in the High Court in the future so that he could have the benefit at an early stage of Senior Counsel's clear and concise advise. And to think that I could have been in the middle of an end-of-week lunch.

As I turned off the light in the consultation room I could just hear the Cathedral bells strike six o'clock. Outside, the February evening had well and truly fallen. The Judge's Yard was a pool of moonlight as Margaret and the tracksuited Stephanie – Margaret had indicated that she wanted a word with Stephanie on her own (I wondered why) – led Arnold and Samantha to the gates. I didn't need a second chance. A hasty wish to everyone to enjoy their weekend and I was gone. Back briefly to my desk, where I packed all those papers that I intended so diligently to look at over the next two days and that I would no less diligently carry back to the Library on the Monday morning, their virginity intact. When I looked out the window to check, my suspicion was confirmed, namely that the consultation was continuing at the gate of the Judge's Yard, so I took the long way around to Hughes' where, in the company of those that I had been unable to join for lunch, I got my weekend off to a belated start.

"Join me for breakfast?" Margaret inquired around ten o'clock on Monday morning. We were not meeting the others until twenty-five past.

"Delighted," I replied, frankly a little flattered by the invitation. Margaret had scarcely recognised my existence up to now. The new Silk wouldn't hear of me paying.

"Leader pays," she announced proudly, at the same time gesturing to me in a magnanimous manner to return my less valuable lucre whence it came. We found a table in the corner from where we could keep an eye on the comings and goings of our colleagues. The Barrister's Restaurant was beginning to come to life.

"Have a nice weekend Dermot?" Margaret wanted to know as she dipped her free chocolate into her cappuccino.

"Not really. It was my weekend on with the twins, on top of which I had quite a bit of paperwork to do. A case of all work and no play, I'm afraid."

"Oh, you poor fellow," Margaret consoled with a sympathetic

air that didn't really become her. "I can't say anything about the twins, but I do remember the paperwork. I remember it well," she spoke almost wistfully, as people do sometimes of something painful which is now safely in the past.

"One of the constant nightmares of Junior Counsel – the undiminishing backlog of paperwork. Burning the midnight oil. Entire weekends spent at the dictaphone. The only time I was ever up to date was on the first of October after the Long Vacation. It was undoubtedly the curse of being a top Junior," she added modestly. "And the great blessing of being a Senior is that all that has gone...for the time being, at any rate. Take this weekend for example. After our consultation on Friday evening, I drove to Galway. Hunted with the Galway Blazers on Saturday and went to their Spring Ball that night. Wonderful weekend. Just what you need after a week in court. Take my advice, Dermot. Take Silk as soon as you can." While this advice might well be worthy of inclusion in Kahlil Gibran's little opus, it was not of immediate relevance to my career. Unfortunately, taking Silk was about as approximate to me as getting on top of her backlog was to our top Junior, as she then was. Margaret intimated that the imparting of this advice was an appropriate note on which to terminate our early morning tête-à-tête, and so we headed off to meet our appealing client.

To my astonishment, minus her tracksuit. I hardly recognised Stephanie. In the Circuit Court and as recently as the previous Friday, one would have been forgiven for not giving her a second look. It wasn't that she was unattractive, simply that the tracksuit treacherously undermined her good looks. On Monday, however, "all changed, changed utterly: a terrible beauty is born". Now you would forfeit a second glance at your peril. Indeed, most of the people passing along the first floor corridor did so sideways. As I approached her I wondered who was the image consultant with whom she must have spent most of the weekend. Time for her to take Silk also, such was her achievement. Or become President of Ireland.

I wasn't sure where to start – at the top or at the bottom. I elected for the latter. Obviously some garment had to replace the tracksuit. It wasn't quite as obvious what that garment was. Like its wearer, it demanded a second look. Eventually after considerable agonising on my part I decided it was a skirt, though to call what Stephanie was wearing a skirt was to so redefine the meaning thereof as to make the Supreme Court's interpretation of the Constitution look almost literal. Clearly the image consultant was unhappy with most of the content of the original garment and decided to reduce it to its bare essentials. What Stephanie was left with might best be described as a pleated pelmet, such that if a door was opened this side of the Phoenix Park her modesty, already severely challenged, would well and truly vanish.

Released from the hibernation enforced by the tracksuit bottoms, Stephanie's legs were able to show themselves off to advantage. Restless and athletic, they jigged and jogged their athletic way up as far as that pleated skirt where, like a train into a tunnel, they disappeared briefly only to emerge on the far side metamorphosed into a bare midriff out of which Stephanie's tummy button stared like a great eye. Further up the page a certain generosity of endowment, wrapped in a tight transparent blouse, put any residual doubt about her gender beyond question.

All of a sudden my day was looking up. And down. If ever there was an advertisement to put tracksuits, especially pink ones, right out of business, Stephanie on this Monday morning was it. All of this was lost on Arnold, who didn't even notice the considerable increase in the pedestrian traffic in the corridor. The two courts on this corridor were popular and busy at the best of times, but even at their busiest they would not attract the volume of people promenading at this hour, many of whom found inexplicably that at a point discreetly beyond where Stephanie was standing they were in the wrong place or had left something behind and so had to retrace their steps.

Arnold was as oblivious as ever. Towering over the two sisters like a redundant lighthouse he stared into the middle distance. Whatever or whoever he was seeing it was neither Margaret nor I as we made our way towards him. In fact, when Margaret wished him good morning he jumped a little as if startled by the greeting. Arnold sprang to life, relatively speaking. "Oh yes, Margaret and Mac, I was worried that you were not coming. *Harmon v. Nicholson,* on now in a few minutes, Circuit Court appeal," as if he was giving us some vital information of which we were not aware. Margaret greeted Stephanie and Samantha, who had not yet bothered to remove either her walkman or her gum and was still chewing furiously to whatever cerebral music was being expelled by Radio Docklands.

"How are we this morning girls? Full of fight?" she inquired.

"Oh yes, Margaret. Full of fight. Any thoughts over the weekend?" Samantha asked.

"In fact, yes. I have been giving the matter a lot of thought and each time I come to the same conclusion, namely, that this case should be settled. The fact is that you were on the road and almost invisible – what chance did the motorist have? I accept totally that you did not get a fair hearing in the Circuit Court and that the judge was biased against you from the beginning, but there is no certainty that this judge – and we don't know yet who it will be – won't have the same bias against joggers. Or he may not be biased and may give you a fair hearing but may still come to the conclusion that there was nothing that the driver could have done to avoid the accident. Now what you've got to remember is that if we can settle this case – and I have little doubt but that we can – you have the certainty of money in your hand and a decree for costs. On the other hand, if you fight and lose again, you will have no money and you will have two orders for costs against you. A bird in the hand is worth two in the bush, Stephanie. In short, what I think you should do is give me authority to see if the offer of ten thousand pounds, maybe twelve thousand pounds, might be reinstated. Obviously I'll do my best to get more for you, but if push comes to shove, then I think that you should be prepared to accept the original offer. What do you think?"

"Frankly Margaret, Samantha and I were chewing it over during the weekend" where Samantha had the room for something else to chew I had no idea "and we began to think that we should take their offer, too. What do you think, Arnold?"

Apparently my view was not a prerequisite to the resolution of the discussion. Arnold, taken aback by this request for his opinion, said, "Well, I have been giving the matter a lot of thought as well...and well...yes...I think that you should...I mean it would be prudent...I'm inclined to agree with you...all of you."

"Well that's it then, we're all agreed." Margaret said. My acquiescence was apparently assumed. "I'll go over to Brendan and see what he says." With that Margaret strolled down the corridor to a bay window where she summoned Brendan from his entourage.

Brendan had been brought in to lead Miriam, despite the fact that Miriam didn't need leading. Brendan Farrell, SC was very much of the old school. It was doubtful if the later decades of the twentieth century had made much impact on him. If the current generation of barristers were interested in turnover and regarded the Law Library as a place where they carried on their business – in much the same way as one might be an undertaker or a distributor of sun-beds – Brendan regarded himself as being a member of a profession. It wasn't a question of how quickly you could dispose of the case and how much you had earned that day. One was briefed to represent one's client in court and that was what Brendan would do. It mattered not to him whether the case settled or fought or indeed whether or not it got on at all that day. In his declining years he was happy enough to have a brief and if it wasn't reached and had to be adjourned to the next appeal List the following Monday, that was not a disaster. Insofar as one can be sure of anything in the legal world, Brendan would be available then also. Polite and pleasant at all times, he was not, however, the ideal opponent if one had decided – as we had here – that one's case had to be settled at all costs. In such a situation one needed an opponent who would put his shoulder to the cause of settlement – in the jargon of the millennium, someone who would be proactive and who for good reason or none would be extolling the wisdom of settlement.

This was not how Brendan saw his role. The client would ask him what his view was. He would respond that he thought the client would win the case. He would then ask the client if he wished to make an offer and the client would reply that in the light of Brendan's advice he didn't think he could and so the case – every case – would fight.

Margaret paraded Brendan to a vacant window. "Delighted you are in the case, Brendan. Between the two of us I'm sure we will be able to come to some agreement. I have a very difficult client but I am confident at the end of the day that I'll get her to take twenty five thousand pounds. It's worth the full thirty thousand pounds but I have to give you some discount for the risks. Do you think that your people would come up to twenty five?"

"I've no idea, Margaret. I haven't discussed settlement with them but I'll certainly see what their attitude is."

"Remember, we're down the List a bit so we may not get on, which will mean next week which won't suit any of us."

"I don't really mind. I've checked my diary and I'm free next

Monday so that's not a problem."

"Oh yes, of course. Anyway, see what you can do."

Brendan was back in a jiffy. "I'm afraid no joy, Margaret. Insurance company wants to run the case. Asked me what I thought. I told them. In the light of what I said, didn't see any justification for settling. On top of which the defendant himself is an important client of theirs and he doesn't think he did anything wrong and they want to keep him happy. Case has to fight."

"Do you think there is any prospect of settlement?"

"No I don't. They seem quite determined."

Margaret returned to our corner and explained what had happened.

"Did you ask them to reinstate the offer?" Samantha wanted to know.

"Frankly, I didn't. I decided to pitch it higher in the hope of doing better than the offer and when Brendan told me they were so resolute I didn't see much point in mentioning another figure."

"Would it be worth trying it anyhow?" enquired Stephanie, who wasn't quite as full of fight after all.

"Nothing to lose," replied Margaret as she headed off in Brendan's direction for a second time.

"Brendan, you know that ten thousand pounds was offered in the Circuit Court with a hint of twelve thousand pounds? My client tells me that she will settle for that now. The twelve thousand pounds, I mean. With costs. It would be a good day's work from your client's point of view. If you go down you'll probably go down for the full whack."

"I don't think I agree with you there. Your client would have to take some of the blame at least."

"Perhaps you're right. It would still be a good settlement from your point of view. Will you see what you can do?"

"I'll relay what you said."

Brendan was back in an even quicker jiffy than the first time. "I'm afraid not. Insurance company feels that you had your chance and you blew it. The defendant isn't helping because when he heard there was an offer in the Circuit Court he nearly had a heart attack. He was furious and my insurance man was left hoping that the offer would not be accepted. So there is no question of them reopening it now, particularly as they won in the court below. Frankly, I think they're right."

"Is there nothing?"

"Nothing."

"We'll go on then." Margaret conveyed the disappointing news. I have to confess to a certain disloyal pleasure at the way things were working out. After all, I had strongly recommended the offer in the Circuit Court and they, all of them, would have none of it. Serves them right. Even Margaret had got it wrong, confident as she was that the offer would be reinstated once the insurance company saw she was in the case. If she was conscious of any of this she didn't show it.

"Nothing for it but to go in and sock it to them!" With this encouragement, Margaret turned on her elegant heel and led her team into court.

Unfortunately, we were down the List and if form was anything to go by, it was quite likely that we would not be reached and Stephanie's appeal would go back to the following Monday.

Stephanie and Samantha took their prominent touch line seats in the empty jury box that ran up the northern side of the courtroom. When he sat, the judge had his back to the Phoenix Park. The usual last-minute communications before his Lordship's entry were interrupted as the communicators focused their Monday morning attention on Stephanie as she arranged herself on the seat normally reserved for the foreman of the jury with an immodest mixture of exhibition and exposure.

Just as the door opened and the crier entered commanding "All rise," Margaret turned round to me and said, "The draw will be very important. I wonder who is hearing the Circuit Court appeals today?" I couldn't believe my eyes. Who bounced out on the Bench with great speed to wish everyone a good morning but Mr Justice Fleming. I wondered to myself how was it possible. Fleming adored Margaret and it was only a matter of time before his loyalties would be equally divided between Margaret and Stephanie. Could Margaret have known all along?

"Now Mr eh...if you would kindly call the List. I see there is a lot of work to get through and there is nothing to be gained by procrastination." As he was speaking his eyes travelled the courtroom. He was a judge whose eyes did much of the work. They were as restless as Stephanie's legs, on which they eventually alighted. For a moment I thought he was about to ask Stephanie what case she was in and to call her first, but if such a thought entered his head it never got beyond that particular location. We were well down the List – tenth out of fifteen. Little chance of being reached and certainly not before lunch. The cases ahead of us were going on: half an hour, an hour, three-quarters of an hour and two all-day cases.

One of my colleagues was in more of the cases than moderation or prudence would allow. In driving parlance he was over the limit. He was for the defendant in each case and the practise was that when the case was called, Counsel for the plaintiff would indicate to the judge that the case was going on and would then estimate the likely length of the case in terms of hours. Usually these observations went unopposed. But not where this particular colleague was concerned. As each time estimate was announced to the court, he would eye first the judge and then his opponent in a fashion that suggested that this might be the most contentious point in the case and that his opponent was misleading the court. Then in a loud and cross voice he announced that the case would take at least twice that length of time. This frenzied ritual accomplished, he would retire exhausted but happy and go outside and settle the cases.

"*Harmon v. Nicholson.*" Margaret rose to her accomplished feet.

"Going on, my Lord. Two hours." Brendan didn't demur.

"Thank you Ms Thompson. Ms Thompson, I don't think I have had the pleasure of your appearing before me since you changed your status. I'd like to welcome you to the Inner Bar and to my court as a Senior Counsel. If you are half as successful in your Silk gown, which becomes you so well, as you were as a Junior, you have a glittering career ahead of you."

"May it please your Lordship. Thank you for your kind words." Even Margaret, who would not have regarded vanity as a matter for the confessional, was a trifle taken aback by his Lordship's eulogy. But it didn't end there.

"As everyone knows who practises regularly in my court, there is a tradition that when a new Senior is on his or her first appearance before me, I take his or her case first." It was clear from the eye contact that was being exchanged by the regulars in Fleming's court that this was the first they had heard of this well-established practice.

"Accordingly, Ms Thompson, when I have finished calling the List, I will take *Harmon v. Nicholson* first."

"May it please your Lordship. Thank you, my Lord."

Then, adding as an afterthought that didn't really matter, "Incidentally, who is for the defendant?"

"I am my Lord," said Brendan, rising to his feet.

"Thank you, Mr Farrell. Does that inconvenience you at all Mr Farrell?"

"Not at all, my Lord. As your Lordship pleases." Fleming resumed the List.

As Margaret had informed him that our case would take two hours, he adjourned the remainder of the List to two o'clock to the silent consternation of all involved. However, that consternation was short-lived because as the court was clearing it became obvious to one and all, and to Mr Justice Fleming, that Margaret's client was the deliciously undressed female in the foreman's seat. The exodus stopped in its tracks. The cocktail of the appealing Stephanie and Margaret on the one hand and Mr Justice Fleming on the other was too good to be missed. This was to be no run of the mill Monday morning.

Margaret opened Stephanie's appeal. She was extremely articulate and would have had no difficulty in opening the case at length but she knew her judge, and while she knew that she would have his rapt attention she was aware that she wasn't the only object of Fleming's attention on this Monday morning. She opted to open the case with brevity. It is important – in fact, one of the principal rules of advocacy – to know your judge. And Margaret knew her advocacy.

With all the solemnity of a sister in religion, Stephanie swore to tell nothing but the truth and sat down. As she crossed her legs, the pleated pelmet she was wearing lived up to everyone's expectations and vanished. She turned towards his Lordship and as she did she rested the upper part of her conspicuous body on the little altar that was provided for exhibits that might be presented to her in the course of her evidence. Mr Justice Fleming's concentration was capable of being immense and already he was giving Stephanie his exclusive attention.

"I think you're the plaintiff in this action, Ms Harmon?" Margaret began.

"I am," Stephanie answered nervously in a quiet, husky voice.

"Would you be good enough to tell the court where you live and with whom?"

"I live at number twenty Woodbine Terrace, Mount Merrion, with my parents and my sister Samantha, who is sitting down there," Stephanie faltered in a voice that was vanishing in the same direction as her garment.

"Now Ms Harmon," his Lordship interjected "there is no need to be nervous. Just relax there and answer the questions Margaret – I mean Ms Thompson – asks you and when she is finished, that nice gentleman down there in the wig and gown will ask you a few questions. You've nothing to worry about in this court. You are in safe hands."

"Thank you my Lord," Stephanie responded.

"Now Ms Harmon, do you remember the tenth day of February 1994?"

"I do."

"Please tell his Lordship what you were doing about six o' clock that evening." Stephanie proceeded to give her account of what happened but unfortunately nobody present could hear a word she was saying so irretrievably vanished was her voice. Now this is often a low moment for a plaintiff and her Counsel, as Stephanie discovered before Judge Doherty. But in this instance Mr Justice Fleming was neither unsympathetic nor impatient. He interjected for the second time.

"Ms Harmon, do you see the microphone in front of you? The registrar will turn that on and if you speak into it and look at me we will all be able to hear your evidence."

"Thank you, my Lord." The registrar turned on the microphone and Stephanie proceeded to implement his Lordship's instructions. She leant forward so that the tip of the microphone was within a centimetre or two of her husky mouth and in a gratuitous gesture, as if this in some way might assist the acoustics, she wrapped first her left hand and then her right around the outstretched microphone. The warm-up was complete and Stephanie was ready to give her substantive evidence to an engaged audience.

Under Margaret's expert direction she told his Lordship everything that happened that unfortunate evening. No detail was omitted, even to the extent that – it had apparently been raining more heavily than she had admitted in the Circuit Court – her tracksuit clung to her every crevice and contour such that she more resembled someone emerging in her wet suit from several days' snorkelling in the Great Barrier Reef. It may not have been his most relevant intervention, but for some reason best known to the judicial mind, his Lordship wanted to know if she jogged in the summer also.

"I jog all year round," Stephanie told him, wondering how this could have a bearing on her case. Margaret had warned Stephanie about cars coming "out of nowhere" so we were spared this particular semantic embarrassment this time around. At the end of her evidence the fat-cat in the Jaguar could not have been fancying his chances.

"If you would just answer any questions Mr Farrell may have for you," Margaret advised Stephanie as she resumed her seat.

Emerging from an earlier era, Brendan rose to his anachronistic feet. He could have phrased his opening question in cross-examination more happily. "Tell me Ms Harmon, could you not have done it better on the footpath?" Brendan enquired. The place erupted. Fleming did his best to contain himself, putting his hand up to his mouth in an effort to prevent himself from exploding. Brendan had no idea what everybody was laughing at.

"What do you mean, Mr Farrell?"

"Ms Harmon, you said you were jogging on the road. Wouldn't it have been better and safer if you had jogged on the footpath?"

"Oh, I see what you mean, but I've already explained to you that the path was all broken up at that point and I would probably have fallen." Brendan's facility for framing questions did not improve. He wanted to know how in those conditions she thought his client could have seen her.

"It wasn't as if you were sticking out, now was it?" he asked, coming to the point. More guffaws. Stephanie explained that she was running towards the defendant and he should have seen her in the headlights of his car.

"Would you at least accept, Ms Harmon, that had you been wearing something transparent, my client would have had a better chance of seeing you?" The television was never as good as this, and on a Monday morning too. What a start to the week. There was enough here to keep the coffee room buzzing for a week. The judge now had two hands over his mouth. He was finding it more and more difficult to avoid joining in the general merriment. All the time Stephanie was giving her evidence she was running her hands up and down the microphone as if, like an udder, it depended on her manual massage for its effectiveness.

"I think you mean luminous, Mr Farrell?"

"I beg your pardon, my Lord?"

"I think you mean if Ms Harmon was wearing something luminous."

"That's precisely the point my Lord, she wasn't wearing something luminous"

"That may or not be so, but the word is *luminous*, Mr Farrell."

"Precisely, my Lord. That's what I said, if she had been wearing something luminous."

"No Mr Farrell, you said transparent."

"Did I? Well I meant luminous." Brendan, who was still quite unclear as to the reason for the atmosphere of good humour in the court, rested his puzzled feet as the transparent Stephanie gave an answer to which no one listened. She made her way back to her place beside Samantha.

"Is that your evidence, Ms Thompson?" Fleming wanted to know, in a tone that suggested that Stephanie's evidence could not be improved upon. Margaret turned to me and asked what we were going to do about the engineer. I explained very quickly that in the Circuit Court the engineer had been a disaster. Margaret took her cue. "It is, my Lord."

"Mr Farrell, presumably you want to call Mr Nicholson?"

"I do, my Lord."

"Do you have any other witnesses?"

"No, my Lord."

Mr Nicholson made his combative way to the witness box. No cigar this time. Pausing on his way to shed his expensive overcoat. He was no fool and knew well that things were not exactly going his way. If Circuit Court prejudices had blown in his favour, the prejudicial wind had changed. He was in the High Court now and the High Court prejudices were of a more elemental nature. However, Mr Nicholson was a businessman and a successful one at that, and he had not achieved that success without encountering adversity on the way. His coat was off and he was not going under without a fight, though he may have underestimated his match, who was still busy visually escorting Stephanie to her foreman's seat.

Brendan asked, "Mr Nicholson, where were you going the evening of your accident with the plaintiff?"

"Wicklow. I had an appointment to meet some friends in Wicklow at six thirty."

"Were you in any kind of a hurry?"

"Frankly, I was because I had left my home in Ballsbridge late, but I had just got through to one of my friends on my mobile and had explained the position to him so that at the moment when the accident occurred I was not in a hurry." Mr Justice Fleming, who had paid no attention to anything apart from Stephanie and Margaret up to that point, suddenly sprang to life.

"Your mobile, Mr Nicholson?"

"Yes, my Lord."

"Mr Nicholson, I wonder if you can explain something to me?"

"I hope so, my Lord."

"Can you explain to me why nowadays every Tom, Dick and Harry has to have a mobile?"

Mr Nicholson didn't like being associated with every Tom, Dick and Harry. "I imagine because they find them useful, my Lord," was his somewhat sarcastic explanation to his Lordship.

"They may be useful but they are also extremely dangerous if used while driving a car," said Fleming, reminding Mr Nicholson that as the judge he had the upper hand. "Perhaps that is why you didn't see Stephanie – I mean, Ms Harmon – in time, because you were playing with your mobile?"

"I wasn't playing with my mobile, my Lord. It is not a toy. It is an essential apparatus for any self-respecting businessman. I was simply making an urgent phone call and I am well capable of doing that without it interfering with my driving."

Nicholson continued with his evidence. How dark it was and how inclement the weather. How carefully he was driving and comfortably within the speed limit when suddenly this black-suited jogger appeared on the road before him giving him no chance at all. All this time while Nicholson was droning on, Fleming's attention was concentrated on Margaret and Stephanie. Once or twice he looked at the witness and when he did he appeared to be muttering "mobile" under his breath.

I was wondering if Margaret would bother cross-examining, it was so clear in which direction the judicial wind was blowing. However, on balance, I felt that Margaret would not be able to resist a moment of glory. I was right.

She rose to her interrogatory feet.

"Mr Nicholson, you were driving along the Bray Road at about six o' clock in the evening in the direction of Wicklow?"

"Guilty, my Lord."

"There is no need to be facetious, Mr Nicholson. You either were or you were not. It is not a question of innocence or guilt. Now please answer Ms Thompson's questions properly," interjected his Lordship.

"It was dark and raining heavily at the time?"

"I've already said so."

"You were late for your appointment in Wicklow?"

"I think we've had that."

"You were on your mobile at the time of the collision?"

"We've had that also."

"The collision was due to the fact that you were driving too fast because you were in a hurry?"

"No. You're adding two and two and getting twenty-two. Any hurry I was in was over once I made contact on the mobile."

"The collision was due to the fact that you were on the mobile at the time and therefore not giving your full attention to the road in front of you?"

"No. Emphatically no. There is no difficulty in driving and making a phone call at the same time."

"Then Mr Nicholson, why did the accident occur?"

"Quite simply because the plaintiff was jogging along a busy main road at night, as Judge Doherty in her wisdom found."

"You can leave Judge Doherty out of this, Mr Nicholson. That was the Circuit Court. She can be of no assistance to you now. I wasn't in the Circuit Court. Indeed if I had been the result might have been different," added Margaret, breaking her vow of modesty for the second time that day. "Well Mr Nicholson, why did you say that you did not see the plaintiff until the last moment?"

"I did not say that I did not see her until the last moment."

"When did you see her then?"

"Em...when did I see her?"

"Yes."

"Em...at the last moment I suppose."

"Why was that Mr Nicholson, did she come out of nowhere?"

Nicholson, who had been listening in the court below, knew better. "Certainly not. I am not saying she came out of nowhere."

"You'd better not be, Mr Nicholson, because we all know that people don't emerge from nowhere," interjected his Lordship again.

"Well, where do you say she came from?" Margaret continued.

"One moment I was driving along and I had a clear road in front of me and the next moment there was the plaintiff right in front of me. I don't know where she came from."

"Mr Nicholson, you were driving the car. You must know where she came from. We have a few facts in this case. First, the plaintiff was jogging along a straight stretch of road. Secondly, you were driving your Jaguar in the opposite direction and you were on your mobile at the time. Thirdly, there was a collision. Now you accept that the plaintiff didn't come out of nowhere. Where did she come from?"

Nicholson was decidedly uneasy. He didn't really feel that someone of his standing in the community should be here at all. The courts were for criminals, not for people like him. He was only here out of a sense of civic duty. Judge Doherty recognised that and had treated him with the respect he deserved. But this was different. It was as if he was on trial himself.

"Maybe she came off the path my Lord. Maybe she had been jogging along the path and just before I arrived she moved out onto the road."

"I object, my Lord," said Margaret. "This is the first we have heard of this suggestion. If this was Mr Nicholson's case it should have been put to my client in cross-examination. It is too late to make this case now."

"I agree," said his Lordship, conveniently ignoring the fact it was something that emerged in the course of Margaret's cross-examination and therefore was entirely admissible. Brendan was not slow to his feet to make this point. But to no avail.

"Well, Mr Nicholson?"

"Well what, Ms Thompson?" Nicholson asked, resigned already.

"Why did you not see Ms Harmon until the last moment?" Nicholson hemmed and hawed. No answer forthcoming.

"Mr Nicholson?" inquired his interested Lordship.

"I suppose...em...I mean...I just don't know. All I know is that one moment she was not there and the next she was. Where she was the moment before she was there I just don't know if...if you know what I mean."

"I'm afraid I don't, Mr Nicholson," replied Fleming.

Margaret, feeling that she had done a good job, resumed her seat. Arnold thought that she had done a good job also and leant across the table between them to tell her so.

"Was that okay?" Margaret, in a spirit of humility, wanted to know when she turned around to me. I could hardly tell her that she could do no wrong in front of Fleming, who found it difficult to choose between her sophisticated charms and the more earthy charms of Stephanie. Fleming would have been happy with the short straw.

"Superbly well," I replied hypocritically. What else could I say? What did she want to hear?

"Mr Farrell, do you have any more witnesses?"

"No my Lord, it is a two witness case."

Mr Justice Fleming gave judgment: "For a while this case gave me some difficulty." Presumably his Lordship was referring to the moment before he was aware Stephanie was the plaintiff. "On the one hand there was the jogger on a dark night, on the other the driver of the Jaguar who was on his mobile. Who was at fault? How could the driver be blamed? But as the case progressed, all became clear so that in the end I have no doubt at all where justice resides. Even if this were a criminal case and I had to be satisfied beyond a reasonable doubt, I would have no reasonable doubt here as to who was responsible for Ms Harmon's accident. I would like to congratulate Ms Thompson for the manner in which she handled her first case in front of me and I might add that colleagues considerably her senior would have been proud of her succinct cross-examination. The key to this case is Mr Nicholson's mobile, one of the great modern menaces. Everyone seems to have one. In cars. Out of cars. In restaurants even. I have no doubt but that if Mr Nicholson had been concentrating on his driving instead of his telephone conversation this accident would not have occurred. I find for the plaintiff. Having read the medical reports and heard Stephanie's very fair, indeed understated, account of her injuries, I have no hesitation in awarding the plaintiff the full jurisdiction. Decree thirty thousand pounds. Now what did the learned Circuit Court judge do?"

The registrar handed Fleming the Circuit Court Order. "I see. The complete reverse. Dismissed the plaintiff's case. Now I wonder how she arrived at that conclusion?"

"If I may be of assistance, my Lord, Mr McNamara tells me that she didn't have much empathy with joggers."

"Ah, I see. That's what it was. Very often the way with new judges. No disrespect to Judge Doherty who will be a fine judge, but sometimes at the beginning of one's career on the Bench it is difficult to approach each case with an open mind. There is a tendency to bring your prejudices with you on to the Bench. She'll overcome that in time. Very well then, decree for thirty thousand pounds."

"Costs, my Lord?" Margaret asked.

"That follows."

"In both courts, my Lord?"

"Of course."

Senior Counsel bowed to the Bench and retired to leave his Lordship free to bring his open mind to the remainder of the cases in the List.

As Stephanie and Samantha congratulated Margaret, I could see just a short distance down the corridor Brendan shaking Nicholson's disgruntled hand. Arnold joined in the congratulations. "Samantha, that was a great idea to bring Margaret on board."

"Well, it all goes back to a case we had about a horse in a park. We were for the plaintiff. I can't remember who our barrister was. One of the regulars I presume." *Me, Samantha. It was me.* "Well, Margaret was for the defendant and she was getting a torrid time from the judge who was a complete misogynist. Any other Counsel would have buckled under. But not Margaret. She stood her ground and eventually the judge who clearly hated her, indeed hated all women, had to find in her favour. Well Stephanie had her accident shortly before that case and I remember thinking we should brief Margaret for Stephanie's case, but unfortunately Margaret took Silk. I just can't remember who was for us." *Don't mind me on the fringe of this fan club. I am not sensitive. Ignore the fact that it was a hopeless case and we gave it a great run.*

"All's well that ends well as someone said once," Samantha said, drawing on her repertoire of literary quotations.

Margaret's modesty was about as transparent as Stephanie's blouse. "A team effort," she announced, "everyone played their part" and after a pause, "even Dermot." We all laughed. I wanted to remind everyone what it had been like in front of Judge Doherty but I knew no one would pay the slightest attention, so I sulked to myself.

Margaret led her admiring entourage down the corridor. A little later as I headed down the quays, I thought of the one important advantage to the outcome: I would be paid. So thank you, Margaret, for small mercies.

The Out-of-Towners

It had been a busy family weekend. On Saturday, the twins were two and Rachel thought we should have a party for family and friends of the twins from the crèche, where, it had to be admitted, they spent most of their time. It wasn't intended to be thus. Thus is simply how it worked out. When we married, it had been our intention, at least I believed it was our intention, that I would support the family and Rachel would rear the children, at the same time playing a not insubstantial, if supporting, role in the matter of providing financial assistance from her practice. Like the Oscars: best supporting spouse.

In the intervening years, however, there had been developments and under-developments. First of all, Rachel had gone from strength to strength in her matrimonial practice. Added to that was her early-married-life discovery that the joys of domesticity and the promise of fulfilment therein were overrated. By contrast, the under-development was simply that I had not taken off with as much rapidity as we expected, or indeed as we had assured Rachel's father. It was not wise, of course, to have married so early on in my career, as he had hinted to me on a number of occasions, but there was not much point in rehashing old territory.

I spent most of Saturday morning purchasing the ingredients for the party tea and attending to diverse household chores. In fairness, Rachel had promised to do her share, but late on Friday night she received a phone call from her best solicitor, wondering if she could attend a consultation on Saturday morning with

Monday's client. She assured me she would be back well before kick-off.

Between cousins of the twins and their friends from the kindergarten university, thirty or so two-year-olds had responded in the affirmative. The well-mannered little darlings. Add to these under-age socialites adoring grandparents, agnostic at best godparents and a sprinkling of less-than-enthusiastic aunts and uncles and there wasn't much change out of fifty guests due at three o'clock in our garden flat by the sea.

On the dot of that very hour, the entire fifty or so guests arrived, or so it seemed, to our scrupulously hoovered apartment. I felt the punctuality of the crèche-goers owed less to good training than to the single-minded determination of their parents not to miss a minute of the Saturday afternoon babysitting facility which we – more accurately *I* – was providing. Their punctuality was in stark contrast to Rachel's, who had phoned on her mobile from her solicitor's office to say that the consultation had gone on longer than expected, but she was leaving at that moment and would be home shortly.

While the partying two-year-olds were having a whale of a time under the baton of their *chef d'orchestre* (Rachel had eventually returned), I was ensuring that the adults were having their share of the whale and wine. I was also trying to ensure that Rachel's parents and mine did not have too much of one another.

We weren't long married when I realised from something Rachel inadvertently let slip that her parents believed that she had married a foot or two beneath her. While growing up, a somewhat protracted and continuing process, I had never felt that there was anything modest about my background. My father had a good job in the bank, my mother was a very attractive woman devoted to her young family, we lived in a comfortable house in Terenure and all in all, I considered myself rather privileged. Until I met Rachel's parents. Her father was a successful businessman who never found his close identification with Fianna Fáil to be anything other than an advantage (to date he had escaped the attention of the tribunals) and her mother loved entertaining and being entertained. Rachel told me once that she never remembered her parents in at night unless they were entertaining. Rachel's parents were constantly saying to mine how they missed them on the cocktail circuit. If Rachel's parents had little time for their grandchildren, my parents had little time for anything else.

It was with considerable relief that I closed the door on the last of our fifty or so guests and poured Rachel and myself a gin and tonic.

As if the party wasn't enough for one weekend, Sunday was the first Sunday of the month, which meant lunch at my in-laws. It was like some tribal ritual, a scene out of the *Forsythe Saga* or a C P Snow novel, as if the monthly reunion gave definition to the family or at least a feeling of self-importance. "We have lunch together every first Sunday of the month, therefore we are a family of substance," seemed to be my father-in-law's philosophy.

The occasion had all the spontaneity of a dental appointment arranged months in advance. My father-in-law would enquire as to how my practice was going, stopping short of asking how much I had made in the previous month. On my way I would reflect on my cases since I had last seen him, picking out the least embarrassing ones and embellishing them considerably in preparation for the inquiry that was as inevitable as the lunch itself. "Any interesting cases, Dermot?" He knew jolly well that I had not had any interesting cases, at least none that would be of the slightest interest to him. The enquiry was entirely rhetorical and bore no relationship to the extent of his interest in my career. He had long since decided that I was never going to be able to provide his darling Rachel with the standard of living to which she had been accustomed during the twenty-four years before she married me.

The juxtaposition of the kids' party and the in-laws' luncheon in the one weekend was too much for this fragile soul, and it was with a good deal of relief that I made my way to Heuston Station that Sunday evening. The joys of Tralee and Arnold's brief beckoned.

At home or abroad I have always enjoyed travelling by train. Even at home I cannot make a train journey without a certain sense of adventure. It may not be quite as thrilling as boarding the TGV or the Orient Express; Heuston Station may not evoke the same sense of romance as the Gare du Nord, but for all that, within a matter of hours, Iarnród Éireann would have me in a new city or a new town or better still perhaps on the threshold of Connemara. Added to all this on this occasion was the thrill of an away fixture, a new Circuit, a new judge, old colleagues in a new environment. I must confess that I have never done a case out of town without returning refreshed and reinvigorated.

The Sunday evening journey to Tralee was a long one – four hours long. My first disappointment arrived when the rather tired and not very interested lady behind the glass window informed me that there was no first-class on the train to Tralee. When I enquired as to why not, having been assured on the phone that morning that there was, I was told rather laconically that it was Sunday. I happened to know that already, so I didn't immediately see why this unflappable official was informing me as to the day of the week. I decided to try again. This time she was more forthcoming: "There's never a dining car on a Sunday." All was still not clear. I couldn't see the logic between Sunday and the absence of a dining car. Perhaps it was a religious thing, but then in post-religion Ireland this didn't seem likely. I abandoned the struggle for enlightenment, simply accepted her word for it and with this disappointment under my belt boarded the train, along with everyone else from Croke Park. I had visions of standing the whole way to Tralee. It was a complete stroke of good luck that just as I was passing a particular seat, its short-lived occupant decided that he would prefer to be in the bar with his friends.

It was no reflection on my mother-in-law that I was beginning to feel a little peckish. After all, there were many hours of invisible countryside ahead of us. We weren't long out of Heuston Station when I decided to go in search of the dining car. Twice I walked the length of the train in case by any chance I had missed it on my first visit. When I had had enough exercise I decided to ask the first official I met if there was anywhere in particular I should be looking. This official was likely related to the female official behind the glass window, for he spoke in the same disinterested, disembodied monotone.

"The dining car?"

"Yes. The dining car. I wonder could you tell me where it is?"

"It's at the front of the train," the official said, pointing in a south-westerly direction. I thanked him for his assistance and made to proceed in the direction indicated by his finger.

"What are you going there for?" he asked me, a trifle enigmatically I thought. At this stage I decided I had conclusive evidence of his relationship with the female official behind the glass window.

"I was hoping to get something to eat," I replied, wondering if I was giving him too much information all at once. Perhaps I should have broken it up and delivered it to him in sections.

"Oh, you won't get anything to eat there," he surprised me by saying. At this stage I had begun to wonder how a visitor could handle this dialogue, particularly a visitor without the second language.

"Is there any particular reason why I won't get anything to eat in the dining car?" I asked in total bewilderment. At this stage, apart from hunger, curiosity was getting the better of me.

"It's closed." More laconicism. More evidence of relationship. Curiosity by now had the upper hand. What on earth was the point of travelling a closed dining car? The official read my thought. "Chef phoned in sick before we left. You knows chefs, temperamental as hell."

"Does this mean that there will be nothing to eat between here and Tralee?" I enquired in a resigned tone.

"Good Lord, no," said the official, plainly aggrieved at this slight on the efficiency of Iarnród Éireann. "There will be a trolley going up and down the train during the journey." It wasn't immediately clear how the trolley was going to make its way up the aisles of the carriages, so crowded were they with those who only a few hours earlier had been roaring encouragement to the Kerry team as they sought to restore the Sam Maguire to the kingdom. Pondering the logistics of a travelling trolley, I returned to my seat.

If I thought that I had escaped, albeit briefly, from the bosom of family, it was only in part true. Opposite me was a jaded looking young mum with a baby on her lap. He had a considerable advantage over me in that he was not dependent on the travelling trolley for his nourishment. I do not claim to be an expert on nipples, but certainly the biggest I had ever seen in my twenty-eight years belonged to his mother who exposed them to the ravages of her young offspring's lips on a more or less constant basis. And to me a little less frequently. With difficulty I did my best to confine my thoughts to the wonder of motherhood. Beside the engrossed mother and son, there was also a little boy about the same age as my twins and beside me his sister, Jane.

At this stage, a tiring Jane who had obviously assessed me according to her best lights had come to the conclusion, notwithstanding the fact that I was male, I had a certain capacity for self-restraint and had decided to take me into her confidence. She demonstrated this by nestling up to me. At first. And very shortly afterwards by climbing onto my lap. Her mother didn't seem so keen on the relationship going so far so quickly. However, Jane was so tired and her mother so busy that there was nothing the three of us could do about it. Jane slept and I snoozed.

We were just approaching Portlaoise when I woke to the feeling of a certain warmth, a certain warm wetness, in the region of my lap. It took me a while to become aware of the full significance of the sensation. Eventually I realised that to my great bad luck, Jane had relaxed totally. What was I going to do? This was my only suit for my visit to Tralee. Mother opposite was oblivious, devoting all her attention as she was to her nipple-obsessed youngster. I decided that I couldn't tell her. She had enough on her hands, not to mention other parts of her anatomy. This would have to be offered up. Portlaoise came and went with hasty farewells and a thank you for the facility of my lap, the mother still not aware of the full extent to which that facility had been availed of by her beautiful daughter.

It is not possible to describe the extent of my discomfort. Jane had made her mark. The train was crowded. No sign of the trolley. Nothing for it but to take out Arnold's brief. At least I could get that read in transit and not have to wait until the early hours in my bedroom. I emptied the contents onto the table in front of me: hand-written covering letter, pleadings, hand-written attendances, glossy holiday brochures, booking forms, invoices, receipts and paper clips which no longer kept their contents bound together. I was about to attempt to put some order on the documents that tumbled out of the recycled brown envelope when my eye was caught by someone walking along the aisle towards my end of the carriage. I thought I recognised him, but wasn't sure. He hadn't seen me yet. Eventually our eyes met. I smiled. He smiled back. Yes, it was him, an older acquaintance from college. I had never known him that well. I assumed he recognised me also. I thought I should say hello.

"Hello," I said.

"Hello," he said back, a little hesitantly.

"Long time no see," I said, to his total bewilderment. Oh no, what had I done? What unnecessary interruption had I brought upon myself?

"Do we know one another?" he inquired.

"I believe we do. UCD, late-eighties," I assisted him. He was none the wiser. Meanwhile my wisdom was expanding. I was beginning to recollect more clearly. Freddie Walker, bore of the year, first-class honours, bored for college against Trinity, won easily. How could I retract my initial "hello"? Too late. He was latching on.

"I'm afraid I don't remember. I have a very poor memory. I meet so many people." *I'm sure you do.* There was nothing for it. I was well and truly stuck.

"I did a bit of debating. L and H, Law Society, that sort of thing. You didn't actually debate, but you were a regular attender. I met you from time to time at the parties afterwards." *How could you forget? You used to pin me up against the wall, fix me with that mad stare of yours and talk the pants off me about the ins and outs of that evening's motion for hours on end. I couldn't get a word in edgeways, even if I had wanted to.* I couldn't believe that he didn't remember me. Obviously I was a conversational equivalent of a sex object. He merely needed me there to talk at and to. It didn't matter who I was. As long as I, someone, anyone was lying up against the wall listening to his boring theories. He probably wouldn't have recognised me half an hour later out on the road, let alone years later on this train journey to Tralee. Why did I say hello?

"I think I have you now," he said, ignorant of the full truth of that observation. By now he had sat down in the seat left vacant by Jane. "You did medicine, didn't you?"

"No, law."

"Are you sure?"

"What?"

"I was sure you did medicine."

"No. Law. From beginning to end."

"Anyway, thank you for stopping me. It's always nice to meet old friends. Especially on long train journeys."

"Where are you going to?" I asked in trepidation. *You couldn't be, could you? Oh, yes you could. The very place.*

"The whole way. Tralee." *Where else?* "I'm delighted to have someone to talk to." *And at.*

"I see you're planning a holiday," Freddie said, helping himself to an eyeful of the glossy female on the cover of the holiday brochure.

"No, in fact it's a case I'm doing in Tralee tomorrow. Have to read the brief on the way down."

"Oh, plenty of time for that. We can have a chat first."

Around Limerick Junction I decided to throw myself off the train, but unfortunately, due to the crowds I couldn't reach the door. As he chattered away about this and that, all the time oblivious to the glazed expression on my face, I contemplated the various ways of disposing of him. The one thing I was clear about was that it would have to be slow. There was no earthly way he should get away with a quick death. It should be long and torturous. And intricate, like his arguments. There should be nothing straightforward about it.

Just when it seemed this journey would never end, we arrived in Killarney. Freddie thanked me for my company. "I really enjoyed the chat. Hardly noticed the journey passing. Funny thing is that if you hadn't stopped me I would never have recognised you." The most unkindest cut. "Glad you did, though. It's a long journey and it is always fun to reminisce. By the way, good luck with your case tomorrow. I have just realised that we were so engrossed that you didn't have a chance to read your brief. *Ciao.*"

"Good luck, Freddie. By the way, when are you travelling back?" Nothing could be left to chance.

"Oh, I'm here for the week." *Thank God for that.*

"Oh, that's a pity. I'll probably get away tomorrow or at the latest Tuesday."

"Too bad we won't be returning together." *No doubt you'll come across another long-lost buddy you don't recognise and bore him to suicide.* At least, based on statistics, I wasn't due to rendezvous with Freddie again this side of the pearly gates.

The train continued its journey to Tralee, where I got off and made my way to the Mount Brandon Hotel. Exhausted by my overexposure to Freddie, I forewent the pleasure of reading Arnold's brief and went to sleep.

My alarm clock call woke me at six thirty, and I immediately got down to reading the brief, which should have been read over the weekend. A letter from the client to Arnold gave me all I needed to know.

Dear Mr O'Reilly,

Thank you for taking my case.

You were recommended to me by an older colleague in my office who remembered you from your rugby-playing days in UCD. He spoke very highly of your prowess on the rugby pitch, not to mention academically. He assured me that you would give me the Rolls Royce treatment. Which I badly need.

Let me begin at the beginning.

Last May, my girlfriend, Ms Karen O'Toole, and I booked a holiday in Majorca. We made the booking through travel agents here in Tralee, called Funshine Holidays Limited. (Incidentally, this is why we had to come to you up in Dublin. We tried a number of solicitors here in Tralee, but they all travelled with Funshine and accordingly felt that they couldn't act against them. So much for the fearless independence of the legal profession, of which we hear so much. Our mutual friend said that he remembered you above all for your courageous tackling, so we will be looking for plenty of that in this case.)

As I've never had to trouble a solicitor before, I am not sure how much information you require. It's a bit like a confessional, isn't it? However, you did say to write to you setting out the complete history of the problem, and therefore in the interest of comprehensiveness, perhaps I should give you a little bit of personal background.

In particular, I think you should know that Ms O'Toole and I had never been away before. Together I mean. In truth, I hadn't been abroad myself. As for Ms O'Toole, she was – and still is – a well-travelled lady, both in and out of the country. Here at home, by way of occupation, she is a courier with Hidden Ireland Limited, a high-class operation conveying wealthy Americans by luxury coach around the country, staying as they go in top-drawer country houses. I'm sure a gentleman of your eminence has heard of them. You can see that Ms O'Toole would know a thing or two about how to look after clients, particularly clients en vacancs, as the French would say. I anticipated certain teething, not to mention other anatomical difficulties due to the infancy of our relationship and so I was all the more anxious that the technical, as opposed to personal, side of the arrangements would go smoothly and according to the brochure.

Having gone so far, I may as well go the whole hog. I was more than a little keen on Ms O'Toole and entertained hopes that our vacation might lead to greater things. Modesty prevents me from adding that I had reason to believe that Ms O'Toole may also have had hopes that were not inconsistent with mine.

Let me say straight away that we have no complaint with Ms Ní Chinneide, who looked after us in Main Street, where Funshine has their office here in Tralee. It might have been preferable if she had had some first-hand knowledge of Majorca or indeed any of the places that we discussed in detail with her. Having said that, a fear of flying is a very common condition, because of which Ms Ní Chinneide told us she holidays every year in West Cork. She finds this very congenial and of course it does not involve flying. She spoke so enthusiastically of West Cork that we, I mean I, am thinking very strongly of going there this year.

Around midnight our plane touched down at Palma Airport. A number of inflight gin and tonics had had the desired effect. We were in a happy and relaxed mood, giggly even, and we were both looking forward to a romantic fortnight in the sun. It was only a matter of minutes before the first disaster began to unfold. We were standing at the carousel along with the other passengers who had been on our flight in the reasonable expectation that our luggage had travelled with us. I am not sure if the brochure said anything about luggage, but a friend of mine who has a Certificate in Legal Studies believes that it is an implied term of the contract that your luggage will arrive with you. Needless to say, Mr O'Reilly, I know nothing about implied terms – I was simply interested in getting my luggage, but no doubt you will be able to say if my friend is right or not.

We waited and waited, but to no avail. The holiday rep, who was more interested in the airport official in the tight trousers than our misfortune, thought that she was being reassuring when she said that this often happened and that we would sort it out at the welcome meeting in the morning. I asked her if it would be all right if we turned up naked to the meeting. On first impression these Majorcans did not have much of a sense of humour.

Eventually, we were prevailed upon to board the vehicle that had 'Luxury Coach' written on its exterior. By now it was one in the morning and fatigue was setting in. According to the brochure the hotel was a short drive from the airport. Either the airport or the hotel had moved in the twelve months since the brochure was written, because it was four thirty before we pulled up outside our "lively hotel". At first glance there was nothing at all to suggest that the building to which the disinterested rep was pointing was a hotel. Not a sign of life. Not a light. Indeed, not even a sign, except the words THE GREEN PARROT written above a modest hall door. We were mortified. We collected our duty-free and made our embarrassed way along the aisle of the luxury coach. No one else was going to The Green Parrot. The remainder of the party was continuing on to the Hilton Hotel, brightly illuminated in the dark Mediterranean night like a Great Gatsby mansion. As best we could, we tried to pretend to those of our travelling companions who were awake and were following our every step with great curiosity that perhaps our hotel was a mansion that they couldn't see on the far side of the road or around the corner. This ruse didn't work very well because the rep with whom by now I had established something considerably short of a rapport walked straight up to the door that to all intents and purposes looked locked and opened it. Our cover was blown and there was nothing for it but to walk into the darkened foyer. Muttering something about the welcome meeting taking place in the Hilton the next morning at eleven, the rep returned to the luxury coach, which sped off to the even more luxurious Hilton, our fellow travellers greatly relieved that they were not joining us in a hotel that had all the joie de vivre of a cemetery.

My assumption that Pedro would be asleep behind the reception desk turned out to be unfounded. But he had left a note, which read:

Dear Señor O'Shea,

Welcome to The Green Parrot. The bus is later than usual. I am gone to bed. This is your key. Please deliver your own luggage. See you in the morning.

The Porter

Ms O'Toole was no longer giggling as we made our way to the lift. To our astonishment when the door of the lift opened there was a body slumped in the corner, to all intents and purposes without life. It would be an exaggeration to say that this body came to life during our ascent to the third floor. However, the owner of this body did satisfy us that as far as he was concerned "the day that Thou gavest" had not yet ended, no matter how perilously close le fin had come. Something that as closely resembled a conversation as was possible with the occupant of the body ensued. Ms O'Toole was in urgent need of reassurance, which unfortunately was not forthcoming. She asked him what the hotel was like. For a moment or two it seemed that he would not be able to furnish her with a reply and then, belatedly, we heard the words, "pretty shitty" in a Cockney accent. He seemed pleased with this combination of words, for he kept repeating them and as we made our way down the corridor to our room, the words followed us as in an echo. We struck up quite a friendship with Dave over the ensuing days and it quickly became clear that his conversational skills rarely went beyond these two words.

Not having any luggage had one advantage – there was no unpacking to be done. As I undressed, I heard what I thought was suppressed sobbing coming from the bathroom. I knocked on the door. I was rather taken aback by what I saw. Not the picture of Ms O'Toole sitting on the loo. After all, that was why she had gone into the bathroom in the first place. But what she was wearing. A shower cap. The reason for this headgear was not immediately apparent, but as I stood there, I received certain clues, one of which was a large drop of water falling from the ceiling onto Ms O'Toole's cap. There was a leak in the ceiling of the bathroom, which coincided geographically with the loo. For Ms O'Toole this was the final straw. She burst out crying. It was not how I had envisaged my first night in Majorca with the love of my life, consoling her as she sat on the loo in a flood of tears and a shower cap.

It had been an inauspicious start, which didn't readily improve.

Ms O'Toole had had her final straw in the bathroom the night before, and mine arrived the next morning. The last thing I had done before retiring for what might be called, in the absence of an alternative phrase, my night's sleep, was to put my shoes outside the door for polishing. Looking back on the entire episode, perhaps this was a trifle naïve of me. When I opened my door the next morning, there were no shoes to be seen. Gone without trace, never to be seen again, by me at any rate. I spent much of the holiday looking at people's feet in the vain hope that the shoes would turn up.

Things really didn't get any better. When we made our humiliated way up the drive of the Hilton to the welcome meeting, we found that the rep from the previous night with the fetish for tight (male) trousers was more interested in her Hilton guests than those from The Green Parrot. When we eventually got to her (last), she only had a moment as she was late for her next welcome meeting. We felt that many of the Hilton complaints (no trousers press in the room, couldn't get Sky Sports on the telly, didn't every Hilton have a masseur or a masseuse?) were not quite as pressing as ours – leaks in the loo, no luggage, no air conditioning in the bedroom and Majorca in the middle of an early summer heatwave. It was difficult to impress our case on the departing rep, who felt that our teething problems would settle down after a few days.

During the day we "explored" our hotel – an expedition that took all of ten minutes. Things got worse. It became clear that Dave had brought most of the factory with him. He and his friends, dressed in little more than their tattoos and armed and legged with pints of the local brew, spent most of their time from early morning until well after sunset around the sunken bath that was the "spacious pool in a Mediterranean setting" of the mendacious brochure. As the day and the local brew wore on, we discovered that Dave's "pretty shitty" mantra was at the more elegant level of their conversational range.

The hotel being in funereal dark and cathedral quiet at the time of our arrival the night before was a little deceptive. We had jumped to the conclusion – not unreasonably on the evidence before us, as you lawyers would say – that the hotel was not a lively place. Far from the truth. The disco in The Green Parrot, which was situated beneath our bedroom and which attracted all the local "Carmens" to minister to Dave and his friends, raved and rapped until 4am, at which hour, on the dot, Dave and his friends fell victim to a synchronised sleep that caused them to slump in whichever corner of the hotel was nearest to them. You might have thought that this would have been our cue for the commencement of our night's slumber, but no. The absence of noise allowed us to focus our attention on the absence of air conditioning, which, in the middle of this early season heatwave, ensured that we got precious little sleep between the cessation of the disco and the opening of the restaurant for breakfast at an unhealthily Germanic hour. The result of all this was that we passed the days in something of a daze, not unlike that experienced by Dave and his friends, if differently induced.

Mr O'Reilly, I could go on and on. Indeed, you may think that I have already done so. But I will not trouble you further. Suffice it to say that the problems with the air conditioning and Dave's factory continued. Our clothes eventually arrived a week after our good selves and the leak was repaired shortly before we were due to depart. We never saw the rep again and the disco rapped on.

Altogether the holiday was a disaster of tragic proportions and when I say tragic, I mean tragic. I refer of course to my relationship with Ms O'Toole and its intended development in the Mediterranean setting. Within a few days, we were at one another's throats and, not to put a tooth in it, on setting out I had had the modest aspiration that we might spend our time at different parts of our respective anatomies. However, for some reason, unknown to me, there is a corelation between disaster and the throat of your loved one. We hardly spoke during the second week and eventually Ms O'Toole negotiated an early flight home.

The bottom line is that I have not seen Ms O'Toole since.

Over to you, Mr O'Reilly. Please advise me. I would like to get back the price of my "holiday of a lifetime". In addition, I would like damages and my friend with the Certificate in Legal Studies says that I am entitled to exemplary damages on account of the breakdown of my romance. However, these are all matters within your expertise and I await your advices.

Yours in grateful anticipation,
Sebastian O'Shea

I had to hurry the last part of my client's letter as my alarm clock call never arrived and I was running out of time. My ever-consistent solicitor had arranged for me to be at the courthouse at nine twenty-five. I made a final assault on my fry and gulped down my cup of tea.

At nine twenty-five on the dot I crossed the threshold of Tralee Courthouse, like many of its siblings around the country, a fine example of nineteenth century architecture. Unlike so many with their neglected and dilapidated interiors such that you would be excused for believing them to be ruins rather than living buildings, where forensic fortune ebbed and flowed, this one had been renovated recently and was therefore considerably more cheerful and congenial.

I was surprised by the emptiness however, albeit at such an early hour. Usually by nine twenty-five you would find a number of insomniac clients lined up against the outside wall of the courthouse, as if for Sunday Mass, in anticipation of the arrival of their legal team. This Monday morning was an exception. Not a trace of litigious life. Either Tralee people took a more casual attitude to their litigation or local solicitors did them the courtesy of suggesting a more realistic time of arrival. On the way to the Bar Room, I poked my nose into a number of rooms that looked as if they had not been inhabited this side of Daniel O'Connell's last visit.

I prepared an entrance just in case, but it was entirely unnecessary. The Bar Room was every bit as deserted as the remainder of the building. Except for a table and a few chairs, little by way of furniture or creature comfort, and a few volumes of dusty statutes that looked from their emaciation as if they coincided with years when the Dáil wasn't sitting. And of course the inevitable en suite where those who sought to wash their hands got about as much privacy as a cattle dealer on fair day.

I robed, left the empty Bar Room and returned to the empty hall. There were three or four gentlemen leaning their furtive figures against obliging pillars. I thought it prudent to do a lap of enquiry, as inconspicuously as my costume allowed, to see if any of them answered to the name Sebastian O'Shea. In general I felt that each of them likely rejoiced in the surname O'Shea, but I was on less sure ground with the Sebastian bit.

"I'm looking for a Sebastian O'Shea," I enquired of the first. Absolutely no response. I may just as well have been addressing the pillar. I repeated, "I'm looking for a Sebastian O'Shea."

"You are, are you?" came the reply, somewhat less than immediately, in a major breakthrough. This one wasn't giving much away.

"I am," I confirmed, unsure as to why confirmation was necessary. Silence ensued. Clearly helping your fellow man was not high on this gentleman's list of priorities.

"By any chance would you be Sebastian O'Shea?" I tried again with diminishing optimism.

"Why?" my friend wanted to know. *By God, they keep their cards close to their chests down here.* I felt as if I was rushing our relationship.

"Because I have an appointment to meet him for court. He is my client," I blurted out, giving everything away in one fell swoop. My new friend wouldn't be impressed by my capacity for a confidential relationship if I dropped my guard as easily as that.

"No, I'm not," he confided in a moment of weakness. Perhaps I had impressed him after all by my openness and honesty. Why he couldn't have told me that half an hour ago I'll never know. I felt I was on a roll.

"Well, by any chance would you know him?" I pursued.

"That depends," he replied enigmatically. I couldn't for the life of me imagine what it might depend on. Was he looking for a tip, I wondered?

"Depends on what?" I asked, my astonishment almost palpable.

"On which Sebastian O'Shea you are looking for." *Of course. The kingdom must be overflowing with Sebastian O'Sheas.*

"The one with the case," I said, not really advancing matters.

"I know nothing about a case," he said. "I'm just standing in here out of the rain."

"Well is the Sebastian O'Shea that you know here?" I ventured, wondering what conversational boulevards this enquiry might lead to. Furtively he surveyed the scene, his hand covering his mouth. His head barely rose to the level of his eyes, which barely opened and yet they did all the work. Without rotating his head as much as one degree, his eyes rolled from west to east taking in the entirety of the hall. There were only another three or four men in the hall, but my friend approached his task with the solemnity appropriate to an identification parade, as if the penalty for wrong identification was summary execution. Eventually, without taking a moment less than was necessary, he interpreted all the information he had received and answered, "No."

I thanked him for his endeavours, wondering before taking my leave if I shouldn't seek to exchange addresses, so friendly had we become in the course of the morning.

I decided against interviewing the other gentlemen in the hall and instead went in search of the Circuit Court office. I thought I might ask what time the court was sitting at that Monday morning. By then I was accustomed to the native refusal to part easily with information and I didn't take it personally.

"What court?" asked the official in the office.

"*The* court," I replied, wondering why the simplest question had to be shrouded in mystery and met not with an answer but with another question.

"District or Circuit?" Oh I see, both courts sit here.

"Circuit."

"No Circuit Court here today."

"And the District Court?" I asked, even though it was irrelevant from my point of view, for the District Court could be sitting all day and it would be no use to me. However, I was getting into the swing of things. Relevance wasn't the only law governing this part of the universe.

"No. No District Court here, not today."

"When is it sitting then?"

"The District Court?"

"No. Circuit Court."

"Next Monday," she said, adding, "you're in plenty of time," delighted with her touch of humour. Oh no. I was about to ask her was she sure, but thought better of it and proceeded on the basis that if the official in Tralee Circuit Court office told me that the next sitting of the Circuit Court in Tralee was the following Monday, she was likely to be right. A nightmarish thought crossed my mind.

"Is the Circuit Court sitting today?"

"Here?" she replied in a tone that suggested that Dublin barristers weren't all they were cracked up to be.

"No. Anywhere." She consulted the office diary.

"Ennis." *Could my case be in Ennis?* I wondered aloud.

"What is the name of your case?"

"*O'Shea v. Funshine Holidays Limited.*" She checked the Ennis List but couldn't find it. Thank God for small mercies.

"Is it listed here then?" She checked the Tralee List.

"Yes."

"When?"

"Next Monday."

Oh Arnold, obviously you meant Monday week, I said to myself and unwittingly to my friend behind the counter.

"I beg your pardon?"

"Oh nothing. Sorry. Talking to myself. Wondering how this misunderstanding arose. Sorry."

"I see. Do you leave Dublin often?" she enquired, clearly wondering if I was fit to be let out on my own.

"From time to time. My practice is mainly in Dublin, though." I think she felt that was probably a good thing. "First time in Tralee," I added.

"Will you be back again next week?"

"Almost certainly."

"There's quite a lot of interest in your case, you know."

"Is there really? I wonder why."

"Local interest, really. Everyone uses Funshine for their holidays and the plaintiff is quite well known. He had a great romance going when he left, but they came back separately. Everyone is dying to find out why." I leaned over the counter conspiratorially.

"Would you do me a favour?"

"I might."

"Well it's just that I would prefer if no one knew about this. About me coming down early I mean. Just a secret between you and me. Do you follow?"

"I do."

"Is it a deal then?"

"It is. Your secret is safe with me," she added with an impish smile that suggested she was about to take a half-page advertisement in *The Kerryman*.

"Thanks," I said and slunk off back to the Bar Room, but not before the entire Circuit Court office waved me off uttering a chorus of "see you next week".

Back in the hotel I checked out and made for the station.

At least on the way back I wasn't going to be troubled by Freddie. At that very moment he was busy boring the pants off his colleagues at the conference in Killarney.

I sat back in my seat. The lunch-hour train was almost empty and I was enjoying the scenery between Tralee and Killarney. We were just creeping out of Killarney when I heard someone saying, "Dermot, what a coincidence. I didn't expect to meet you again so soon. What happened? Did your case settle?" I couldn't believe it. Freddie. Who said lightning doesn't strike twice?

"Yes," I lied. "Quite a good settlement, actually. What about you? In fact I was just thinking of you. I thought you were boring a conference – I mean at a boring conference for a week."

"So did I. And so I was until I got a call to return to Dublin. Something urgent at the office. Heady stuff. Can't talk about it. Confidential. You might be reading about it next week in the papers. Well it looks like we'll have plenty of time to discuss those topics we didn't reach on the way down." Four hours, to be precise. I settled down. What else could I do?

The week passed. Rachel was not very impressed by my error. I told no one else, not even Arnold. At nine twenty-five on the correct Monday morning I strode through the portal of Tralee Courthouse for the second time in eight days.

"Ever been here before?" Arnold wanted to know.

"No. Never. Very first time," I lied. "It's always interesting to visit a new courthouse and see how the local Circuit conducts its business." As I completed this observation, the cock, in the form of the entire Circuit Court office staff, crowed: "hello Dermot", "welcome back to Tralee", "better timing this week".

"You seem to be better known here than you think," Arnold commented, who was in a particularly alert and perspicacious mood that morning.

"Oh, just friends messing," I lied for the second time. "Knew them in college." The third. Arnold smiled.

We met Mr O'Shea, discussed his case and on the dot of ten thirty entered the courtroom. My task was an unenviable one: hired from outside to represent Mr O'Shea in his grievance against the local and popular travel agent, upon whom everyone's holiday depended. As in so many cases, much was likely to depend on the identity of the judge. One of the advantages of life on Circuit was that the Circuit had its very own judge – a forensic fixture as it were – so that the task of advising your client as to the likely outcome of his case was that little bit easier. Appearing regularly before the same judge, one came to know his strengths and weaknesses and dare one say it, dare one suggest that the judicial body and mind might be tainted with the frailty of prejudice and foible.

On this South-Western Circuit, the judge was, and had been

for twenty years, Judge Gibson, a judge held in high esteem by the barristers and solicitors practising before him. He was a painstaking judge whose motivation was the just and fair resolution of the dispute in front of him and not the supermarket principle of turnover espoused by many of his colleagues. It may be true that the latter principle, which was often wrapped up and conveyed to an unsuspecting public under the guise of the legal maxim "justice delayed is justice denied" better suited the bank balances of barristers, but the fact was that parties, even defeated parties, who had their cases heard by Judge Gibson emerged from his conscientious court comfortable in the knowledge that their case had had a full and fair hearing uncomplicated by fear or favour.

Insofar as the folklore of the South-Western Circuit had reached the Law Library, it suggested that if Judge Gibson had a flaw, it was that he was a little elderly at this stage and a little out of touch. He wasn't really in tune with the pace and colour of life in the nineties. It was for this reason and no other that I felt that he may not be the best judge to hear Mr O'Shea's case. I thought it unlikely that he would ever have been on a package holiday, and if he had it wasn't with Ms O'Toole or anyone who wasn't wearing a wedding ring. However, we were on the South-Western Circuit and Judge Gibson was our judge.

The door to the judge's chambers opened and out ran the crier, followed in close pursuit by his judge. It had all the appearances of a race between them to the bench. "All stand," commanded the ex-army crier, delighted with the authority he had over the assembled multitude. I couldn't believe my eyes. Judge Rogers down for the day from Dublin. For some reason, Gibson wasn't sitting and had arranged for a replacement. Perhaps he, too, booked his holidays with Funshine. Maybe I wasn't going to be playing as much away from home as I had thought. At least Arnold and I were no longer the only out-of-towners.

We were well down the List and looked unlikely to get on that day or indeed the next. Arnold had no difficulty with his self-esteem and believed either that because he was Arnold or because he had travelled all the way from Dublin that the Listing procedure should be rearranged to accommodate his case being taken first. He had already spoken to me about seeking priority. When I asked him on what grounds I should look for priority, he said he would leave that to me, that he was sure I would come

up with something. I tried to explain to him that the days when the local judge and the local practitioners deferred to Counsel travelling from Dublin were long since gone, and that it was more likely that the plaintiff would be penalised for briefing people from off the Circuit. He wasn't having any of it.

"Ms O'Higgins, please call the List." Once again Arnold was at me to jump the queue. I didn't and eventually *"O'Shea v. Funshine Holidays Limited"* was called, well down the List.

"Going on. About an hour, my Lord."

"Welcome to Tralee Mr McNamara, and also Mr O'Reilly."

"Thank you, my Lord. Indeed, the welcome is mutual."

"You have been sitting there very patiently. I have a practice, Mr McNamara, when I am sitting on Circuit and it is that when Counsel arrives from off the Circuit I hear his case first. Accordingly, I will take your case on the completion of the call over." Arnold gave me the thumbs-up. This was an unnecessarily triumphant gesture on Arnold's part, which did not go down well with his colleagues from the Circuit.

"I am extremely grateful to your Lordship," not to mention chuffed that for once my patience and tactics paid off.

Martin O'Gorman, BL, my opponent for the day, had been leader of the South-Western Circuit since before many of his colleagues were born. He had decided many years earlier that he was not going to take Silk but would remain a Junior on the Circuit. He had a very comfortable home outside Tralee and didn't fancy the move to Dublin, which would be part and parcel of the decision to take Silk. This home-birdness and lack of adventure on Martin's part did not endear him to his colleagues on the Circuit, by whom it was expected that senior men and women on the Circuit would come, and in time, prosper and then go. It was never part of the deal that they would remain forever. Their departure was essential to their continued popularity and indeed to the continuity of the Circuit, to which, once gone, they would return as elder statesmen attending annual dinners and the like and making pompous speeches about their days on the Circuit with stories about their mentors, long since dead, and no longer of interest to the inheritors of the Circuit. If the senior men didn't let go, what chance had those behind them?

The call over of the List continued to completion, whereupon the registrar announced *O'Shea v. Funshine Holidays Limited.* Judge Rogers took the appearances and I opened the case to him

briefly. From my experience of Rogers in Dublin, not to mention my disastrous outing to Letterkenny with my coconut case, where Rogers turned up out of the blue much to my disadvantage, I knew that he cherished brevity.

"I'll call the plaintiff, my Lord. Come up, Mr O'Shea." I turned around for the purpose of indicating to my client the direction he should take in order to arrive at the witness box. To my astonishment the courtroom was full. Usually once a case starts, the court clears. Those not involved in the case at hearing disappear to more lucrative pastures or to coffee. Contrary to the belief of friends and neighbours, a barrister's interest in the cases of others, like the concentration of Americans, is limited in the extreme. Obviously this case was an exception. As the girls from the Circuit Court office told me a week earlier, there was quite an interest in Mr O'Shea's case against Funshine.

I took the plaintiff through his evidence, sticking more or less to the sequence of events set out in his letter to Arnold. The lost luggage, the nocturnal introduction to The Green Parrot and to Dave, the leak above the loo, the stolen shoes, the air conditioning, Dave's factory *friends-sur-mer*, the bruit from the disco and of course the romantic hopes. I had no complaint with Mr O'Shea or the manner in which he gave his evidence. He did so in a self-effacing, low-key way with not a hint of anger or exaggeration. If ever there was a witness who was telling the truth, the whole truth and nothing but the truth, he was it. It was difficult to see why Funshine was contesting the case. Having said that, Martin was vastly experienced and was sure to have something up his sleeve apart from his handkerchief, which he kept there in priestly fashion.

Martin rose to his pre-Council of Trent feet.

"Mr O'Shea, you have a number of complaints with Funshine Holidays Limited arising out of your two week holiday in Majorca last year. Isn't that so?"

"Unfortunately it is, Mr...?"

"O'Gorman. Mr O'Gorman."

"Thank you. Unfortunately it is, Mr O'Gorman."

"You have told his Lordship about each of these complaints individually."

"I have."

"I wonder, Mr O'Shea, if any one or more of these complaints stands out above the rest? For example, is it the lost luggage or

the stolen shoes that gives rise to this action? Or perhaps one of your other complaints, or is it the cumulative effect of all of them?" The plaintiff thought for a moment. I couldn't really see where Martin was going.

"I don't think it was any one complaint, Mr O'Gorman. Unless perhaps the air conditioning or the din from the disco. It is very hard to enjoy your holiday without a night's sleep. Maybe either of these on their own or perhaps together would have driven me to take this action. But in fact I don't think so. I think it was, as you say, the cumulative effect of all of the complaints."

"Very well, Mr O'Shea. Let's take each complaint individually. First of all, the luggage. Do you accept that lost luggage is part and parcel of air travel, that it is a risk you take?"

"Frankly, Mr O'Gorman, I hadn't been abroad before, so I didn't realise that there was a likelihood of arriving without one's luggage."

"I didn't say a likelihood, Mr O'Shea. What I said was a possibility."

"Well, a possibility then. I didn't realise this was a possibility. But if you tell me that this is a risk of travelling by plane, then I'll accept what you say. You're a much more experienced traveller, I'm sure. However, it would have helped if your representative had told us earlier that we could buy replacement clothes and that they would be paid for by the insurance. We were there a week before she told us that. A week in the heat going around in the same clothes."

"Mr O'Shea, that is not what Ms Garcia will say. She will say that she told you that on the first morning in your hotel."

"I'm afraid that is not correct Mr O'Gorman, for two reasons. The first is that she never came to our hotel and the second is that she has as little English as I have Spanish, so she couldn't have told me anything. In fact, we only met her on two or three occasions after the airport. The night at the airport when we were trying to explain to her about our luggage the entire focus of her attention was the gentleman in tight trousers who seemed to be in charge of customs. Thereafter we met her at the Hilton when her attention was devoted to those holidaying in that establishment. Ms O'Toole's difficulties with The Green Parrot and mine were very far down her agenda."

"As for your first encounter with The Green Parrot and Dave, Señor Pedro...eh, I just can't find his surname, Pedro the Porter will be here to say that he stayed at his post until approximately four in the morning when, as it was the second night in a row that bus and plane had been delayed, he decided that it was not unreasonable to retire for the night as he was going to be on duty again early the following morning. He left you a welcome note."

"Indeed he did and the welcome note was timed at midnight."

"Dave will say that he had been in great form at the disco, but that suddenly after it closed something he had eaten earlier in the evening disagreed with him and he became unwell and collapsed in the lift, which explains your surprise encounter on your way to your room."

"All I can say is that Dave and his pals must have eaten something that disagreed with them most nights, because invariably around four in the morning you would find them slumped in various corners of the hotel. I know because as I was unable to sleep due to the noise from the disco and the lack of air conditioning. I used to take a stroll around what the brochure euphemistically referred to as the "hotel complex". It was of necessity a short walk. Judging by the smell of alcohol from Dave and his pals throughout the fortnight, it is more likely that they drank themselves into a state of unconsciousness such that had someone amputated both legs, they would not even have woken up."

"As for the shoes, Mr O'Shea, the management has no idea why you left these outside your door and can only assume that in your exhaustion after the journey you forgot them. The management says that while it has been advised that it has no legal liability, it will reimburse you the reasonable cost of a pair of shoes. With regard to the leak above the loo, Pedro will say that he fixed that."

"If he fixed it he did so on a number of occasions and usually when Ms O'Toole was taking a shower. He always seemed to time his repairs for when I was out and Ms O'Toole was in the shower."

"Pedro will say that the air conditioning was working. It was just that you were unlucky enough to arrive during the worst heatwave for twenty years."

"That may be so, but when I touched the radiators in the middle of the night they were boiling hot, so that we had the heatwave, defective air conditioning and central heating in the middle of June."

"Is it your evidence, Mr O'Shea, that Dave and his friends

should not have been allowed to stay at The Green Parrot?"

"Of course not. It is just that they were constantly drinking, their language was unacceptable and of course the disco went on until about four. We could hear every song."

"Mr O'Shea, do you recall a conversation with Ms Ní Chinneide on Main Street before you left?"

"I do."

"Ms Ní Chinneide will say that the one facility you were most anxious about was a disco. You specifically requested to go to a hotel with a disco."

"Quite correct Mr O'Gorman, but I wasn't expecting my bedroom to be right over it."

"Now Mr O'Shea, moving on to another topic for a moment. Ms Ní Chinneide will say that when you first came in to see her, you asked her for her cheapest holiday. Is that so?"

"I may have indicated to her that I had no desire to go to Hawaii but I don't think I put it quite as you suggest."

"Ms Ní Chinneide is quite emphatic. You requested her cheapest holiday."

"I was bringing Ms O'Toole with me and I don't think I would have chosen the cheapest resort for her."

"What did the fortnight cost?"

"I believe it was two hundred and ninety nine pounds each for flight, accommodation and half-board."

"Mr O'Shea, you wouldn't get two weeks in Butlins for that."

"Butlins, Mr O'Gorman?" enquired his alert Lordship.

"A not very up-market holiday complex in north county Dublin, my Lord. Your Lordship is unlikely to have stayed there," I said.

"Thank you, Mr McNamara."

"It was a cheap holiday, Mr O'Shea?" Martin resumed.

"That was because we were taking it at the last moment. At least that is why I thought it was so cheap."

"You do agree at last that it was a cheap holiday?"

"I agree it was good value."

"And it was a cheap holiday because that's what you asked for?"

"I don't think so."

"Don't you think that you got good value having regard to the price?"

"No, I don't."

"In summary, that you were looking for Hilton value at Green Parrot prices?"

"Certainly not."

"Mr O'Shea, something you said in your direct evidence has been bothering me. You see, I understood that you travelled with your wife, but I understand from an answer you gave to Mr McNamara that in fact Ms O'Toole was a friend and not your wife. Is that correct?"

"It is, unfortunately."

"Why do you say unfortunately?"

"Because I had high hopes for our relationship and in fact I was hoping to propose to Ms O'Toole while in Majorca."

"Do you not think that what was unfortunate was that you chose to go away with someone you were not married to?" The packed court stiffened. This was what they had delayed for. His Lordship hadn't said a word up to this point, but this last question was too much for his visiting Lordship.

"Mr O'Gorman, did I hear you correctly?"

"I have no idea, my Lord."

"Did I hear you suggest to the witness that he should not go away on a holiday with someone to whom he was not married?"

"You most certainly did, my Lord."

"Mr O'Gorman, is this not a matter strictly between the plaintiff and his companion?"

"I submit not, my Lord."

"Surely the plaintiff and his companion can go away on holidays to The Green Parrot or wherever they like without being stopped by the courts?"

"Your Lordship is quite correct. The courts cannot stop them, but if they have recourse to the courts arising out of a contract that involves their relationship, then that contract cannot be enforced by the courts."

The audience was loving this exchange. Most present had heard Martin's views umpteen times over a drink or coffee, but they never thought they would have the opportunity to hear him articulate them in court. The feeling was that it was more fun in front of Rogers. Gibson, after all, might have agreed with him. As for me, it had never occurred to me that I might need the Constitution in Tralee. I hadn't even brought a textbook on Contract. All I could manage was a recent publication on holiday law. Quietly, but in vain, I was scanning the index to see if there was anything under "Constitution" or "marriage" or, as a last resort, "unmarried."

Rogers wasn't finished. "But Mr O'Gorman, what happens if two men, or two women, go away together and share a bedroom?"

"Well, my Lord, if they are homosexual or lesbian, that would be wrong and if one of them sought to sue on a contract that countenanced such a relationship, then the court could not enforce such a contract. To do so would contravene the law of Contract and the Constitution itself."

"But Mr O'Gorman, if two men go on holidays together and share a bedroom, how would you know that they were homosexual? Have a member of staff peep through the keyhole or listen at the door?"

"Certainly not, my Lord. I do take your Lordship's point that there is a practical difficulty where homosexuals and lesbians are concerned."

"Unless, of course, they admit as much in the contract documents, but then I do not think there is a question dealing with the sexual orientation of those going on holidays?" asked the judge.

"I don't think there is, my Lord."

"The mere fact that two men or women share a hotel bedroom doesn't make them gay, does it Mr O'Gorman?"

"No, my Lord."

"Well that's a relief. Surely, Mr O'Gorman, the same difficulty arises in the case of a man and a woman sharing a bedroom? Who is to say whether or not they are having a sexual relationship?"

"With respect, my Lord, we are living in the real world and I submit that if a man and a woman share a bedroom, then it is most unlikely that they are not having a sexual relationship."

"It may be unlikely Mr O'Gorman, but is that sufficient? No, Mr O'Gorman. I'm against you. I will not allow you to continue this line of cross-examination." The crowd, which had been augmented by the girls from the Circuit Court office, had been enjoying the debate and had been looking forward to the raising of the quasi-matrimonial veil. His Lordship's ruling was greeted with barely disguised disappointment.

"Very well, my Lord. Mr O'Shea, may I put it to you that it is because of your disappointment at how things have worked out between you and Ms O'Toole that you have brought this action against Funshine and not because of any failure on the part of Funshine?"

"No, Mr O'Gorman. I do accept what you say about my disappointment at the ending of our relationship in Majorca, but this is not my motivation in bringing the action. First and last I have brought these proceedings because the holiday was a disaster from start to finish. This was Funshine's fault and I am seeking damages against them. In addition, I have a friend who has done a diploma in Legal Studies and he tells me – "

"Mr O'Shea, the court does not require any assistance from your friend with his diploma in Legal Studies. We have enough experts here," Rogers chided.

"Very well, my Lord."

"You may go down now, Mr O'Shea," I instructed the plaintiff.

At half-time the case was going quite well from the plaintiff's point of view. He had retained his cool at all times while giving his evidence. If anyone had made a misjudgement, it was O'Gorman, who had allowed his extra-curricular convictions to infiltrate his advocacy. Insofar as he had attempted to place Mr O'Shea beyond the moral and constitutional pale by insisting on the immorality of his sharing a bedroom with Ms O'Toole, he had managed to antagonise his Lordship. Unfortunately from O'Gorman's point of view, the last-minute change of referee had worked to his disadvantage. Gibson would undoubtedly have been more sympathetic to his antediluvian arguments. What worried me about the defendant's case as gleaned from O'Gorman's cross-examination of Mr O'Shea was the allegation that he was looking for the cheapest holiday available. If the judge accepted that, he might not look too kindly upon the plaintiff's complaints and might feel that they were no more than he had a right to expect given the price of the holiday.

Over to O'Gorman. He directed Ms Rosa Garcia to the witness box. She took *The Bible* in her right hand and slowly, in a mellifluous, broken English repeated the oath after the registrar. She sat down. Majorca may have produced daughters more beautiful than Rosa, but they had yet to be seen in Tralee. On the other hand, if her intelligence reflected the intellectual wealth of that Mediterranean island, then Arnold would be well advised to open a sub-office immediately in Palma. Even he could spot her inadequacy in that regard. "All her eggs in one basket...and not her brain," he remarked to me later in one of his rare insights into his fellow woman.

She had an abundance of long, midnight black hair. On any girl of average attractiveness, this would have been an outstanding feature. But on Rosa, lavishly endowed as she was, this feature was easily beaten into second place by her eyes. Her lashes were long and dark and flaky and drew on her lazy and sensual eyelids like tassels. Most of the time, her eyes seemed reluctant to open, as if to behold what the world had to offer would demean her in some way. Occasionally she looked out from behind half-open eyelids, which gave her an air at once superior and seductive.

Any thoughts that Ms Garcia may have had of seducing Judge Rogers were way wide of the mark. Rogers had two interests in life – golf and work – and sex was not one of them. Unlike many of his colleagues, he was impervious to the wiles of woman. Rosa could cross her legs as many times as she liked and all Rogers would remember would be her evidence. He was happily married in that soulless sort of way that characterises men who like to wash their cars on Saturday and read the newspapers on Sunday. Passion, except where golf was concerned, was not a word that was likely to feature in his vocabulary. He was as unlikely to be caught on the floor of his sitting room, even with his wife, as Arnold was to be accepted for *Mastermind*.

It went without saying that Rosa's silken charms went unnoticed as far as O'Gorman was concerned. He was still wondering if he could reopen the Constitutional argument. That left me and the male constituency of the Tralee Bar to appreciate the Majorcan presentation. As an audience we did her proud.

Ms Garcia prepared herself for Martin's direct examination. Unfortunately she was at a disadvantage when she was not simply repeating what was said to her, as in the case of taking the Oath. One truth quickly became clear and it had the advantage of bearing out what the plaintiff had said, namely that Rosa had not a word of English. She was in trouble immediately.

"Ms Garcia, I think that you were the representative of Funshine Holidays Limited in Majorca. Is that correct?"

"Excuse me?" she replied in her fragmented English. Martin tried again, this time breaking up the question into syllables. To no avail. Her articulation of "excuse me" was destined for improvement. He tried pointing at her to indicate that the "you" in the question referred to her and she eventually got that. He accompanied his repetition of the question with gesticulation worthy of the stage but that got him nowhere. She decided to repeat the question after him to see if that would effect a breakthrough, but without success. This was his star witness. The defence was experiencing one of its lower moments. Rogers was becoming impatient.

"Surely, Mr O'Gorman, an interpreter should have been proofed in this case?"

"I respectfully agree with your Lordship and I regret that I must take the blame for the omission, but in fairness my Lord," O'Gorman added, having become infected by Rogers' impatience, "I assumed, wrongly as it turns out, that someone in Ms Garcia's position would have fluent English."

"What can we do, Mr O'Gorman? Obviously, Ms Garcia cannot understand your questions. Do you wish to persist with her as a witness or do you apply for an adjournment?"

"My Lord, it occurs to me that there may be another possibility."

"What's that, Mr O'Gorman?"

"I am instructed that Mr Neligan, who is the Managing Director of Funshine Holidays Limited, has reasonable Spanish and is in court. Would your Lordship allow Mr Neligan to act as interpreter?"

"It's a little unusual, Mr O'Gorman, to have your client acting as your witness's interpreter."

"It is, my Lord."

"Mr McNamara, can I take it that you would have no objection to this course?"

"No objection whatsoever, my Lord," I answered, believing that a nod was a good as a wink. Mr Neligan was sworn in.

After that unpromising start, Rosa got into her stride with the assistance of Mr Neligan. She may have had difficulty with English, but she needed no assistance in her native tongue and, as with many of her compatriots, gesticulation vied with the flow of language for the interpreter's attention and all the time she looked out from behind her half-closed eyelids. I was beginning to think that my tactic of going along with the judge's suggestion of allowing Mr Neligan to interpret was about to backfire.

It was my turn to shed some light on the operation of Funshine

Holidays Limited in Palma, Majorca.

"Ms Garcia, Mr O'Shea's first complaint is that you showed no interest in his lost luggage. Is that correct?" Having asked the question, I then had to wait for Mr Neligan to translate into Spanish, listen to Rosa's answer in Spanish and then wait for Mr Neligan's translation back into English. At this rate we would be here for the rest of the week. However, in this first instance, Rosa was able to answer in English.

"Yes," she answered to my astonishment. Perhaps this wasn't going to be too difficult after all.

"So you agree with Mr O'Shea that you were not too interested in his lost luggage?"

Mr Neligan translated.

"Oh no, Mr Macamara. I agree with you that Mr O'Shea's first complaint is that I wasn't interested in his lost luggage." I wasn't sure what to make of this answer. Was she trying to be clever? Or was she whatever the opposite of a lateral thinker is, so that she answered the precise question even though that clearly was not the question being asked? Or should I put it down simply to the difficulties inherent in translation? I decided on the latter course. I tried again.

"Ms Garcia, I suggest to you that you showed no interest in Mr O'Shea's predicament?"

"That's not true Mr McNamara, and Mr O'Shea knows it. I looked everywhere for his luggage."

"Mr O'Shea says that you were too busy with the head of customs to be of any assistance to him. What do you say to that?"

"That's good coming from Mr O'Shea. He was so busy in a corner of the airport lounge with his wife that he didn't notice the luggage coming through in the first instance."

"That wasn't his wife," interrupted O'Gorman, unable to shake off his disapproval of Mr O'Shea's relationship.

"We've had that, thank you Mr O'Gorman," Rogers warned.

"Whoever she was, she and Mr O'Shea nearly missed the coach to the Hilton with their canoodling. They didn't seem too interested in the luggage themselves."

"You said the Hilton, Ms Garcia? Were not Mr and Mrs O'Shea –"

"They weren't married! That's my point," interrupted O'Gorman again.

"I'm sorry, my Lord. I'm becoming confused myself at this

stage. Weren't my client and Ms O'Toole staying at The Green Parrot?"

"No. No lo creo, Señor Macamara. Hace ya un anyo que el Funshine no manda clientes al Green Parrot. Tuvieron unas malas experiencias borrachos y cosas de ese estilo. La clientela del Green Parrot ha empeorado bastante," Ms Garcia replied in her native tongue. During this reply to my question, Neligan was looking decidedly uncomfortable and it surprised me when he translated simply "Yes". His Lordship was quicker off the mark than I.

"Mr Neligan, Mr McNamara has just asked Ms Garcia if his clients were not staying at The Green Parrot. Now I don't speak Spanish but I thought that the first word of Ms Garcia's reply was 'no' and she then went on to give a rather lengthy answer which you translated monosyllabically as 'yes'. Now I may be wrong, Mr Neligan, but I wonder if you have translated what Ms Garcia said accurately? Please remember you are on oath and you are required to translate as truthfully as if it were your own evidence." I'm not sure when the phrase 'body language' was invented but of course it merely gave contemporary terminology to a means of communication that had existed as long as man himself. Presumably even in the time of the Ceide Fields, a fellow's shiftiness under cross-examination could give the game away just as he was verbally denying that anything had been going on between him and his neighbour's wife at the Saturday night hop. It didn't require a psychiatrist to tell us of Neligan's discomfort as Rogers spoke.

"If your Lordship will allow me to ask Ms Garcia the question again," which he did, and she replied and he translated, this time less loosely, "No, I don't think so Mr Macamara. Funshine stopped sending clients to The Green Parrot the year before. They had some bad experiences. Lager louts and all that. The clientele at The Green Parrot had got a bit rough," concluded a greatly embarrassed Managing Director of Funshine Holidays Limited.

"Now, Mr Neligan, if you wouldn't mind sticking to the script you are presented with. It doesn't require embellishment from you or from anyone else."

"Yes, my Lord. Sorry, my Lord."

I saw a little opening. "My Lord, I would respectfully ask your Lordship not to take any more evidence from this witness. We are relying totally on Mr Neligan's translation and as we now know that is not so reliable."

"What do you say, Mr O'Gorman?   This is your witness."

"Well, my Lord, I accept that what has happened is far from satisfactory, but I would suggest that your Lordship hear the evidence in full and then it is a matter for your Lordship as to what weight you attach to it."

"Unfortunately it is not quite as simple as that. It is not just a question of attaching whatever weight I think appropriate to Ms Garcia's evidence. It is a question of whether or not I am receiving her evidence at all. I'll hear the evidence as translated by Mr Neligan – hopefully now with greater accuracy – *de bene esse.*" Everyone was immensely pleased with this solution to the problem, as everyone usually is when the words '*de bene esse*' are invoked. These three harmless, unifying words usually have a little something for everyone. O'Gorman was pleased, from his client's point of view of course, that Ms Garcia didn't have to go to the airport just yet and I had the intuition that really Rogers was not going to pay much attention to her evidence as fashioned by Mr Neligan. Only Rogers himself knew the true meaning of the words in the given context.

"Please carry on Mr McNamara. Now where were we? Oh yes. Ms Garcia was explaining the deterioration in the calibre of clientele at The Green Parrot and how the defendant wasn't sending clients there anymore." Just as I thought.

"Thank you, my Lord. I can tell, you Ms Garcia, that Mr O'Shea and Ms O'Toole were not staying at the Hilton. They were, in fact, staying at The Green Parrot."

"If you say so. I'd just forgotten that," she replied.

"You do agree with me that those staying at The Green Parrot ...how will I put it...were from a lower socio-economic grouping than Mr O'Shea and Ms O'Toole and spent their time at the pool singing and drinking until the disco opened?"

"My recollection is that your clients did not spend much time at The Green Parrot. They spent all their time at the Hilton. They didn't mix much. Seemed like quite a romantic couple."

"Well that's not Mr O'Shea's evidence. He said that the romance was ruined by The Green Parrot and by Dave and the drinking chorus. You mentioned the disco. That's another of his complaints, that they couldn't sleep because of the disco."

"From what I saw of Mr O'Shea and Ms O'Toole they were never home from the disco at the Hilton before four in the morning, so that I don't think that the disco at The Green Parrot would have bothered them."

"And the leak in the loo and the central heating?"

"They never mentioned them to me."

"And if they had, would you have understood what they were saying?"

"I did English at school. Of course I would have understood. And anyway couldn't they have pointed them out to me?"

"Thank you, Ms Garcia. I have no more questions for this witness, my Lord."

"You may go down Ms Garcia. Thank you for attending court and a safe journey back to Majorca."

"*Gracias.*" With which Ms Garcia, for the first and only time, opened her eyes fully. Perhaps before going she wanted to feed her brain and her memory with one last and comprehensive impression of the scene as she saw it from the witness box in Tralee Circuit Court for the folks back home and for Majorcan posterity. When she had her fill, her eyes resumed their semi-open position. She uncrossed her legs and returned to the well of the court and anonymity. She had brought summer to a mid-autumn day in Tralee and sent many of those present home via the defendant's office to pick up next summer's holiday brochures.

Unfortunately, Pedro the porter had missed his flight and was therefore unable to give evidence. Judge Rogers enquired somewhat irregularly as to what his evidence was to be. I didn't complain because I had a feeling that the learned judge was merely going through the motions and was anxious to give the defendant every opportunity before finding against them.

"My Lord, according to my instructions, Señor Pedro was going to say that he couldn't wait any longer for the coach, that he was puzzled as to why Mr O'Shea left his shoes outside his bedroom door in the first place, but nonetheless had organised a thorough search for them without success, which left him wondering if Mr O'Shea might in fact be mistaken and perhaps he had not brought that particular pair of shoes with him." This prompted an incisive note from Arnold, who wanted to know if Pedro thought that Mr O'Shea had travelled from Tralee to Palma in his socks.

"As for the leak in the loo, he fixed that eventually. The first two occasions Ms O'Toole called him up to her room, Mr O'Shea was not there and Ms O'Toole was in the shower so he couldn't repair the leak on those visits, but he did return and fix it as soon as was possible." This prompted another missive, this time from Mr O'Shea himself. It read: "What is the witness suggesting?"

Martin continued, "Señor Pedro would say were he here that the air conditioning was working. It was just the fact of the severe heatwave in the face of which all air conditioning was less efficient. There was no mention of central heating, but that, my Lord, is presumably because today is the first time we have heard of this complaint. There is nothing in the plaintiff's pleadings about it. I am not taking a pleading point my Lord," *of course not Martin, perish the thought*, "it is just by way of explaining why Pedro doesn't deal with that particular complaint. My instructions are that were Señor Pedro in court his evidence would be along these lines."

"Thank you, Mr O'Gorman. It is helpful to know what he would have said even though I am not entitled of course to take his evidence from your instructions. Have you any more witnesses Mr O'Gorman, or is that your case?"

"One more witness, my Lord. Ms Ní Chinneide, who has returned from her holidays in West Cork especially to give evidence. She won't take very long, my Lord."

"Ms Ní Chinneide please." Ms Ní Chinneide had her assets in reverse order to Ms Garcia. In other words, her strengths were intellectual. Appearances can be deceptive, but I doubted if she would have the same interest in the Head of Customs with the tight trousers in Majorca as Ms Garcia. If the preparation of the glossy brochures were to be left to Ms Ní Chinneide, I reckoned there would be a lot less photographs and a lot of small print and they would be little read. She made her way to the witness box. Many felt it was time for coffee.

Martin took Ms Ní Chinneide through her evidence. She really only had two points to make and she made them tellingly. Mr O'Shea wanted the cheapest holiday available and a disco in the hotel. He got both. There seemed little way round this evidence, chilling in its clarity.

I really thought we were home and dry but this evidence, late in the day, worried me. How could I undermine it?

"Ms Ní Chinneide, how many clients would you deal with in any one day? On average, that is." The witness thought for a moment.

"On average...I would say...about twenty...some days more, some days less...but on average about twenty."

"Five days a week?"

"Yes."

"That is about one hundred clients a week."

"On average I'd say about that."

"And in a year, that means that you have dealt with approximately fifty thousand clients. I'm not saying that that number of people actually book holidays with you, but you would have assisted about that many people?"

"Mr McNamara, numbers?" interrupted his Lordship.

"I beg your pardon, my Lord?"

"Your mathematics, Mr McNamara. I think you've over-calculated."

"Have I my Lord?" I said, jotting down one hundred and multiplying by fifty. "Oh, your Lordship is perfectly correct. It should be five thousand."

"That's more like it, Mr McNamara."

"In fact, allowing for a fifty-two week year and deducting three weeks for holidays, the figure should be four thousand nine hundred. That is my assessment of the number of clients I might assist in a year, taken on an average basis," Ms Ní Chinneide corrected, flexing her intellectual muscles and no others, in confirmation of my first impressions. Neligan's wife must have chosen Ms Ní Chinneide for the job, I reflected as I wondered where this cross-examination was going.

"That's a lot of clients," I said weakly.

"It is," Ms Ní Chinneide agreed. "Mr Neligan runs a successful business."

"It is so many clients, Ms Ní Chinneide, that I fail to see how out of four thousand nine hundred clients, even allowing for approximation, you could possibly recall any one of them with any great particularity?"

"Training and experience I suppose, and I have a very good head for faces and names."

"O'Shea is a common name in Kerry, Ms Ní Chinneide. You would meet a lot of O'Sheas."

"You would indeed, Mr McNamara, but fewer Sebastian O'Sheas."

"Whatever about remembering Mr O'Shea, I suggest to you that it is stretching credulity to ask his Lordship to believe that you could recall the detail of a conversation with one of the four thousand nine hundred clients, especially when that conversation took place almost a year ago. How do you explain such recall?"

"I'm not sure, to be honest. It may have been his embarrassment. When I asked him how many were going, he dropped his voice in answering 'two'. When I asked him who was travelling with him he looked furtively left and right, up and down the counter, then leant over towards me and mouthed his companion's name four times without emitting a single sound. Eventually I asked him to write it down. It may have been his insistence on the cheapest holiday I had that struck me as a bit mean, particularly when he was bringing his girlfriend. He was well dressed and I felt he could have afforded something more expensive. Or it may have been his insistence on a disco. He struck me as a bit old for that. After all, he was no spring chicken." *Nor indeed may I say are you Ms Ní Chinneide*, I thought to myself in one of those unhelpful, intrusive thoughts that come to ones mind when one is desperately looking for an opening in cross-examination. "Generally he was a bit agitated, in a bit of a hurry. He had to fly out the following week. All in all he was not your typical customer and that is why I remember him so well." Ms Ní Chinneide had built up a plausible profile of Mr O'Shea. There was no doubt she remembered him. Probably no doubt also that she remembered her conversations with him. Indeed, come to think of it, it was unlikely that her social life was much of a whirl and she probably stayed on late in the evening compiling notes of her dealings with each client. I wasn't sure where to go next.

"Ms Ní Chinneide, were you in court when Ms Garcia gave her evidence?" Rogers enquired, giving me a little time to think up my next direction, as I doubted if I was going to make any headway with this one.

"I was, my Lord."

"Did you hear her say that the clientele in The Green Parrot had deteriorated and that Funshine had stopped sending their clients there the year before Mr O'Shea's trip?" *Nice one Judge, why didn't I think of that? Good old Rosa and the drooping eyelids.*

"I did, my Lord."

"Well, how come you sent Mr O'Shea and Miss O'Toole there?"

"Well my Lord, what happened there was that earlier that morning I had received information about a cheap deal in the Hilton for two weeks as long as you could fly out the following week. Would have suited Mr O'Shea down to the ground. Disco and all. Mr O'Shea was delighted. Unfortunately when I went to get it, one of the two seats was gone, so it was no use to Mr O'Shea. We had very little at that time at short notice, so I spoke to Mr Neligan. He said to try The Green Parrot. I reminded him that we had dropped The Parrot the year before because, as Ms Garcia said, of clientele difficulties. He said not to worry and to go ahead and book The Parrot. It was early season and things would be relatively quiet there. That, my Lord, is how Mr O'Shea came to be sent to The Green Parrot."

"I'm sorry for interrupting Mr McNamara. It was just something that crossed my mind and I felt it should be cleared up. Please resume your cross-examination, Mr McNamara."

"Not at all, my Lord. In fact I am grateful to your Lordship for bringing it up. I was about to myself had your Lordship not got there first," I lied most sycophantically. "Following on from what you have just told his Lordship, Ms Ní Chinneide, may the court assume that you informed Mr O'Shea that The Green Parrot where you were sending him had been dropped by your office the year before and the reason why?" Ms Ní Chinneide hesitated. The first sign of any unsureness in her evidence.

"I would be interested in the answer Ms Ní Chinneide," assisted his Lordship, turning the screw another notch. Ms Ní Chinneide was in no hurry.

"No I didn't, my Lord."

"Why not, Ms Ní Chinneide?" enquired his interested Lordship.

"Well, my Lord, as I have already said, Mr O'Shea was very anxious to be fixed up and unfortunately we were a bit low on alternatives at that time."

"That doesn't explain not warning him, Ms Ní Chinneide. Wouldn't it have been fairer to have put him in the full picture about The Green Parrot, and he could then have made up his own mind?" asked his Lordship, who was getting some more experience at turning the screw.

"Yes my Lord, it would have been fairer."

"Why didn't you warn him then?" I asked in an animated tone, deciding to turn his Lordship's interrogation into a duet.

"Because if I had warned him he probably would not have gone so that I would have been left with one disappointed customer and from the office's point of view, no sale."

"And of course no commission" I added, breasting the tape.

"Yes, no commission," Ms Ní Chinneide agreed, having lost some of the composure with which she started out.

Game, set and match.

"Thank you, Ms Ní Chinneide. I have no more questions," I concluded, resisting the temptation to punch the air with my fist. Instead, as I resumed my seat I flicked back the tails of my gown in a modest and I felt more appropriate gesture of triumph, like a concert pianist at the beginning of a great performance.

"Is that the evidence, gentlemen?"

"It is, my Lord" we responded in unison.

"Very well then. I was very impressed by Mr O'Shea and the manner in which he gave his evidence, although I was some-what surprised that Ms O'Toole wasn't called as a witness. Perhaps there are other reasons for not calling her which are not germane to the issues I must decide. In relation to Ms O'Toole, I have to say that Mr O'Gorman's argument about the invalidity of the contract has no merit whatsoever. Maybe ten or twenty years ago but time has moved on. I was not impressed by Mr Neligan's attempt to flavour Ms Garcia's evidence. Initially I thought that Ms Ní Chinneide's evidence about the cheapest holi-day might undermine Mr O'Shea's case, but clearly he should have been told the full story about The Green Parrot. I have no doubt that had he been told, he would not have gone. I find the defendant negligent and in breach of contract and Mr O'Shea entitled to damages. The question is how much. First of all there is the price of the holiday at two hundred and ninety nine pounds. There is no claim for the price of Ms O'Toole's holiday. I would assess the general damages at two thousand five hundred pounds. However, there is an additional element in this case, as Mr O'Shea said his romance came to an end because of this holiday. This was entirely foreseeable and the defendant will have to make this up to Mr O'Shea by way of exemplary damages. This is what Mr O'Shea's friend with the diploma in legal studies had in mind. Of course it is impossible to put a figure on a broken romance, but doing the best I can I will round the general damages up to ten thousand pounds."

"My Lord, I would ask for judgment for ten thousand two hundred and ninety nine pounds."

"That seems to be correct Mr McNamara. Sums correct this time."

"Thank you, my Lord. And costs, my Lord?"

"That follows. Thank you, gentlemen, for your assistance."

Arnold was in a high state of excitement. He stood up, turned around to face the judge and, in a most deferential manner, bowed so low that he almost struck his forehead off the Bench. I gathered up my things and turned to Martin to sympathise with him but he was already gone. The court had filled up again in anticipation of the next case and so I made my way through my thronging colleagues who were generous to the out-of-towners in their congratulations.

"Mighty men," was all that Mr O'Shea could say as he grasped our hands and almost shook them off.

"Well done, Dermot," greeted the chorus of girls from the Circuit Court office, "the early run over the course obviously paid off," they joked.

"What on earth do they mean?" Arnold wanted to know.

"Oh, just a little in joke," I answered. We said goodbye to Mr O'Shea, who had had his best day since the break-up of his relationship.

It was coming up to one o'clock.

"Dermot, what about a spot of lunch? And then we could go out for a round of golf. I hear you've been playing recently."

"Smashing idea Arnold, only I warn you, I'm no good."

"I know that. Any other objections?"

"I've no clubs."

"I've a spare set in the boot. You can have those."

"Excellent."

"And then, depending on the time, we can drive home or maybe have dinner and spend the night here. How does that sound?"

"All right with me. I'm in no hurry. But you, don't you have a closing tomorrow?"

"Oh no. I knew we'd be here for a few days. Kept the day free. Free as a bird, in fact."

"Me too," I said as we ambled into the Mount Brandon.

The *maître d'* showed us to a window table with a view of the mountains. Arnold poured a glass of Chablis.

"That was a very impressive win today, Dermot, and away from home, too. Well done."

"Thank you, Arnold. A team effort, as Margaret would say." I savoured the win and the wine and Arnold's compliment. Sipping his Chablis and looking out at the mountains, Arnold continued, "You know, Dermot, I've been thinking about my panel lately."

My eye may have been on the menu, but I was really wondering if Arnold's "A" team was beckoning at last.

AN EYE ON THE WHIPLASH

Henry Murphy

Dermot McNamara, BL, stands on the threshold of a great career at the Bar. Or so it seems to him. A highly successful college interlude behind him, his devilling year completed, he is more than ready for his first brief when it arrives - somewhat belatedly - well into his second year in the Law Library.

At last the future beckons. Only a matter of time before he sprints up the ladder of success, eventually to join the leaders of the Bar within the inner sanctum of Senior Counsel. His anticipation knows no bounds. Even at this remove he can dimly make out the name on the door leading to his chambers - Mr Justice Dermot McNamara.

Dermot had not reckoned on Arnold, however. J Arnold O'Reilly - a solicitor well beyond the threshold of a career that by no stretch of the imagination could be called great. Arnold was from another world. It was a forensic wonder that he kept his practice going - which was, of course entirely due to his friendship, from rugby-playing days, with Mr Wilkinson, now the Claims Manager of one of the country's leading insurance companies. Dermot's father is a golfing friend of Mr Wilkinson who is responsible for Dermot's first brief and for introducing him to Arnold.

These hilarious accounts of a young barrister just starting up in practice give us a great insight into a mysterious profession.

THE AUTHOR
Henry Murphy is a practising barrister who lives in Sandymount with Mary and their children.

140 pages; 1998
1-901658-10-4; £9.99; pbk;
1-901658-11-2; £16.95 hbk;

THE FILES OF FLYNN DE COURCY

Anthony Philpott

See just why the Irish publishing community was provoked into an unseemly bidding frenzy by the decision of Flynn de Courcy to offer his revealing correspondence for publication. These amusing letters from the eccentric solicitor build up into a record of some of the weirdest - and most incredible - cases in Irish legal history. You won't believe that some of them are true - and maybe they're not!

Read about the legal tribulations concerning the untimely embalmment of Mrs Agnes Stuns, the story of Galapagos Duignan, the results of Miss Eileen Bletch's surgery and the attempts to maintain the privacy - and the dignity - of Mr Eoin Hely-Childers TD.

THE AUTHOR
Anthony Philpott is Creative Director with Ogilvy Mather, based in Dublin.

260 pages
1-901658-22-8 £17.95; hbk: November 1999

The above books can be purchased at any good bookshop or direct from:

BLACKHALL PUBLISHING
26 Eustace Street
Dublin 2.

Telephone: +353 (0)1-677-3242
Fax: +353 (0)1-677-3243
e-mail: blackhall@tinet.ie